ONCE AGAIN, WITH BLOOD

THE ISLAND SERIES,

BOOK 2

LARRY WEINER

Cover Design by Larry Weiner

Previously self-published as *Once Again, With Blood*, 2014

This is a work of fiction. Names, characters, places, brands, media, and incidents are either
the product of the author's imagination or are used fictitiously. Any resemblance to similarly
named places or to persons living or deceased is unintentional.

Print ISBN 978-0-6927-2751-5
Library of Congress Control Number: 2015909179

For the Boys

"Sucking or licking one's own blood from a wound is also a behavior commonly seen in humans, and in small enough quantities is not considered taboo."

—*Wikipedia*

"I had a stick of CareFree gum, but it didn't work. I felt pretty good while I was blowing that bubble, but as soon as the gum lost its flavor, I was back to pondering my mortality."

—Mitch Hedberg

PROLOGUE

"LOOK AT YOU, YOUR FACE ALL TWISTED UP, squealing like a sewer rat, red foam around your lips, holding on to that wooden stake as if you could pull it out. Boychick, in all honesty, it's embarrassing for your kind."

Noam Wysocki sat in the tall grass on a hill that overlooked the North Atlantic. It was a full moon, so he could make out the undulating waves as they lapped repeatedly, endlessly on the shore. It would be dawn in about twenty minutes, give or take. The vampire known by his colony simply as "Idiota" lay next to Noam, writhing. It was a simple kill. Noam hadn't even planned on it. He went to that spot when he needed to quiet himself, feel the breeze on his wrinkled cheeks, for Noam was old. Not too old that he couldn't slam a wooden stake through a vampire's chest, but old enough. And out popped Idiota, leaping above the tall green grass, his mouth agape, fangs flashing, though after seven centuries the fangs were looking more like butterknives, then the pathetic little "*Screeeeeeee!*"

Noam had waited for Idiota to land and simply picked up the stake that sat beside him. He knew enough to carry one at night. He'd leaned forward from his sitting position and jammed the stake through the vampire's dead heart. Idiota had let out another

"*Screeeeeee!*" then crumbled down beside Noam and commenced with the theatrical presentation of vampire death on a small island in the North Atlantic, scene one, act one.

"It didn't have to go like this, Idiota. You know I never had any trouble with you. None of us did. Sure, the children often dumped cow dung over your grave and captured you in an overturned wheelbarrow with some dead rat bait. But you made it too easy for them. We all knew, for a vampire, you were a little touched in the head, but we also knew the last thing you killed was the three-legged dog that hung around the dump."

More gurgling. A large foam bubble grew out of his mouth then popped. Noam shook his head.

"And I suppose your higher-ups are gonna learn about this and, from my mouth to God's ear, Idiota, and this isn't a slam, it just is—they ain't gonna miss you. But you do give me some worry. It was a bold move on your part. Kind of outta character for you. Covering the window of my deli with vampire saliva as if to 'mark' your next kill—that was old hat. But this, this leaping out the grass to attack me, of all people. *Me*? You had to know it wasn't a fair fight. It was almost as if you were ordered to do it. And when vampires start handing out orders, well, to quote my favorite dead Nazi playwright, Hanns Johst, 'Whenever I hear the word culture, I reach for my gun.' It's not the actual wording, but I like the sound of it. Right? Well, Idiota, whenever I hear a vampire make plans, I reach for my stake."

Idiota's gnarled hands scratched and pulled at the wooden stake, mouthing something.

"What was that?" Noam said. He leaned over toward Idiota's face.

"Thaid homing," Idiota hissed.

"Thaid homing? I can't—say it again."

"Theyerd ccchhoming."

"I dunno what—you know what? Forget about it."

"Thaayerd Coh-ming."

Noam heard it that time.

"They're coming."

Idiota threw back his head with momentary relief over Noam getting the words right.

"Of course they're coming, Idiota. They always do. And we always beat them back."

Noam got to his feet with a little effort and dusted off his backside. He leaned over Idiota placing one hand on the stake. For a moment, Idiota made a last grasp for Noam's hand. It was weak at best and slid off onto his unbreathing chest.

"Listen, the sun'll be up very shortly. You'll bake like a Passover brisket. Not that the stake didn't do the job, but you seem to want to stretch this out, so."

Noam regarded the vampire who, once, centuries ago, was a human being. What were the origins of Idiota? Who would make a vampire out of such a wretch? But he wasn't mortal any longer. He was one of them that left Noam with a hole in his own heart to this day.

"I'll be needing this," Noam said. He pulled on the stake. It slid out easily, like a thermometer on a roast beef. "Forgive me if I don't say kaddish. Enjoy the sunrise."

CHAPTER 1

"**YOU'RE A NEWBIE. I MEAN, LOOK AT YOU.** That look of terror. I've seen it before. Of course, it was during a zombie invasion, but still. Whoops! That last sentence freaked you out. S'okay. Let's focus.

"First, you're doing it wrong. All wrong. You gotta calm down or you're not gonna survive it. I'm about to make your life easier. I'm babbling right now because I've had a slight psychotic break. Not really a break, more a sabbatical from reality. It's okay, they'll give me a new drug cocktail plus some *Law & Order*, and I'll be back in action.

"Back to you. Here's the way it works. Used to be that when you got a patient in who was out of his mind, whether from psychosis or crank or whatever, you'd strap him down with his arms at his sides and cart him off. Problem was, these tortured souls would pull on the restraints so hard, it'd dislocate their shoulders, and then the real howling would start—not to mention the potential litigation. Now, since they're in pain, they're gonna smack their heads on the gurney repeatedly. Let 'em. It's a padded gurney. They'll end up with a terrific headache. I suppose you can give yourself a mild concussion. Anyway, it's the shoulders that were the problem. So someone, and I don't know who, but someone, maybe a yoga instructor or a cop, came up with the idea of strapping the crazies one hand up by the side of the head, one down by the hip. Did they demonstrate that to you? They should, along with the Fleet enemas. Try some of that shit, chief. See what I did there? Focus. One hand over the head, the other by the side. Now you're talking incapacitation. Right? Such a simple solution. Almost elegant.

"So listen, you're the new guy and seem reasonably intelligent so I wanna give you some tools to utilize while working the psych ward. Here they are. First, let them masturbate excessively. They're burning off angst and energy and if you stop them they'll do shit like stab each other in the eye with a plastic knife. There are not a lot of ways to blow off some steam in a psych ward. In fact, you might want to suggest they pass out hand lotion with toothpaste. You see a lot of awkward gaits around here—part of the reason is because they're walking around with chafed cocks. Next, obsessively watching a TV show does not a crazy person make. It's the repetition and predictability of the characters that provide comfort. A patient feeling safe is one who won't try to hang himself off a doorknob. Lastly, tell everyone, regardless of how fucked up they are, that things are going to be okay and they're gonna get through this. Even the thrice-admitted homeless paranoid schizophrenic meth addict. You tell 'em they're gonna be A-OK. Even if you know that it's bullshit. It'll make things go a lot smoother and you'll breathe a little humanity into an otherwise inhumane situation.

"Remember, your job is to get 'em back on their feet and get them the hell out of Dodge. That's it. I'm sure you have questions, but it's been a long day for me and I could really use some *Law & Order SVU*. It'll help with the coming down. They've gotta process my paperwork. It's gonna take a while before they even get to me. *Law & Order*. It'll be on TNT, Bravo, and USA. Possibly on NBC. There are a few constants in the universe. One of them being that at any given time an episode of *Law & Order* is running somewhere on Earth. The lounge is off to your left. Why don't we go hang out in there for a while? Don't put me next to someone with their hands jammed down their pants. I'm in no mood for that shit. Watching that is like pissing out my soul. You'll see."

The orderly, a young man with thick horn-rimmed glasses, stood over Kyle Brightman, a little unsure of how to proceed. Kyle was right. The young orderly was in fact into his third day on the psych ward and had not yet mastered the skills for telling which patients had lost their way versus which patients were the truly batshit among them. Kyle seemed near normal, though he was brought in for beating a tourist couple at Pike Place Market with a twenty-five-pound salmon. The tourists, Scandinavians, had cut into a line that Kyle had been in for ten minutes. When Kyle let them know there was a line, the Scandinavians waved Kyle off.

But how could the Scandinavians know that Kyle Brightman had seen some things this past year, things they wouldn't believe, and had just come out of a broken relationship that smashed his heart into a million pieces? True, he instigated it by running away, but still. He looked like just another Seattleite, not someone who had survived a zombie war in the Caribbean and a subsequent relationship with a zombie woman. There were a great many things they didn't know about Kyle, chief among them that there were moments when he knew he was about to do the wrong thing but felt compelled to do it anyway. So, they cut in line and Kyle grabbed the first thing he saw, a gigantic Copper River salmon, and commenced beating the Scandinavian tourists with it. The rest was all screams and a bin of mussels thrown at the bewildered Scandinavians when the salmon fell apart. It was meltdownville after that, and, once again, Kyle found himself at St. Eligius, fifth-floor psych ward.

It had been little over a year since his last visit.

After the paperwork, Kyle was shown to his room, where he found his clean pajamas on the bed. The bed next to him was empty and still made. Kyle had hoped he would have the room to himself. The last time, he ended up with Oscar Pilson, ex-military, ex-Halliburton mercenary and eventually a good friend who now shared a life in the Caribbean sunshine with the woman-with-no-name and her talking Chihuahua. The very sunshine he had abandoned to come back to the Northwest and lose his shit once again. Just like Cate said he would.

At the time he said Cate was full of it, but in the back of his mind a tiny voice had said, "We'll see you soon." She was right about everything: escaping to Seattle, feeling his old ways seeping back into his life and, eventually, the meltdown.

As Kyle slipped on his pajamas, which felt like paper, he thought about where he was in his life. Thirty-three, unmarried, unemployed, bipolar, and alone. Well, the alone part wasn't totally true.

He did know people around town: former friends and work associates from his days as an art director in advertising. Maybe he could land a gig? He knew enough people to call on. It'd only been a year. He wasn't aged out of the job market yet—or was he?

It was time to formulate a plan. First, a few more hours of *L&O*, maybe some ice cream—he hoped it was still stocked in the cafeteria freezer—followed by a nap, then the introductions to the staff counselors and doctors who would mess with his meds and try to impart some coping mechanisms to stop the assaults with seafood.

*   *   *

"Take it down a notch," Dr. Jason Applebaum said to the group. "Doesn't that have a release to it? Hmm? It gives you a chance to just step back and think about things for a moment. To take a mental inventory of your thoughts and feelings and, hopefully, for that one moment, change the course of your life. You breathe deeply and you look around you. In what moment in time do you exist? Is it your reality? And if it is, then to quote Robert Frost, 'Two roads diverged in a wood, and I—I took the one less traveled by, and that has made all the difference.'"

Kyle sat with a certain car-wreck pleasure. He was three days into his hospital stay and in group therapy, this one about coping skills in stressful situations. The therapist, Dr. Applebaum, was going around the circle of people asking each of them to relay an experience in which a coping mechanism failed them as they tried to solve a problem. In between stories, Dr. Applebaum served up some food for thought, a way to punctuate the stories of despair with a tinge of hope. What could it hurt?

"Ahmed, would you care to share a story with us about standing in front of diverging roads and the one you chose?" Dr. Applebaum asked in what really was a wonderfully soothing voice. Ahmed nodded thoughtfully.

"It was when a co-worker took credit for something I had done that my company profited from."

"And how did that make you feel?" Dr. Applebaum asked.

"I felt just awful, like someone had removed my genitalia and lit them on fire," Ahmed said with a heavy Indian accent.

"So you felt physical as well as emotional pain, correct?" Dr. Applebaum asked.

"I could almost smell my genitalia burning on the taupe-colored carpet in our office," Ahmed said. "It was a horrible, horrible feeling."

"Clearly you felt dismayed over what had transpired," Dr. Applebaum said.

"Yes, dismayed. I was dismayed over what Ralston had done to me, that Anglo-Saxon whore."

"Ralston being the man who took credit for your report. What happened next?"

"I defecated on Ralston's desk."

There were a few stifled giggles. Kyle felt sad and entertained.

"You actually defecated on your co-worker's desk?" Dr. Applebaum asked.

"Yes, I shat on Ralston's desk. On a copy of the report I had written, for which he took the credit."

"What happened next?" Dr. Applebaum asked, his curiosity getting the better of him.

"I was still feeling very stressed out," Ahmed said. "I defecated on the CEO's desk, the CFO's desk, and the CEO's secretary's desk because she never treated me well. Then I microwaved a stapler, which started a fire. After that, I began to feel relief at long last."

"Okay. Thank you, Ahmed. Would anyone care to give their input on how Ahmed might have handled the situation differently?" Dr. Applebaum asked the group.

"Man, how you control your ass to shit like that, all off and on like a garden hose?" Cedric asked.

"What might have Ahmed done *differently* in what was a very stressful situation?" Dr. Applebaum jumped in with. "Nancy?"

"I'm sorry, but I agree with everything Ahmed did, which is why I guess I'm in this goddamned place to begin with."

"Thank you, Nancy."

A hand tapped on Kyle's shoulder. It was a nurse. She bent close to Kyle's ear. "You have a visitor."

"Can it wait?" Kyle asked. "This group rocks."

"Visiting time is almost up," the nurse said.

Kyle rose from his chair with a heavy sigh. It wasn't often that group had any entertainment value beyond watching people cry, so when a good scene came along, it was a prize to behold. Kyle followed the nurse out of the room, as *"Take it down a notch!"* was yelled out behind him. Kyle turned the corner and was met by the beautiful yet somber face of Cate Hendricks, the undead woman with whom he had a relationship back on St. Agrippina when the sun shone every day, the sex was good, and Kyle thought he could finally go off his meds. Things had gone south at an alarming velocity.

*   *   *

They sat in the TV room, which was empty save for the elderly homeless man in a catatonic state who sat in a wheelchair in front of the big screen that was set to *Jeopardy* as if it might restore the old man's consciousness. They sat in plastic-covered recliners that were easy to wipe down and faced each other, the glow of Alex Trebek flickering across their faces.

"So, how are you feeling?" Cate asked.

"I feel great. Plenty of ice cream. *Law & Order* on four channels. Group therapy rocks. It's all good," Kyle said.

"I see. And what about your meds?" Cate asked.

"I have new pills now. Or I should say, *more* pills now."

They were both doing their best to keep it civil. *"Rhymes with colostomy for one hundred, Alex."* That turned both their heads to the screen.

"Kyle, what happened?" Cate asked, her eyes still on the TV.

"There is no word in the English language that rhymes with 'colostomy.' It's like 'orange,'" Kyle said. "Maybe lobotomy?"

"I'm trying not to kick you in the balls here," Cate said.

"I know," Kyle said. "Same old song and dance. I get to a happy place and figure I don't need the drugs. It seems to be a lesson I keep relearning."

"I mean, Kyle, you just vanished. I could still see the cloud of dust swirling where you once were."

"It's fucked up," Kyle said. "I can't believe you're here."

"I agree," Cate said. "I should've just thrown away a year-and-a-half relationship and started over with one of my kind. But then who would I have around to kick in the balls whenever they pissed me off...?"

"Now that you mention it, you've got a kind of addiction to caving in my testicles," interrupted Kyle. "Was the sex that bad? You could've just said so instead of getting physical about it."

Cate sat back in her chair, the plastic cover squeaking. *Why did she come after him?* Okay, she loved him, but really? That was enough? Took three planes to get here to, what? Bring him home? Was that even a possibility? Chasing after men was never Cate's style. She was the heartbreaker.

"Heartbreaker, dream maker," she sang in an almost whisper.

"Love taker, don't you mess around with me," Kyle finished.

They smiled at each other.

"I should just eat your brain right here and now and be done with it," Cate said. It wasn't often that she made zombie references. It was still volatile terrain to walk across. Some days she had a hard time working past the idea that she had risen from the dead, much like Zac Efron, on a daily basis.

"It was more than the meds," Cate said. "Percy really tripped your wire."

"Yeah, he did," Kyle admitted. "It was like a borderline serial moron was teaching me how to dismantle a bomb."

"So I see you're over it," Cate said.

"Look, the guy's a douchebag. We had a sweet deal, being our own bosses, our own creative directors. Suddenly there's this brown-shirted haircut in the conference room judging our creative? C'mon. You know how many years I had to put up with running the gauntlet of approval. They don't tell you that when you work in a profession that is remotely creative there will always be someone to ram a telephone pole of criticism up an already worn-out ass, like Jack McCoy..."

"Who's Jack McCoy?" Cate asked.

"Jack McCoy. Manhattan District Attorney, Jack McCoy? Played by Sam Waterston?"

"This *Law & Order* fetish, it's no good," Cate said.

"Said the woman addicted to *Downton Abbey*."

"Kyle, here's the deal. I love you, probably more than I should. I know you love me and I know you have a disease to do battle with. But I can help you with it if you let me. Normally I'd tell a guy to go fuck himself, pulling a stunt like you did."

"After kicking him in the balls."

"Shut up. I'm being serious here."

"I know."

"I'm willing to travel across three time zones to see if we can make this work," Cate said. "And that's a big deal for me. But we have something and I'd like it to continue. Would you?"

Kyle's immediate answer in his mind was "*Hell yes!*" but he also had the deep, dark fear that it would only be a matter of time before he ended up in the psych ward again. But good god, this woman was everything he ever wanted—except for the being-a-zombie part, which really didn't matter so much. He always assumed that sooner our later he'd let her take a bite out of his ass and join her for all eternity or until all the flesh on their bones was replaced with new and exciting composite plastics. Hunter S. Thompson whispered in his ear: *Buy the ticket. Take the ride.*

"I'm in," Kyle said. "I'm so in."

Cate smiled. They lunged for each other. She felt so cold to the touch. It was perfect.

"Here's the thing," Cate said. "You can get your old job back. We've got a new assignment."

Kyle unclenched her.

"Don't fuckin' say it, Cate," Kyle said.

"Six weeks, tops," Cate said. "It'll be like opening St. Agrippina. Remember the excitement of that? Launching a new resort?"

"There's no way I'm working with Percy Shitballs to open one of his resorts," Kyle said. "And as for it being exciting, you seem to forget that we lured hundreds of unsuspecting civilians to an island to be a hot lunch for zombies. Also, there were explosions and gunfire. Can you promise me the same for this? Because I'd love to duct-tape some C-4 across Percy's mouth. Why the fuck did Dory get into bed with him to begin with?"

"Take it down a notch," Cate said.

"Oh, no you di'int," Kyle said.

"Just listen to me," Cate said. "Dory wants to expand the St. Agrippina brand. She needed a partner with cash and land. She found one. Percy's just a suit, not the partner. And it was easy. Why? Because a couple of awesome creatives put together an ad campaign that filled a resort to capacity in a week's time. Sure, it was for nefarious reasons—which we corrected. But nonetheless, we did good."

That was how it worked in advertising. Create a talking Chihuahua to sell cheap burritos for Taco Bell. People line up to get them, not taking into account the lard content that hardens arteries and puts a drain on the healthcare industry which in turn has a field day charging whatever price it sees fit—but so what, the creative worked *and* won a shit ton of awards. That made Kyle think about Dog, the talking zombie Chihuahua that was Woman's sidekick. He would never sell out like that. Fuck sellout-talking Chihuahuas.

"I'll do it on condition that I'm never in the same room with Percy the Taint Weasel," Kyle said.

"I can present the creative," Cate suggested.

"Okay," Kyle agreed.

"Most importantly, we're gonna keep a close watch on your health. This means lots of exercise, eating well, group therapy and taking your meds."

"Okay."

"Let's get you back on your feet and get out of here."

"Can we do it tomorrow? Bravo's got a *Law & Order* marathon running and it's my favorite *SVU* episodes."

"Sure," Cate said. "If you could just stand up long enough for me to smash your balls in with my Chuck Taylors."

They both smiled behind the fear and trepidation.

*   *   *

Topo Bogomil, having just drained the blood of an Austrian tourist, sat in Café Patrocinio, sipping espresso and thinking about all the various postings he'd been given and how each one seemed to represent how the powers that be felt about him. South of France? They felt he was doing a pretty good job. Same for Spain, the Netherlands, and Northern Ireland—though that one could've been an early sign of things to come. It wasn't easy gauging their reaction to his work. It was a lot like putting a suggestion in a suggestion box that emptied into a black hole. It wasn't until things were wrapped and it was time to move on that he got an inkling of how well he had ared. The next posting, surely; but sometimes there'd be a small token of appreciation: an attaboy pocket watch or maybe some extra-filthy lucre in his bank account.

But there was none of that after the Sao Paulo debacle. Things got messed up fast and when the smoke cleared, there was nothing but carnage and empty hands. Not entirely Topo's fault, but still, shit rolls downhill. It felt bad from the start. The mark was too big a fish; the surroundings too unstable; his crew was jumpy about it from the get-go. Topo didn't listen to his gut on that one and paid the price. He had that same feeling as he sat in Café Partrocinio with his bitter espresso and throbbing gut.

"So this is what 'go fuck yourself' looks like," Topo whispered as he took a sip from the small white porcelain cup. He looked out of the window. The moon waxed crescent, reflecting on the calm waters of the North Atlantic. In the distance, a buoy rang lazily through a light breeze. In a way it was a shame to build such a whorish resort on such a pristine island.

"So it goes," Topo said, quoting Kurt Vonnegut, one of his favorites.

* * *

Xavier Wishburn, formerly Jimmy Dank, felt serenely joyful as he piloted his Grumman G-64—one of nine that he owned as the CEO/pilot of West Indies Air—through the bilious clouds and azure sky. His good friends Kyle Brightman and Cate Hendricks sat in the cabin, listening to Derek & the Dominos (at Cate's request) as they headed home. Business was good for Xavier since the oft-called Zombie Land Rush & Barbecue. St. Agrippina did bangup business and now, with the new resort opening, Xavier was about to make a serious purchase— three CRJ Series regional jets, aircraft he wasn't even instrument-rated for. It was a big deal, which Dory was backing because the Grumman's capacity had become woefully outsized by recent client volume. Though the cruise lines were the bulk of tourist transportation, air travel was still a viable way to get to the island—or now, *islands*.

But for the moment, Xavier was pleased to have Kyle and Cate back. He knew things had been rough for the both of them, but deep down he knew they'd find a way to make it work. Kyle had mentioned to him that they were getting the band back together, which struck Xavier as sincere and maybe a tad overzealous. Probably the meds. It didn't seem to affect Kyle's bullshit detector any. They both thought Percy Merriweather to be a cubicle thug with a grasp of "out of the box" verbiage and an odor of indifference to authenticity. He too wondered why Dory had partnered up with someone who let Percy be the mouthpiece. True, it was a cash infusion and the acquisition of another property, but still, couldn't there be some venture capitalist out there who wasn't a complete charlatan? Nonetheless, it was good news for West Indies Air—something Percy had suggested a name change for.

"The North Atlantic Line, perhaps?" he'd mentioned to Xavier over cracked crab.

"Sounds like a railroad," Xavier had told him, though in actuality, it sounded pretty regal. Xavier took note of his soul departing for greener pastures.

"Ladies and gentlemen, we are now on our final approach to St. Ledo," Xavier said in his soothing pilot voice. "The North Atlantic Oscillation fluctuation at this time is positive, with warm winds coming out of the zonal systems of the South Atlantic. We ask that you please put away all electronic devices. Flight attendants, prepare doors for arrival, crosscheck, and all-call. At this time, if you could remain seated with your belt buckles securely fastened, allowing enough movement to bend over and kiss your asses, I've had too many vodka martinis, God have mercy on us all, here's a little Foghat to send you into the valley of the shadow of death."

Slow Ride blasted out of the cabin speakers. Kyle turned to Cate with a wide grin. "We're getting the band back together!" he shouted over the engine noise, giving a thumbs-up. Cate gave the thumbs-up back, wishing he'd stop saying that.

* * *

Dory Parthenia sat behind her Plexiglas desk, taking a moment to choose her words carefully as she looked at Kyle's bright blue eyes. He did have nice eyes, like shards of broken glass arranged in a circle. But what a pain in the ass. Okay, he was worth the pain. He did good work. The chemistry between him and Cate generated great ad creative despite their drama. It'd taken a while for Dory to learn the *Guidebook for the Caring and Feeding of Kyle Brightman*, but once she did, he never let her down. If anything, being with Cate had a calming effect on him. Domesticity tames the restless mind. That, and sixty milligrams of Citalopram and one hundred and fifty milligrams of Lamotrigine. She was surprised that Cate went after him. Would she do the same for someone she cared about?

She'd built a four-star resort, Dory had. After the reconstruction following the Zombie Land Grab & Barbecue, St. Agrippina had become a premier getaway for middle management and up. She was able to recruit undead from various parts of the globe interested in a 401(k) with "maintenance benefits" in the Bahamas. She also did a fair bit of recruiting from colleges that spewed out grads with useless degrees who kept open minds about working alongside personnel who ate brains. Doing the deal with Percy Merriweather's people would expand the St. Agrippina brand. Dory's hope was to be the South and North Atlantic island destination when the Azores proved too expensive and Aruba was too full of dentists.

But first, get the creative back on track.

"Look Kyle, it's me you're mad at, not Percy. And I get it. I don't blame you. I should've given you a heads-up," Dory said, to disarming affect.

"Yeah, you should've," Kyle said, his selfrighteous indignation deflated by Dory's admonition. "He's like the feeble uncle at Thanksgiving who keeps dropping his dental partials in the mashed potatoes. You can't just kill him, but he was almost unbearable to put up with."

"He's a businessperson just like me, though not as smart," Dory said with a wink. It was true even if it did sound vain. "So whaddaya think? Wanna open the next asskicking resort this side of the West Indies? Be a nice change of scenery for you and Cate. Get you off this island for a bit."

There was a knock at the door. It opened and Cate stuck her smiling face in.

"Just in time," Dory said, waving Cate in. "I was just filling Kyle in on the new resort."

"Awesome," Cate said, closing the door and taking a seat on the second Eames recliner facing Dory's desk. Though she ended up caving in her mentor Atria's skull, Dory retained Atria's style, using the same décor for her office.

"Let's get to it," Dory said. "The new resort is called 'St. Ledo,' named after the Patron Saint of Happiness and Good Hygiene. Anyway, about the hotel…"

"Hold on, D," Kyle said. "We're opening a resort called St. Happy that will appeal to those with good grooming habits?"

"Okay, I didn't pick the name," Dory said. "St. Ledo was a Portuguese saint. The island is situated in the North Atlantic, between Bermuda and the Azores. Percy thought it appropriate given the location."

"That part of your sentence—'Percy thought'—yeah, that makes me wanna staple my large intestine to a race horse," Kyle said.

"I like it," Cate said. "Short, easy to say. We can sell the happiness angle."

"Exactly," Dory said. "The place is a confluence of cultural and historical significance. Okay. I'm quoting Percy, but he's right. The island's a melting pot of influences, from Portugal to Britain on Bermuda to—honest to God—Sephardic Judaism coming out of Spain and the Azores. It's bigger than St. Aggies. Even has a small village, Oliveira, with shopping—very old-world charm meets tiny streams of revenue."

"Didn't the Inquisitions start in Spain?" Kyle said.

"Bygones," Dory said. "The main hotel is smaller than ours, but we'll be offering timeshare cottages situated throughout the island. We're going to cater to a more upscale clientele. We're looking to attract those avoiding the Jimmy Buffett lifestyle. We want Eastern seaborders, Canada, Portugal, Morocco, Miami. We wanna pull from the south, the north, Greenland—this could be big."

"Do you want me to send you back to where you were—unemployed—in Greenland?" Kyle said.

"Come again?" Dory said.

"*Princess Bride*," Cate said.

So that's why she went after him.

"So we're getting the band back together for another big push," Kyle said.

"That seems to be the case," Dory said. "You two ready to rock it?"

Kyle winced.

"What?" Dory said.

"Nothing," Kyle said. "It's just when C-level types make with the hep dialogue I expect us all to jump up with high-fives and a freeze-frame." Kyle rose out of his chair. "Which sounds like a pretty good idea!" He raised his hand, waiting for the others to join them.

"So we're clear," Dory said. "You actually went after him?"

*   *   *

Sari Wysocki sat on the deck of *Candido*, her thirty-foot sailboat, thinking about slicing up cow tongue for human consumption. Working at a deli involved slicing up various kinds of meats and that was something Sari found pleasant—even meditative—but there was just something about cow tongue that repulsed her. It wasn't so much the part of the cow, but what it represented. It was more anthropomorphism than anything else, such as believing a cow could talk. It was similar to the effect one might have naming an animal then having it turn up on your table. To Sari Wysocki, cow tongue represented civility and humanity.

Van Morrison's *And It Stoned Me* rose above deck, putting Sari in a relaxed mood, as if she were a character in a summer read. She made busy work, knitting an orange and gold caftan for the mild weather that slowly took hold of the island formerly known as Queixa. Freakin' developers. Someone made a deal and now her beloved northern island was about to be transformed into another Sandals resort. "St. Ledo?" Wasn't *Ledo* a Boz Scaggs song? Or was it *L.I.D.O*? Whatever. They were promised that business would only improve, which meant working longer hours and spending less time on her boat.

Sari, along with her father, Noam Wysocki, owned the island's only deli. How a Brooklyn-style deli came to be located on an island between Portugal and New York wasn't such a mystery, at least not to her father. He'd married a woman from Lisbon, Catalina Guarda, whom he had met in his father's deli in Flatbush when she came in one day and asked if they sold Francesinha, a Portuguese sandwich. Noam was instantly swept away by the exotic request. It helped that it came out of the full lips of a brunette with deep brown eyes and a figure that his father, Max, called "the origins of sin," which was how he described a comely woman who entered the deli.

It was Catalina's idea to be closer to home and she convinced Noam that pastrami, kugel, brisket, and Francesinha would do well in her part of the world so long as they provided strong espresso to go with it. They relocated to Lisbon but found the city to be too much city. That's when Catalina mentioned an island northeast of the Azores that already had a decent-sized population bound to be grateful for a new dining choice. So they moved to Queixa with one cold case and some deli furniture and opened Koufax's Delicatessen, named after Noam's favorite left-handed pitcher for the Brooklyn Dodgers, Sandy Koufax (there were no Los Angeles Dodgers in Noam's mind). Which was fine with Catalina, as she got to take control of the décor.

Sari was born on Queixa and had an idyllic childhood on an island that had a mixture of culture, religion, and coffee. She was raised Jewish and Roman Catholic, thus cornering the market on Jungian symbolism and food rich in meats and spices. She attended college at Cornell, majoring in anthropology, and ended up with a job in public relations at Edelman, which blackened her heart.

"Whaddya gonna do in Manhattan? Promote the next energy-drink crap you kids love so much, as if coffee weren't enough? Come home, work with your parents. There's no shame in working in the family business. It's an investment. One day your mother and I are gonna set sail for Australia, and we'll need someone reliable to keep things going here," her father had intoned. As timing and the universe would have it, her mother, Catalina, died before Sari made her decision. Sari was told that it was a heart attack. Catalina was standing there next to the crate of salmon on ice in the backroom, and then she was on the floor, dead. They buried her with a simple headstone on a small hill facing the Atlantic Ocean. Noam visited daily, but as time went on and Noam's heart got back on its feet (with a pronounced limp), the visits became weekly, with Noam giving reports on the goings-on in his life, just like you would after a day of work.

Sari came home, choosing to live aboard the Candido, which was docked in the village of Oliveira, a town built of adobe, maple, and stone, on an island full of olive farms. Oliveira was a vacation destination for those who searched hard enough—most travelers opted for the Azores or drifted south to the West Indies—and its town center was a mix of tourist shopping and practicality for the locals. The merchants were swollen with excitement at the prospect of a resort opening on the island. The chamber of commerce on Oliveira had decided to give the village a facelift, with planters hanging from every light pole and lots of streaming lights that advertised, "You're somewhere exotic—spend accordingly." Noam was pleased in that buying-a-used-car kind of way: glad to have it, but would it be trouble down the road? As for the name change, it was universally accepted that renaming an island after a minor saint who was a big fan of flossing was typically American and therefore completely off the mark.

"So it goes," Sari said. She sat aboard Candido, listening to her Van Morrison channel stream in and knitting as the boat lolled slowly, seagulls overhead, the blueish-green Atlantic reflecting the light. It was a good life on the island, no matter what it was called. Maybe the resort would yield a few dates? God knows she could use a little sex, though not so much the romance.

CHAPTER 2

BECAUSE THE RESORT WAS STILL FINISHING construction work, Kyle and Cate's base of operations was located atop Koufax's Delicatessen, in a studio flat that overlooked the bay. It was decorated with plaster walls painted bright orange and aquamarine. Turkish rugs were splayed about, and wooden furniture from what looked like the ninth century dotted the small space. The windows were made from lead glass shaped into arched maple framing. In the center of the studio was a twelve-foot bamboo table with legs scooped out and left unfinished. On it sat two Mac workstations, the industry standard for advertising and design. Kyle's station had two twenty-one-inch monitors while Cate had a laptop—creative penis envy. There was also a digital camera set up with a Mamiya 645DF that had a Leaf Credo back, which Kyle had spotted and got and instantly had given him a boner. There was a fully stocked bar, which, according to Cate, Kyle would not be partaking of since it didn't mix well with his meds, or so the third-year resident had said back in Seattle. Since when did mood stabilizers not include a well-mixed Moscow mule? One thing Kyle did note with disgust was the bright green yoga mat.

"What the hell is that?" Kyle said, pointing to the mat.

"You do yoga now," Cate said. "Also, you hike, swim, and jog."

"Jesus, Mary and—seriously? That's a lotta workin' out. I thought we'd take some nice strolls around town, maybe get something to eat, an Americano perhaps? That's rehabilitation, right?"

"I intend to get your heart rate pumping for at least thirty minutes a day," Cate said. "The only antidote to mental suffering is physical pain."

"Schwarzenegger?"

"Karl Marx."

"In the ballpark."

"We're above a freaking deli!" Kyle said. "How awesome is that? You get the name? Koufax? As in Sandy Koufax? That means it's a New York-style deli. Might even be kosher, not that it matters. Unless you keep kosher. Do Hasidic Jews eat only kosher people? Fuggit."

"You'll be on a strict, two-thousand-calorie-a-day diet consisting of vegetables with protein," Cate said.

"One pound corned beef, mustard, sauerkraut, Russian dressing piled high on fresh rye—the New York reuben—side of macaroni salad, kosher dill, Dr. Brown's root beer. Sweet Jesus, I love this new gig."

"Six ounces of lean corned beef, mustard, sauerkraut, kosher dill, no dressing, no bread, no macaroni salad, mineral water."

"How do you eat a reuben without bread?"

"On a friggin' plate, you chazzer!"

"Don't do that," Kyle said.

"What?" Cate said.

"Curse in Yiddish."

"Why not? You do."

"Yeah, but I nail it."

"Yes, because the Northwest is chock-full of Yiddish."

"Don't be a nishgutnik."

"What's that?"

"Look it up, you Vilde Chaya."

* * *

Sylvia Woodcock had been warned about Kyle and Cate. A loose cannon and a zombie…?

She worked at BBDO in Manhattan. She could handle this. As far as she was concerned they were in-house low-level talent. She was an account supe in the big leagues. She had her own little fiefdom. People jumped to attention when she walked in. Maybe not jumped, but surely took notice. Yeah, it was a perfect setup, except for the part where she told a client that it was absolutely crucial that they understand in no uncertain terms that their piece-of-shit product (another revitalizing skin cream) was not ever going to stick in the minds of the masses beyond the too-good-for-them campaign her agency had put together.

Sometimes in advertising, you speak your mind and are branded a maverick. Other times, they have you escorted out by security forty minutes after the meeting. It was fine with Sylvia. She needed to get out of the city for a while and when her roommate told her about an account job on an island promoting a resort, well, how bad could it be? Hospitality wasn't her category—she'd done her time on T-Mobile—but they were impressed nonetheless. She could handle the whole zombie thing, though she told her friends back in the city that they were Eastern Europeans, most likely Russian. Sylvia Woodcock had lost the ability to be shocked back in early 2007 when she learned that a certain cleansing product used human armpit cheese as an ingredient. That, and seeing the head of a small crocodile sticking out of her toilet. Zombies barely registered. She once dated what she was certain was a Golem. Zombies? Please.

Sylvia stood in front of Koufax's deli, checking her hair: jaw-length blonde, powerful. The kind of haircut that says "this woman doesn't wear scrunchies." Blue-eyed, medium build; she looked down upon the stick women with their tri-athlete ways and crossing their legs just so and marrying mild.

She regarded the deli sign with a smirk. Really? New York deli on an island that celebrated salmon yearly? The name so obvious it could belong to a chain? She went in and ordered an everything bagel with lox and cream cheese and a double espresso, which they called a "Bica"—to Sylvia's mind quaint and pointless. The girl behind the counter told Sylvia the lox was caught from the Tungulaekur River in southern Iceland. "That's impressive, hon," she'd told the deli girl.

She took her order to go, went back outside, and found the door next to the deli that led to the second-floor apartments. The intercom next to the door was labeled *Swordfish*. A nod to the Marx Brothers. Nice. She pressed the button. A moment later the door buzzed and she went in.

* * *

"Sylvia Woodcock wins name of the week," Kyle said as he, Cate, and Sylvia sat around the small round table near the kitchenette. Sylvia was enjoying her bagel and feeling the effects of strong coffee.

"Heh," Sylvia said, sipping her coffee.

"So, BBDO," Kyle said. "How did you fall from grace and end up here?"

Cate shot Kyle a look. The no-filter thing could be tiresome.

"Good question," Sylvia said. "I was shitcanned. How did you step up your game to land this gig?"

"For the win," Kyle said. He decided right then, Sylvia was gonna work out fine. Plus, she was hot in that stiletto-heeled-dominatrix/account-supervisor kind of way.

"So, I've had a chance to look over your work on the flight out here and have to be honest, it's pretty good," Sylvia said. "I understand from… Dory, is it?"

"Yeah, Dory."

"As in *Finding Nemo* Dory?" Sylvia asked.

"Right." Kyle said.

"Anyway, Dory told me that the campaign was a big success, that you had the occupancy rate filled within a week. Was that true?"

"It was," Cate said. "It helped that we were offering package deals that were crazy cheap."

"So I saw," Sylvia said. "How was that affordable?"

Kyle and Cate looked at each other. Should they tell her about the Zombie Land Rush & Barbecue? She already knew about the zombie thing.

"Building brand awareness," Cate said. "They were willing to spend to get it."

"Uh huh," Sylvia said. "Now, you're a zombie. Do I have that right?"

Jesus, these New Yorkers, thought Cate. "Dead as a doornail," she replied.

"I could tell from the handshake," Sylvia said. "Well, anyway, you look amazing. Not at all what I expected. Same for Dory. What's your secret? Because I'd love to get some of what you use."

"It's the quality of brain matter that gives me my healthy sheen," Cate said drolly.

Sylvia gave Cate a knowing smile then took a huge bite of her bagel.

"So, did they mention how much time we had on this?" Kyle asked.

Sylvia nodded with her mouth full and pulled out a file folder from her leather Fendi bag, she slappeing it on the table, opening it, then passing out two pieces of paper.

"Here's the timeline," Sylvia said, mouth still full of bagel. "It's a little tighter than I'd like but doable."

Kyle and Cate reviewed the timeline. Sylvia was right: there was time but not much for procrastination. She also handed out a rationale complete with audience survey and target messaging. Kyle felt the slight tightening of his sphincter as he read the rationale. It sounded dangerously close to being told what to do.

"Boilerplate," Sylvia said. "You guys nailed it the first time around. I assume you know what's expected and what has to be executed."

"Yeah, we're pretty clear on that," Kyle said, feeling his angst float away.

"Good. Then, what say we finish up here and go find the bar you two will be working from."

"I love you, Sylvia Woodcock," Kyle said.

"Kyle doesn't drink," Cate said.

"He does if he works in advertising," Sylvia said. "Unless he's a boozehound. Are you a twelve-stepper, hon?"

"I'm on some meds," Kyle said.

"Paxil? Zoloft? Citalopram? Wellbutrin? Never mind. I'm on enough Lexapro to kill a fat elephant but I still gotta have my Dark 'n' Stormies to get through the day."

"Again. I love you, Sylvia Woodcock."

Cate frowned. Was it that easy to slide off the program? Was she gonna have to play nanny, constantly reminding Kyle about the rules?

"He's fresh from the psych ward so it might be a good idea that he follow doctor's orders," Cate said, her eyes burning through Kyle's.

"The loony bin, huh?" Sylvia asked.

Kyle was shocked and a little bit hurt. How could she blurt out something like that? Something so personal. Did she not have a filter? He would never have done that to her.

Actually, he would.

"I can order a Shirley Temple while we work," Kyle said, smiling at Cate.

Sylvia turned to Cate. "So it's like that between you two, is it?"

*   *   *

Rupert Jagger (venture capitalist) aka Louis Pasternak (textiles importer), aka Giles Millford, (shipping magnate), aka Tor Jurgenfrost (whaling captain), aka Milos Gabichon (poet), aka Liev Lev (Province of Riga Mayor), aka Lolo Bentencourt (landowner), aka Viscount Falmouth of Bhurtpore aka King Ferdinand II of Aragon (Royal Scrivener) sat outside Café Renaldo, sipping an espresso and feeling calmed by the night air that wafted gently across his closecropped Van Dyke. It was rare that he had a chance to sit quietly by himself and admire the stars, the occasional laughter from nearby tables, the clicking of heels on the cobblestone street, and the way a string of bare-bulb lights swayed lazily.

The last year had been nothing more than architectural plans plus meetings with contractors, landscape designers, restaurant supply reps, flatware reps, alcohol distributors, linen manufacturers—this was his first foray into being a hotelier and already he was wondering if this was the right investment. But then, it was more than an investment. It was an obligation. The lottery numbers had been called throughout the centuries and, after all of this time, his number had finally come up. Which was something he'd dreaded all of these years.

And then there was the dubious success of St. Agrippina. True, many zombies were killed off during that feeding frenzy, but that was mostly due to poor planning and the lack of vision by the resort owner, Jackson Farraday. Still, the numbers of people it brought in were hard to ignore. The St. Agrippina case study was a complete success and failure, and his people wanted to duplicate it. Modern-day marketing at its best. Duplicate the failure right up until the failure part. Zag instead of zig. Swoop and poop. Ahead of the skis. Plug and play.

It was never like this back when he ruled Sicily.

"Flash feeding," they called it. Populate, feed, move on. Leave no witnesses, no transformations, no minion creations, pure smash and grab. He'd formed a partnership with one of the zombies who had survived and flourished, Dory Parthenia; he had plans to repeat her success right down to using the same marketing team. Zombies already had a reputation;—"Doveryai no proveryai" aka "Trust but verify"—but Dory seemed hellbent on success at any cost, and that was a kind of corporate ruthlessness he could exploit.

So Rupert Jagger was now in the resort business. He sipped his Brazilian espresso. The Portuguese coffee culture had made its way to St. Ledo. He worked diligently to call the island by its newly branded name—a gift of the marketing genius, Percy—and enjoyed the offerings of the Iberian peninsula, even the heavy Roman Catholicism that Rupert had admired through the centuries for its iconography and pageantry and blood. Soon, he'd be back in his world of meetings and phone calls and email and texting and the myriad ways people of the modern age said, "I'll be there in five minutes." God bless them and their precious plasma.

* * *

The second tavern would be called Saint Bobo's in honor of Saint Bobo, who vowed after warring with the Muslims at Fraxinet around the 980s that he would renounce war and become a pilgrim devoted to the wellbeing of widows and orphans. Thierry Delassix was stressed but excited about opening another tavern on another resort island. His current tavern on St. Agrippina's was doing well, and his small-batch bourbon, St. Bertold, was still highly touted and difficult to find, as intended.

Did he really want to expand his empire to include another tavern? Dory had sort of talked him into it and now he wondered when it was he had decided to be a spirits whore. It wasn't for the money, half of which he donated to various charities in the West Indies; it was more the adventure of it. Since the Zombie Land Rush & Barbecue, life had seemed a bit wanting. Sure, firing large-caliber weapons was fun, but it was the camaraderie he missed. When he learned that Kyle and Cate would be working on the new resort as well, he was all in. He didn't see them that often, as St. Agrippina kept them busy and well, time had passed, and habits had changed. Plus, Kyle had left for a while.

Thierry needed help opening the second tavern and found it in Xavier's cousin, LeRoi Wishburn, a recent Howard graduate with an MFA that rendered him completely useless in an already tight job market. LeRoi was hyperactive and could juggle composing an opera and cooking coq au vin (for LeRoi was skilled in the French culinary arts, as a hobby) while expounding on the differences between Cro-Magnons and Neanderthals (we're Cro-Mags; *Fox & Friends* are Neanderthals). This worked well with Thierry's laissez-faire style of management.

So sat Kyle and Cate inside the walls of St. Bobo's, with its adobe and cedar beam confines that were lit by gas lanterns, and decorated with checkered tablecloths and a bar carved out of African sapele. Affixed to a beam at the end of the bar was a brass bell salvaged from the French frigate *Flamand*, later renamed *Arc en Ciel*, built in 1667. Below it, etched in a brass plate: EN CAS DE UNFRIENDLIES MORTS-VIVANTS, aka IN CASE OF UNDEAD UNFRIENDLIES.

The sun had just set as Cate sipped a Moscow mule from her copper cup while Kyle drank a Shirley Temple from a straw, deciding that if he couldn't drink he was going to fart as much as possible because, fuck it. Kyle had his pad of newsprint on the bar, his fine-point black Sharpie twirling in his hand. Cate had her laptop. The wi-fi in St. Bobo's was excellent.

"Why can't we just lift the concept from the St. Agrippina campaign and call it a day?" Kyle asked.

"Yeah, that's one approach," Cate said. "Gimme more."

"Give you more—listen to you with your alcohol-fueled work ethic. This Shirley Temple's not inspiring me, but go ahead, imbibe."

"Stop being such a pussy and give me a concept," Cate said.

"Here's one: '*Come to St. Ledo's because it's not full of zombies.*'"

Cate wrote it down. "We're in the beginning stages of desperation."

"So we're not going after poor people, aka the flyover states," Kyle said.

"Listen to you, you classist."

"Is that a real thing?"

"Hold on," Cate said, Googling it. "According to Wikipedia, Classism is 'prejudice or discrimination on the basis of social class.' Let's use it in a sentence. 'My name is Kyle Brightman and I feel inferior to others because I've never found the clitoris and have a world view dominated by classism.'"

"That's fuckin' classy," Kyle said.

"We're skewing upscale here…"

"Define upscale," interrupted Kyle.

"People unlike us who can afford luxury vacations."

"Continue."

Cate took a sip of her Moscow mule.

"How's your Moscow mule?" Kyle asked.

"Delicious," Cate said. "We're selling upscale luxury comfort on an island in the North Atlantic, a place not known for exotic luxury, with various influences ranging from Portugal to Delaware. The weather, like the culture, is a mixture of temperate and humid sub-tropical, the cuisine is fish, fish, and more fish along with olives and a wide assortment of baked goods. Also, there's a deli. Several cafes, shopping brand names, historic sights…"

"Are there?" Kyle asked.

"A place this old? C'mon."

"What music do have in your head right now?" Kyle asked.

"Y'mean what am I listening to?"

"Yeah."

Cate pulled up her Spotify screen.

"I'm still stuck in the seventies…"

"Jesus H…"

"Hold on. I'm swinging the pendulum away from the pop hits to the heavier and more grassrootsy thing. I've been swapping out playlists with Xavier."

"Seventies rock. How *Reservoir Dogs* of you," Kyle said, tapping his Sharpie against his half-empty glass. "Zep?"

"Check."

"Aerosmith."

"Check."

"Heart. Alice Cooper. The Sab. Sweet?"

"*Ballroom Blitz.*"

"That skirts the pop thing," Kyle said.

"Van Halen, Tull, you forgot The Who…"

"Not sure on the Van Halen."

"Seventies and beyond rock," Cate said. "I can't help my pop ways."

"Boston."

"'I see Marianne walking away…'" Cate sang.

"Grass-rootsy… Creedence?"

"CCR."

"Not The Dead. I don't get The Dead," Kyle said.

"Then you're alone in the universe," Cate said.

"The Stones?"

"Goes without saying."

"Thin Lizzy, yo!"

"Check."

"So that's the soundtrack to the campaign," Kyle said. "Stoner music."

"I've got *More Than a Feeling* stuck in my head, which isn't unique," Cate said.

"Hmm…"

"'…More than a fee-lain,'" Cate sang in a higher voice.

"Could be something there," Kyle said, writing the song title down on his pad. He drew a small mountain range with a sun and a church tower then scribbled down the lyric Cate had just sung.

"What about another song?" Kyle said. "'I can see for miles and miles and miles…'"

"'So many people have come and gone,'" Cate countersang. "'Their faces fade as the years go by.'"

"How about 'St. Ledo's Calling,' right? Instead of *London's Calling*."

"That just hurts to hear it mentioned."

"Yeah," Kyle said. "That never happened."

From a table in the back, Topo Bogomil sat with his whiskey sour, wincing along with Cate. *St. Ledo's calling*? As keen as his hearing was, he'd been able to hear their work session from the back of the room and found the whole of it painful. These were the ones behind the St. Agrippina success? What was Rupert thinking? Topo felt he could do a better job and soon found himself thinking about promotional ideas. So much so that he took a pen out and began jotting them down on his cocktail napkin. The magic of advertising conceptualization was in the air.

* * *

The tattoo artist was nearly finished. It had taken four hours of a second sitting to complete it. It helped that the tattoo was going across a back of considerable size and—to the tattoo artist's delight—hairless.

The tattoo was a quote: *The Marines I have seen around the world have, the cleanest bodies, the filthiest minds, the highest morale, and the lowest morals of any group of animals I have ever seen. Thank God for the United States Marine Corps. –Eleanor Roosevelt, 1945.* At the top were two flags crossed, the stars and stripes and a flag with the Special Forces insignia on it.

"We're done," the tattoo artist said, leaning back in his chair.

"Great. I thought you said it would hurt," Oscar Pilson said.

"*Pft,*" said the partially paralyzed talking Chihuahua, Dog, shaking his head.

"Howzit it look, hon?" Oscar asked Woman, who sat in a nearby chair flicking a page of *People* magazine.

"Did you know Kim Kardashian has a degree in economics?" Woman asked.

"We gotta keep you off the mainland, hon. It's doing terrible things to your brain," Oscar said. "So? The tat?"

"Hmm? Oh. Yeah, looks great. Nice sentiment," Woman said.

"I just got an Eleanor Roosevelt quote inked across my back for all eternity, and you're telling me about celebrity goings-on? What is it?"

"I'm bored," Woman said, licking her thumb then flipping a magazine page.

"I told you getting a tat was like watching paint dry," Oscar said.

"I'll take that as a compliment," the tattoo artist said, spreading plastic wrap across the tat.

"I'm not bored about that," Woman said.

"Kee-righst, do we have to have this conversation again?" Oscar asked.

"Yes, we do," Woman said, tossing the magazine onto a side table. "I know you're full of shit when you say you don't miss it."

"I don't."

"Like hell. You're a warrior, not a complacent small business owner."

"I'm a *retired* warrior and the small business is now medium-sized. Isn't it enough to march terrified ordinary fuckin' citizenry through dank jungle and be well paid for what we call a Sunday morning stroll? Not all soldiers yearn for the kick of an M-14 in their golden years..."

"You are not in your 'golden years'," interrupted Woman. "Why don't we go shopping for walkers while we're in Miami? Maybe some Depends? They might make 'em in camo."

"Aw hon," Oscar moaned.

"I haven't shot anything since that rabid warthog, and even then, it was outgunned."

"What would you have me do, hon? Get us inserted into some hot spot in Afghanistan? I hear Syria's got some action on the ground."

"Could you?" Woman asked with too much enthusiasm.

"Don't even," Oscar said. "Look, we got a good thing going in the West Indies. We live in a tropical paradise, business is good, we have a 401(k), you and I are solid."

"Maybe we could catch a few Haitian gunrunners?"

"You'd want to go down to Santo Domingo, where the Ozama River outflows. There's action going on there."

"So you do have an itchy trigger finger!" Woman said.

"Aw, hon."

"Just consider it," Woman said. "I knew you weren't out of the game. It's who we are. We have the rest of our lives to sit on a beach, sipping Coronas. Just not now."

"Speak for yourself," Dog said.

The tattoo artist stared at the talking Chihuahua and decided to lay off the amyl nitrate.

*　*　*

Luria de Graciosa, as far as hospital administrators went, was an agent of mischievous altruism. She'd been with St. Hermens Clinic for nine years and had not once toed the company line, despite what it cost her in promotions and friends. It was a medium-sized clinic with the politics of a major hospital.

Often the subject of both ridicule and fear, Luria saw herself as the patron saint of getting shit approved. Due to her efforts, St.

Hermens was the first hospital in the North Atlantic to get an MRI machine. She did it by putting together a three-hundred-page cost/benefit analysis and population growth index based on age, sex, income, malady, weather conditions, housing, and tidal charts, and then had those findings endorsed by Johns Hopkins, Massachusetts General, Mayo Clinic, Cleveland Clinic, UCLA Medical Center, Northwestern Memorial, and the Barcelona Centre for International Health Research. She gave speeches at town halls, gathered signatures and wrote editorials. By the end of it, the members of the St. Hermens board of directors (all three of them) begged her to get an MRI machine—top of the line, equipped with personnel to run it.

That, for Luria de Graciosa, was amateur hour.

Luria sat at her desk located in the morgue of the hospital—a petty torment by her supervisor, which, much to his chagrin, Luria loved. She brought in hydrangeas that she kept lit with thousand-watt magnalume lamps, put up prints by Picasso, Rauschenberg, and Renoir, and added an overstuffed leather chair and a Turkish rug. She loved the quiet, mixed with the low volume sounds of Maria Callas (whom she resembled) floating by the cold chamber doors that held the cadavers in their post-mortal-coil state.

In Luria's hands was a vial of blood. Her respect and awe of such a natural element of the world was also the cause of her stress, for not a day went by that there wasn't a complaint about the desperate shortage of blood at St. Hermens and the local clinics in the surrounding area. They did blood drives that helped somewhat. But still, the small hospital on Queixa—Luria refused to call it by its new name—had barely enough blood on hand to cover the local township.

How could the entire country of Portugal be short of blood? For that matter, Spain and Morocco? She'd gone as far awa as the States for blood, but they were tight, as well. How, in a world overflowing with humanity, could there be such a short supply of forearms to take a pint from?

*   *   *

The township of the island formerly known as Queixa had a population of eighteen thousand. Each family who resided there seemed to have a unique story as to how they ended up on a smallish

island formed from volcanic rock that spiraled from the depths
of the North Atlantic. Encircled by the Gulf Stream, the North
Atlantic Drift, and the Canary Current, Queixa was historically an
island used for replenishing supplies for whalers and smugglers.
Entranced by the tropical climate and mild winters, many who came
to re-stock ended up staying. Folklore had it that several treasures
were stashed throughout the island which might explain the wealth
of a few local families who claimed to have made their money in the
whaling and olive trade.

Once largely unpolluted by tourism, Queixa's cobblestone
streets became lined with shops and bed-and-breakfasts that created its own tourism economy, thanks to such publications as *AARP*,
AAA, and adventure pubs like *Outdoor* and *National Geographic
Expeditions*. Art galleries, two general stores, gift shops, a high-end
salon and spa, brand-name clothing shops, a smoke shop, several
restaurants, two movie theatres, a playhouse, more than dozen
cafes, and a rug merchant (known to be a money-laundering front
for Eastern European mobsters) occupied colorful adobe storefronts
with placards that dated some of the buildings to the 1600s. There
was a local historical society where you could trace the history of
Queixa; it displayed artifacts from as far away as Greenland and
Nova Scotia, the Western Sahara and Portugal. The food on Queixa
was fantastic—and now there was a Brooklyn–style deli!

One might ask, with such a melting pot of cultures, how exactly
did vampires enter the equation?

*   *   *

"It doesn't blow," Sylvia said, looking at the wall of work Kyle and
Cate had pinned up.

Kyle sucked heavily on his straw causing his Shirley Temple to
gurgle as the final sip went into his mouth. He'd become addicted
to Shirley Temples to the point of buying his own ginger ale and
grenadine to keep at the studio. Cate had informed him he could be
more manly and drink an Arnold Palmer or Roy Rogers, but Kyle
said a Shirley Temple was the only one, among the three, with a set
of balls. Cate had no idea what that meant, but let it go.

"'Sat right?" Kyle said, already prickly.

"You've got some interesting thoughts going on here. I wonder if you shouldn't take them farther," Sylvia said.

Kyle gave Sylvia his dead-eyed stare. *Just who is the creative director here, huh, Sylvia? Because it sure as shit isn't you.* The pain Kyle felt was real. Would he ever escape the opinions of those who were less than capable of having them? He didn't care if Sylvia played in the big leagues. Kyle knew what good creative was, and there was some good creative tacked up on the wall. *It doesn't blow. Know what does? You, Sylvia Woodcock. You blow.*

Cate could feel the internal combustion building in Kyle. "I think we have some good direction here," she said. "Pretty good for a first round."

Kyle swiveled his head toward Cate, his face taking on a tint of red.

"We definitely have some things worth fleshing out," Cate said.

"Agreed," Sylvia said. "I like the whole 'Boston' thing. *More than a feeling.* I doubt we could get the rights, though."

"Yeah. I dunno. Just couldn't shake that vibe," Cate said. "More the words than the music—something about it being more than a feeling. I dunno."

"No, I get it," Sylvia said. "I would keep going with that one. Okay, Kyle. You can quit calling me a know-nothing amateur in your head and spill it."

"Who died and made you C.D.?" Kyle spat.

"What else?"

"We've made a good run of it without any fucking 'creative direction.' Sure, we might be operating in a vacuum, but fuckin' A, it works. Now we gotta put up with your shit because you got bounced from the bigs and now you're gonna position yourself as the firewall to the client, who, by the way, has already given us carte blanche to bang out whatever we see fit. Goddammit sonofabitch motherfuckin' shit!"

"Anything else?"

"Fucking fuckity fuck!"

"Finished?"

"Cockballs."

"Good," Sylvia said. "You gotta let that shit fly."

Kyle took a deep breath. He felt relief. Sylvia got it. She was one of us. Glad to have her.

"I'm on your side," Sylvia said. "But Percy Merriweather is not. And you're gonna have to put work in front of him. Correction. Cate's gonna have to put work in front of him. I'm not letting you in the same ZIP code as Percy."

"Agreed," Kyle said.

"There's some good stuff up here," Sylvia said. "But you know you gotta push it. I mean, you get that, right?"

"We do," Cate said.

"Kyle?"

"I'm good," Kyle said. "But we've got some good stuff to work with, yeah?"

"You do," Sylvia said. She was impressed with Kyle's bipolar train of thought. From enraged to being on board in, what? Thirty seconds? Mark of a true creative. She was glad to have him off the sauce. Cate obviously knew how to handle him. And her work was a nice counterbalance to Kyle's mess of ideas. *I mean, really. "St. Ledo calling?" Jesus.* However, the idea about being the only place on earth to eat matzah ball soup and buy a handwoven sweater from Iceland was good. Could make for some fun headlines.

"Get your asses back to Saint Bobo's and give me a second round, then," Sylvia said. "But first, let's get some deli."

"She's all right, this one," Kyle said to Cate, his thumb pointing toward Sylvia.

Cate just looked at him and wondered how she'd fallen for such an amalgam of psychosis.

CHAPTER 3

SHE HATED IT, SLICING UP COW TONGUE. No matter how she did it, Sari would never get used to it. Gutting fish? Separating cow ribs? It's all good. Her dad thought it was funny to have her slicing tongue because what she didn't realize was that, as she sliced, her own tongue hung out just beyond her lips. To Noam, that was funny.

Sylvia, Kyle, and Cate had taken a booth at Koufax's and were awaiting their orders. It was of note to Sylvia that both Kyle and Cate gave Sari the once-over when she took their orders. Him, he was easy to get. He was male. It's what they did. But Cate? Perhaps there was more to her than even Kyle understood? Sexual-identity fluidity went with ad agency life like Ryan Seacrest and taupe hotel carpeting. It wasn't a woman looking over her possible competition. No. It was more a look that one would associate with hunger. She was a zombie. Perhaps a bisexual one?

"Kyle, order up!" Sari shouted from behind the cold case. Kyle leapt out of his seat.

"Someone's hungry," Sylvia said.

"Aaand how," Cate said.

Sari had the plates of food ready next to the register.

"Lean pastrami, Swiss, no bread. Rueben and the lox with olives," Sari said without looking up.

"I should Instagram this," Kyle said.

"That would be original," Sari said. "Not a lot of pictures of food floating out there."

Well, that was a lousy line. "I'm kidding," Kyle said. "I meant, for after the lunch."

He didn't mean that. It just… came out.

"Oookay then," Sari said with a tight grin.

"How long has the deli been open here?" Kyle asked, trying his level best to erase the previous twenty seconds.

"Before I was born," Sari said. She had orders to fill.

"So, in the nineties," Kyle said.

"Would you like a side of horseradish with that line?" Sari asked.

"Not a line. Just curious about a deli on an island hundreds of miles away from New York."

"They have delis in California, you know. Even the flyover states."

Kyle smiled at the flyover-state reference.

"Point taken," Kyle said. "And yes, I'll take the horseradish."

"I'll bring it out to you and your girlfriend, is it?" Sari asked.

Kyle looked over his shoulder. "Try *girlfriends,*" he said.

Sari found that a decent recovery. She smiled at him and went for the horseradish. Noam had picked up on the conversation.

"Give me the horseradish," he said. He wasn't about to let some two-timing sad sack put a move on his daughter. That's how he referred to Kyle in his mind. Noam still used idioms from New York in the fifties. "Sad sack," "weisenheimer," "cornball," and "sap" were all words Noam used with frequency and just the right amount of East Coast to make them work.

"Horseradish for the eyeball," Noam said, setting down a small serving dish containing the white substance. He gave Kyle a look that said, "Schmuck."

"Thanks," Kyle said, wilting under the glance.

"How do you like the olives?" Noam asked Sylvia.

"Fabulous," Sylvia said.

"They're locally grown," Noam said.

"What isn't farm-to-table these days?" Sylvia asked.

"Ah, but these are different," Noam said. "These olives, they're blessed."

"Really now?"

"Really," Noam said. "They've been grown on hallowed ground, these olives. The first olive trees were planted in 1641 by St. Irene of La Guardia, a patron saint of brine and protectorate of blood."

"Hold on," Kyle said. "Irene of an airport?"

Cate backhanded Kyle's shoulder.

"St. Irene of La Guardia came from the Campo de La Guardia, one of the regions of Spain most heralded for its winemaking. The vintners of Vino de Pago often referred to their wine as part of themselves, their blood."

"So, St. Irene, protector of wine," Kyle said. "I can get behind that."

"You. Cram some sandwich in that cakehole of yours. We're learning here," Sylvia said. "Sorry about my friend. He works in advertising."

"Ah," Noam said, as if that in fact explained the rude outbursts.

"Please, continue," Cate said.

"Irene of La Guardia spent several years abroad, in Italy. She was to be a nun, dedicating her life to Christ, and was to remain a virgin. A monk, one of her teachers, made advances on Irene one night as they prayed. She refused him. Being a virgin was rife with complications, including telling your boss that no means no. The monk was angry and gave Irene a drink that bloated her stomach. He then told people she was with child. Talk about sin. But this monk was more than a letch. He decided that if he couldn't have her one way, he'd have her another. He came to her at night—some say he never showed his face during daylight. He came for her soul, but she drove a wooden stake through his heart, destroying his soulless being, instead. Irene returned to Spain, where she swore she would be a protectorate of blood. But not wine. No. The blood of humanity."

Silence. Kyle's legs pumped up and down as if he needed to urinate. He looked around the table, begging for permission to speak.

"Go on," Sylvia said.

"She drove a wooden stake through a monk?" Kyle asked, surprised. "First. That is awesome. Second. We're talking about vampires, right?"

Noam looked into Kyle's eyes.

"Trust me on this," Kyle said. "I can handle the truth. Boy, can I handle the truth. Cate, tell him. Seriously. I'm all about the paranormal."

If Cate had blood running through her veins instead of a unique mixture of formaldehyde and a patented bonding element, she'd have been red. She gave him a serious pinch on his thigh.

"Why are the olives in need of a blessing?" Sylvia asked.

"The olives, for the people of Queixa, are a symbol of life. So long as the olives continue to grow, there will be life," Noam said.

"Getting back to the monk-staking," Kyle said.

"Dad? Hello? Customers here," Sari shouted from behind the counter. Noam gave a broad smile and quick wink to Kyle then went to make food for the masses.

"You know what this means?" Kyle said.

"I do," Sylvia said. "Olives make a good pairing with Pinot Noir and it sounds like we've hit the jackpot for both."

"Pairings... no!" Kyle said. "I can't believe this shit is happening again. We have to stop work on the resort campaign immediately."

"No, no," Cate said, shaking her head. "It's not what you think. That was an anomaly. Things are different here..."

"How are they different?" interrupted Kyle. "Huh? How are they different than what happened on St. Agrippina? I'm telling you, last time was zombies. This time—vampires. We're working for vampires. We're ringing the dinner bell for a bunch of bloodsucking cretins. I'm out. I'm out. I had this feeling deep in my gut. 'Haven't you been down this road before, Kyle?' I ignored it. It's not the bipolar mishigas talking. I have to get off this island, like, right now. All of us do. Right now. Don't even finish your sandwiches. I'll go get Xavier and we can catch the next flight out of here. C'mon. Get up, we gotta go!"

Kyle was out of his seat, motioning the others to join him. Sylvia popped an olive in her mouth while Cate rubbed her forehead vigorously.

"Let's go, let's go!" Kyle said.

"Don't make a scene, Kyle," Cate said.

"Don't make a scene?" Kyle hissed. "Look around you! All of these people? They're gonna lose their blood. It's gonna be drained out of them like blood draining out of a congressman's dick after a glory-hole session. We have to go."

"Now, *that's* an analogy," Sylvia said. "Listen, hon. Sit down. I don't care if the ghosts of the Mongolian Horde are invading, we're gonna get that campaign locked down and ready for launch. Cate, I think now's a good time to break the no-alcohol vow of chastity and get this kid a drink."

"I agree," Cate said. "Maybe several. Kyle, you need to take it down a notch."

"Are you kidding me?" Kyle asked. "You're springing that on me, now?"

"Now's the perfect time," Cate said. "Listen, your undead girl-friend's not denying the existence of vampires, just ones running a resort on an island in the middle of the fucking…"

Then it dawned on Cate, like the buildup of pain from a dentist's drill. Kyle might be right. She felt the room turn on its axis. It was surreal. In what felt like moments but was, in reality, half an hour, she found herself on a bar stool in St. Bobo's nursing a Moscow mule with Kyle and Sylvia, the room finishing its spin, the cool mix of ginger beer and vodka running down her throat.

"Keep drinking. Both of you," Sylvia said. Kyle and Cate obeyed. Sitar music ebbed and flowed around them as they set down their drinks on the bar, looking like kindergartners at a lunch table with their hands resting in their laps after a sip of chocolate milk. It was a messy business getting the two of them out of the deli and into the bar. Sylvia felt like she was in charge of a couple of patients post-elec-tro-convulsive therapy as she ushered them to a couple of barstools. Joaquin, the bartender LeRoi had hired to work at St. Bobo's, looked up from his laptop as Sylvia ordered Kyle and Cate to sit on the stools.

"Moscow mule," Cate had muttered.

"Same," Kyle had followed with.

"Make it three," Sylvia had said, taking a stool. "You guys have a thing for this drink."

And there they were, drinking, possibly hallucinating the sitar music—which they weren't; Joaquin was a fan of Ravi Shankar—and trying to find a solution, any solution that had a different outcome than their reliving St. Agrippina all over again. Whatever took place on that island had done quite a number on them.

"So it wasn't a gas line explosion on St. Agrippina?" Sylvia asked, feeling pity for the mess of humanity on barstools that sat before her.

"It was zombies," Cate said. "My people."

"Bad zombies," Kyle said, eyes on the bar. "Very bad zombies. Hungry, too."

"So what was the plan? Eat a bunch of tourists?" Sylvia asked.

"Not a bunch," Kyle said. "A shit ton. Our campaign was a success."

"Ahh," Sylvia said.

"We can't let it happen again," Kyle said.

"Like you're the first ad creatives to come up with an ad campaign that's success had an adverse reaction on the general public and world at large?" Sylvia asked. "Please. McDonald's? Ford? Tampax? Take a number, kids. The list is long."

"Tampax?" Kyle said.

"Toxic shock syndrome," Cate said.

Good. They were coming back to the world. Sylvia had had a moment's pause when she thought she might have to farm out the work, which would have made the deadline impossible.

"That's the business we're in," Sylvia said. "There is virtually no product on earth that we shill for that doesn't have an opposite and equal repercussion on people, the environment, even legislation."

"What about UNICEF?" Kyle asked.

"UNICEF has a CEO. 'Nuff said," Sylvia replied.

"Damn. That's cold," Kyle muttered. He took a sip from his copper cup. "I like this drink very much."

"Course you do, hon," Sylvia said. "So? What do we have in the way of proof that the island is covered with vampires, other than the word of a deli owner? Hm?"

"How about for starters, me," Cate said. "You could've had this same conversation about my kind last week."

"I *did* have that conversation last week," Sylvia said. "And I thought it was bullshit until I met Dory. I can only make assumptions until I have proof."

"That's crazy," Kyle said. "Do you think Uma Thurman exists?"

"She does. I met her."

"Is she tall in real life?"

"She is. Gorgeous skin, too. Bitch."

"You know what I mean," Kyle said.

"I don't," Sylvia said. "I believe what's in front of me. The rest I take on faith and what side of the bed I woke up on."

"So you're good with zombies, but vampires are no fucking way?" Cate asked, incredulous.

"It's a simple rule for living," Sylvia said. "So, about the campaign. We've got more work to do."

"What if meet an actual vampire?" Kyle asked. "Then can we leave the island?"

"Depends on the vampire," Sylvia said. "Cate here's a good zombie. What do you say to that."

"Okay, so if we meet an asshole vampire, can we leave?"

"If they're an asshole AND a vampire, then we'll consider an exit strategy," Sylvia said.

"Pinky swear?" Kyle said.

"Shut up and drink," Sylvia said. "Now that you're back on the sauce, I expect better work."

*　*　*

From Joaquin's drink blog, *Beba!*

"Mau Boa Mistura" or "Wicked Good Mixture."

Whenever I feel like the North Atlantic is sending me indoors to escape the tidal chill, I like to put together what I call, "Calma Fervoso." Take one part type O negative (or zero south of the equator), mix with jigger of Agave Dos Mil Tequila Blanco Grand Reserve (or similar), two Galega olives (pitted), a dash of kosher sea salt, and a pinprick of hot sauce. I use "The Demystified Archangel" for that subtle kick. Now, for the truly adventurous, place contents into a steel butter-melting pot (or similar), run it through a warm room, then serve in your favorite coffee mug. "Mais vale prevenir do que remediar" (better safe than sorry).

*　*　*

"We're travel pimps, but when we book, say, Leonardo and guests for ten days on a yacht anchored off the coast of, I dunno, Ascension Island in the South Atlantic, we become pimps with million-dollar spiked heels."

Rolf Nesbitt had no idea what that meant. He nodded as if he understood, but he was clueless. He'd been warned about that when he took the job. That Philomena, whose name he doubted was real, would spit out idioms, analogies, metaphors, similes, euphemisms, colloquialisms, and epithets at an alarming rate. It was a prestige gig, being the assistant to a travel agent for the idle rich and famous. How it got him a step closer to selling a screenplay, he wasn't sure. His friends thought it was a great way to make connections. Rolf thought it was a great way to get discounted travel.

"So, what's this new account, St. Ledo's?" Rolf asked. He and Philomena were at Dan Tana's for lunch. Wine bottles hung from the ceiling in woven baskets, which set Rolf on edge. Who puts wine bottles over the heads of customers living in an earthquake zone like Southern California? It was one of many hangouts for celebrities. Kevin Bacon was at a nearby table with someone not famous. Rolf wondered if someone he knew knew the guy having lunch with Kevin Bacon.

"Yet another island resort," Philomena said, shoveling chicken parm into her mouth. Philomena was like that. Thousand-dollar earings and the table manners of a longshoreman.

"Are we booking it yet?" Rolf asked.

"We're about to," Philomena said. "I'm thinking along the lines of Sarah Jessica and Matthew, a few Gettys, Kathy Griffin."

Rolf wrinkled his nose.

"Not a fan?"

"How about Zach Galifianakis?"

"He's a handful," Philomena said.

An agent from CAA walked by, smiling at Philomena. "Roger," she said as he passed, then to Rolf. "Bestiality."

Rolf almost spit out his mineral water.

"It's true," Philomena said. "Ask around. This whole town is like one big preschool full of twitching little bodies lacking any impulse control."

Rolf wondered if one day he'd be lucky enough to be one of those preschoolers. Philomena sighed. That meant she wanted to be asked what she was thinking. By now, Rolf knew to follow through.

"What's weighing on you, dear?" Rolf asked.

"Oh, it's nothing," Philomena said. "I'd like to do something different, something for the good of something. Something… to be proud of besides the money."

"You donate to 'Save the Marmot,'" Rolf said. "There's the new LaCrosse Field charity event at Harvard-Westlake that you spear-headed. You do a lot of good for the community."

"I'd like to step up my game," Philomena said. "Those things were about writing a check. I'd like to do something more signifi-cant. Or with more panache."

"Celebrity involvement?"

Philomena winced. "Not just another charity—though I do want that aspect of it. But I'd like to create an experience of some kind. Like Make-a-Wish but without the earnestness of the dying."

"Hmmm, yeah," Rolf said, feeling like he had just agreed to a thoughtful reason for torture.

"A good pairing," Philomena said. "Like a Vermentino with fresh herbs. Ginger and Fred."

"Hitler and Pol Pot," Rolf said, unable to help himself.

"Good," Philomena approved.

"What about a celebrity with… a less fortunate person. A child, perhaps?"

"Nothing terminal," Philomena said. "Too much guilt."

"Autism?"

"Gauche."

"MS?"

"That's a possibility. What's that disease where the child is born old? Like *Benjamin Button*?"

Rolf whipped out his smartphone and began Googling "old children."

"You're thinking of progeria," Rolf said.

"Progeria…" Philomena trailed. "Progeria. Children of progeria. The cure for progeria."

"It says one in eight million births, a very low incidence rate," Rolf said. Didn't matter. Philomena was in brand mode.

"You could imagine the photo-op possibilities," Philomena said. "Pairings. The young celebrity with the progerian. Is that how you say it? Progerian? They're weird looking little bastards, right? Make for some good visuals."

Sure, what the hell. "Hutchinson-Gilford progeria syndrome, HGPS," Rolf read off his phone.

"HGPS... Help fight the battle against HGPS," Philomena said. "When you give, give generously. HGPS. I like it. It has a real humane quality to it."

"It's terminal," Rolf said. "Most children don't make it past the age of thirteen."

"Oh, so what? Everything kills in the end. HGPS. What can we do with that?"

"A charity event of some sort, I'm guessing?

"Obviously," Philomena snapped. "What *kind* of charity event."

"A run? A walk? Limo wash?"

"A vacation."

"Y'mean, like Disneyland?" Rolf asked. "That's been done to death, pardon the pun."

"No, no," Philomena said. "What if we gave them the gift of living like a celebrity for a week? Luxury. Spoils. Entitlement."

"In an exotic locale?" Rolf said, hating himself for playing along. The phrase, *Don't hate the player, hate the game*, sprang to mind, but he knew it was more *In for a penny*. Or more so *Shake hands with Satan, you wretched swine*.

"Something new for both celebrity and HGPS," Philomena said. "'Come to St. Ledo and live in the moment.' Something like that. I dunno, put somebody on it. Find a TV writer. They're good at the cornball. But *that*. That is how we fill rooms *and* publicize this new playground for the rich."

Beaming with pleasure, Philomena stuffed more chicken parm into her mouth. She made a mewing sound as she ate. Rolf felt his soul leave his body and move slowly down Santa Monica Boulevard, eventually landing at the bottom of the ocean for all eternity.

* * *

While dreams of HGPS and celebrity were being played out in Philomena's mind, Luria sat in Percy Merriweather's office discussing a charity that would benefit the citizens of (take a breath, Luria) St. Ledo: A blood drive. It had taken five phone calls and numerous emails to get the meeting with Percy, who had assumed it was yet another local griping about deforestation or the raping of a culture—things for which Percy had a phalanx of stock retorts. But this woman Luria proved relentless in her efforts to have her five minutes with him. Fine.

Percy kept a Newton's Cradle on his desk, this one with an ivory base, which he set in motion while Luria talked, the clicking of the balls on thin wire punctuating his intent to not listen.

"Blood supplies are at a bare minimum on the island," Luria said. "It's not just us. The Azores, Lisbon, the States—there's need all over the North Atlantic. This could be a real chance to stock up."

"You're asking that each occupant of the resort donate a pint of blood as part of their vacation," Percy said, incredulous at the mere mention of it.

"What if one of those occupants were to have an accident?" Luria asked. "Moped riding. Windsurfing. Jet skiing. Boating. The phrase *boating accident* exists for a reason, y'know."

Percy harrumphed, but it did create a tiny bubble of concern in his head, right next to what C-list guest he could bang.

"Why don't we just have a drive for the citizens of the island?" Percy asked. "Surely there's enough of a population," (Percy knew the exact number), "to cover the blood supply. I don't see why we have to tap the resort guests."

"Your hotel has three hundred and fifty suites," Luria said.

How did she know that?

"If each suite held two people, that's seven hundred pints of blood. Three lives are saved with one pint. You can tell your guests they lose a pound for every pint."

"Is that true?" Percy asked, suddenly interested.

"Completely," Luria said. "Call it a charity event. You can call it that indefinitely. Your guests don't book, on average, longer than five days."

Again, how did she know that? She was right on both counts.

"The charity angle could be great PR for the resort," Luria said. "Matt Damon does water. St. Ledo's does blood."

"Oooh, I don't like the sound of that," Percy said, reminded of the Zombie Land Rush & Barbecue.

"St. Ledo does living. I dunno—you have a marketing team for that," Luria said.

Percy stopped the clicking of the Newton's Cradle. It would make for some great PR. Do it for a week and see how it plays out. What's the worst that could happen?

"I think we might be able to do something with this," Percy said. "I'd love to help the community, as would our guests."

Luria smiled. Actually she clenched her teeth.

* * *

He was weird. Weird in that *Blue-Velvet,* underbelly-of-society, secretive-and-dangerous-and   someone-you-want-to-run-from-as-quickly-as-possible kind of weird. At least they were in public. Dory couldn't handle this guy, Topo Bogomil—*what the hell kind of name was that anyway?*—alone in her office. She thought of the Warren Zevon song, *Werewolves of London:* "…And his hair was perfect." He wore a white Guayabera shirt with tan khakis and sandals, and had a face without a hint of beard.

Yes, it was good to meet in public. The café was perfect. She sipped her triple espresso, trying to understand what he wanted. He had told Dory's assistant that he was a shareholder of the resort and was checking in on things. "Checking in?" Send an email. Read the regular status updates. Ask around. But meet in person, at night, with the co-owner of the resort? She knew they had shareholders, paid mostly in oceanfront suites, but this guy, she would've remembered his name.

But then she'd never met Rupert Jagger either. It was always Percy with the details. Jagger lived in castle or a sleek modern post and beam, *Dwell*-magazine-type house located atop some mountain overlooking rolling hills and snowcapped peaks. He was driven around in a black Mercedes or Audi. His women were young enough to be daughters. He owned many watches. His money was good—at least clean, as was his history of real estate acquisitions and partnerships. So what if she never met the man? If only Percy weren't such a damned… *Percy.* And now, this Topo guy?

The thing was, he seemed as thrilled as she was about the meeting. It felt as if he were fulfilling a contractual obligation to meet the new boss. He seldom made eye contact and his face conveyed a sense that his thoughts were far off topic, which made Dory feel the slightest hint of comfort in that they both felt the same way. She wondered if she looked as odd to him as he did her. After all, no matter how much work was done to Dory, she was still a zombie, and that meant things seemed a bit off with her, as well.

The night air was warm. That's what Dory overheard the couple at the next table say. Her skin was dead. No weather stories to tell. She was grateful her tastebuds were still intact. Why that was true, though, she had no idea. This whole undead thing was still fraught with mystery and discovery.

"It seems almost a desecration to build the resort in such a timeless setting," Topo said, looking out over Bom Dia Bay. Dock lights cast shadows over various moored yachts and sailboats that bobbed with the slow-moving tide.

"A rising tide lifts all boats," Dory said, her eyes on the same vista as Topo's.

"Such is the march of progress," Topo said wistfully, as if the words were meant more for him than her.

"So how has making the transition to being undead been for you?" Topo asked, taking a sip of his espresso.

Dory wasn't often caught off guard. That did the trick.

"I, uh... well I'm not—what exactly?... Wait..."

"I apologize," Topo said, capping Dory's verbal stumbling. "It's merely a curiosity. One doesn't often conduct business with, well, with your kind. To be frank, I'm fascinated by it. I hope I haven't offended."

Dory stared blankly. Offended? She supposed not. Would she be if he had asked what it was like to be Jewish (which she wasn't). Maybe this would be an interesting meeting after all.

"It wasn't by choice," Dory said. "And I won't go into detail how that occurred, if that's what you're after."

"No," Topo said. "We're all born. Then we die. And for some, we're born again, literally. No, I'm interested in your perspective on life now that it is something you can be part of for centuries. Certainly things have lost their sense of urgency for you."

Truer words... "Some mornings, I wake up and I'm excited by the prospect of watching progress over such a long span, of being part of that progress. Other mornings, I wake up and wonder if I still have soul."

"For defying the will of God by rising from the dead?" Topo asked.

"Something like that," Dory said. "I was never a religious person, but when you rise from the dead, as you put it, you begin to formulate certain questions."

"The hows and the whys," Topo said.

"Right. How can this happen? Why me? It fucks with your head."

"Are you ever angry about it? About losing your mortal self?"

"Yeah. After the shock and fear came the anger. I'm still angry about it."

"Why?"

"Why?" Dory repeated. "Why… because you're not supposed to rise from the dead."

"Lazarus did," Topo said.

"If you believe that sort of thing."

"Do you?"

Dory scoffed at the notion.

"According to the gospel, Lazarus did rise and continued to live his new life," Topo said.

"And people wanted him destroyed because of it," Dory said. "Okay, I did go and read that part of the bible after this happened. Didn't provide much comfort though."

"I imagine not," Topo said. "If they knew about you, they would kill you. For those who do claim to know, they become hunters."

Dory studied Topo. How could she have missed it? Topo was undead. Still foreboding, but not because he was undead. It was his personality that felt menacing, even though they'd just had a fairly philosophical discussion that did provide Dory with some level of relief. Not a lot of therapists specialized in being undead.

"What's your story?" Dory asked.

It was Topo's turn to scoff.

"You seem to have a keen insight into the inner workings of my kind," Dory said.

"I have a vast knowledge of sailing vessels, but a captain that does not make me," Topo said.

"Way to be evasive about it," Dory said, a bit stung by Topo's maneuvering. This time Topo chuckled and it evaporated the menace in him.

"From your status updates it seems that we're on track to open sooner than expected," Topo said.

Dory nodded her head. It was like being on a blind date that suddenly went sour with one question.

"So it's gonna be like that," Dory said. Topo smiled. His teeth were perfect. Zombie. "Um, yeah. Things are going well. For the first time in recorded history, contractors have delivered on their promises."

"And your marketing team?" Topo asked.

"Same team as St. Agrippina," Dory said.

"Right. The resort that had the unfortunate gas leak," Topo said.

Dare she bring him into the fold with what really happened? Chances were, if he was undead, he already knew.

"Crisis handled," Dory said.

"Apparently so," Topo said. "Your resort has a six-month waiting list."

Dory smiled. *Damn right it did.*

"We expect similar, if not greater, results with St. Ledo," Topo said. "At least, that was what I was told to convey."

Well, look at the flirt. "I promise you, Mr. Bogomil…"

"Topo. Please."

"I promise you, Topo. I always deliver."

Topo wanted to add an "I bet you do," but refrained in the event he had to kill her.

*   *   *

Kyle winged his dart toward the wall of newsprint. It landed firmly in the middle of a sketch of a family running in the surf.

"There's your winner," Kyle said to Cate.

"And that's how we do that," Cate said, rising out of her chair, removing the dart, and turning it in her hand. "I'm tapped out. I got nothing. I've been to the well and the well was dry."

"We're fried. We've given 'til it hurts. Let's go to the movies," Kyle said.

"Sylvia's gonna stop by to check on things."

"Who gives a shit? C'mon, at least let's go to St. Bobo's."

"No can do."

"Let's have sex then. It's been three days."

"No want to do."

"How can you turn this down?" Kyle said, motioning to his body as if he were a model on *The Price is Right* showing off a new Frigidaire refrigerator.

"Alcohol, movies, sex," Cate said. "What a complicated man you are."

"I'm serious, we need a break," Kyle said.

"Nope. We gotta power through it."

"What? What's left? A resort for the rich and famous. What needs to happen here beyond showing some beach and a hotel suite? This is travel: show the perfect bodies in the pool and the open fire pit patio at dusk with the white drapery moving ever so slowly. That's a wrap."

"We did that," Cate said. "So did everybody else."

"Know why? Because that's what you do in this category. Remember back when Lexus did car commercials without showing the car?"

"It failed," Cate said.

"Because they didn't show the fucking car. We have to show the car," Kyle said.

"Yeah, but isn't there a way to do it differently? Make it stand out?"

"No. There isn't."

"Bullshit."

"Fine. Show me the campaign that didn't show the resort," Kyle said. "Hmm? We got a whole stack of *CA*s to go through. See if you can find one."

CA stood for *Communication Arts*, the publication that published award-winning advertising. Getting your ad into it meant at least a 5K bump in salary. Also, it's where you stole ideas from.

Cate hit a key on her laptop. *More Than a Feeling* began to play.

"Oh, for fuck's sake," Kyle said. "You know that one's dead in the water. It's already been used in an ad for Barclaycard. Never mind that, though. Douchebag Mike Huckabee used it as a campaign song. Tom Scholz—the founder of Boston—ordered a cease and desist. God, this seventies rock thing you've got going on—you had Xavier blasting Foghat!"

"*Slow Ride* is pure awesomeness," Cate said.

"I haven't heard any Rush. Hmm? They released *2112* in '76."

Cate clicked off Boston and put on the familiar outer space whoosh that opened *2112*.

Kyle nodded his head. "Tha's what I'm talking about."

"Happy?" Cate said. "Have a helping of *Temples of Syrinx*."

They listened for a few moments. Then Kyle jumped out of his chair. "*Temples of Syrinx*!"

"Yeah, and you thought getting the rights to a Boston song would be hard," Cate said.

"A temple," Kyle said.

"With high priests, even," Cate said.

"Your body is your temple," Kyle said.

"You're getting biblical on me here."

"Not that. Think mind and body as your temple."

Cate did so. "Your temple of the soul," she said.

"How do you treat your soul?" Kyle said.

"Like a temple. Where's the temple? In your soul? Is it a place?"

"Like a resort?"

"Reclaim your soul. Rediscover that temple. Rediscover your soul."

"Is that cheese?" Kyle asked.

"I dunno," Cate said, typing quickly. "It's another way in."

"Pink Floyd."

"What?"

"I haven't heard Pink Floyd in your mixes," Kyle said.

"Focus," Cate said. "Temples of the Soul."

"Pink Floyd's *Behold the Temple of Light*."

"Don't know that one."

"It's an obscure instrumental Never mind. Temple of the Soul."

Kyle got out his pad of newsprint and began sketching while Cate typed. "Behold," he said while he sketched. "Like that word."

"Behold, the temple of your soul," Cate said. "Temple of or temple for?"

"Behold the temple for your soul," Kyle said.

"Behold, the temple for your soul awaits."

"Dunno about 'awaits,'" Kyle said.

"What about luxury?" Cate asked.

"Oh, we're gonna have the money shot," Kyle said, turning his pad to Cate. On it was a crude sketch of an altar with a photograph resting on it. There was a seashell and some other trinket-type things adorning the photo, including a lit candle.

"That could be something," Cate said. "Have different shots of the resort and change out the little doo-dads."

"Right? Kind of a nice, spiritual thing. Rich people are always getting into Kabbalah 'n shit like that. Buddhism. Right? All that money in exchange for their souls. They freak out, want their souls back. We offer that. Print out your headlines, throw it up on the wall."

Cate hit print and went over to the printer to get the headlines while Kyle ripped out the sketch. Together they put the pages up next to each other then stepped back for another look.

"This could be something," Cate said.

"I told you we had more," Kyle said.

The studio door opened and in came Sylvia with a bag of lettuce and carrots.

"I think we have something," Kyle said.

"'Sat,' right?" Sylvia asked, setting the bag on the kitchen counter. She walked over to them and studied what they'd just put up. No head nod. No facial expressions.

"Well now," Sylvia said. "That doesn't totally suck."

CHAPTER 4

MINUTES FROM THE CREATIVE PRESENTATION

IN ATTENDANCE: Percy Merriweather (Jagger & Associates), Dory Parthenia (CEO), Sylvia Woodcock (Head of Accounts), Cate Hendricks (Senior Copywriter), Lisa Polinksy (assistant to Dory).

Sylvia presented demographics, reach, media strategy and costs. Dory was in agreement. Percy wanted to know about cutting costs; Dory said it was a conversation to be tabled. Percy insisted that costs should be a consideration when viewing creative. Sylvia suggested the presentation be shown, then address concerns about costs. Percy was adamant about reviewing costs. Sylvia inquired as to how one could determine costs for something they haven't seen yet.

The meeting proceeded with Sylvia reviewing the case study for St. Agrippina then going over the strategy statement. Percy questioned the strategy statement, wondering if there might be a disconnect between the strategy statement and what they were about to look at. Sylvia asked how there could be a disconnect if the work hadn't been shown yet. Percy further inquired that the strategy may need revising. Dory questioned Percy's input, stating the strategy had been approved by Jagger & Associates. She then produced the strategy document with the proper signatures. Percy mentioned that his name wasn't on it. Dory said that it was for the C-level management team and that, once again, they had approved the strategy.

Dory then suggested Cate present the work. Sylvia asked for comments to be held until three campaign directions had been presented. Cate opened with the recap of the strategy statement, adding information in regards to what the target audience felt about vacation time based on research Sylvia had completed. She also talked of the media buy, which would be print, radio, and web. Percy inquired as to why there would be no TV. Sylvia said that there wasn't time and the costs would be prohibitive. Percy said he wasn't concerned with costs but wondered if the time frame could be doable. Sylvia suggested that they continue.

Cate presented the first campaign, entitled "What's Your Time Worth?" and focused on the narrow amount of time people in positions of power had when it came to vacations. The second campaign was called "Temple of Your Soul." Its focus was on reconnecting with your truer self in a place made for such things. The third concept was called "St. Ledo Is Calling." It presented St. Ledo as a four-star resort on an island full of shopping and dining choices. Percy questioned the size of the logo, assuming that it would be made larger. Dory felt they all achieved their objective and gravitated toward the "Temple of Your Soul," because she felt it captured the belief that those with minimal time on their hands that took them away from the things that mattered was a positive, even aspirational message, that the resort understood its clientele and was there to help. She made no comment on the third execution. Percy stated that the third execution, "St. Ledo Is Calling," was the right direction to go with. Dory and Sylvia disagreed, stating that it was too similar to other industry campaigns and offered nothing new in the way of messaging. Percy disagreed, stating that it as a safe approach guaranteed to fill rooms.

Dory referred Percy to the St. Agrippina campaign, which used humor to address the needs of the consumer dollar rather than focus on the resort amenities. Dory reminded Percy of the success of that campaign. Dory decided to go with Temple and wanted to know how fast we could move into production. Percy voiced his disapproval, wanting to meet with Jagger & Associates to consult further. Dory said that was fine, but she was given full creative authorization. Percy exited. Temple will now move into production.

* * *

Ricky Sheflet sat in the chair his father had designed for him. It looked like a chair that might be found inside a mode of transportation in the year 2045. His father, Bert, called it "the chair of solitude" after Ricky's love of comic books, particularly *Superman*, which most of his friends thought too pop and not obscure enough to render it cool. Ricky didn't care. Any guy who had to hide his true self by taking on a weaker form and hanging out in a fortress of solitude was A-OK with him. The chair, better known as a zero gravity chair—but with a sleeker design utilizing the latest in microfibers, alloy, and NASA-grade memory foam—was where Ricky went to do his thinking. Also, it took the crushing power of gravity that he felt with every joint and sent it somewhere else for a while.

Ricky had the rarest of diseases, progeria. To make it easier on people whom he met for the first time—for there would be questions, always questions, as if it were brave of a stranger to ask them—Ricky would tell the inquisitor that he was born one hundred years old. It was an oversimplification, but then, like TED talks, it dumbed things down for the lowest common denominator. He rarely went into detail about the physical ailments stemming from progeria unless he found himself in a situation in which he'd rather be any place else. Listing the symptoms and effects of the disease made people uncomfortable, and for Ricky, it was a surefire way to get someone out of his sphere of existence rapidly.

Ricky was using Skype to talk with two other kids with progeria, which was a small club, being that around three hundred and fifty kids on Earth had it. Ricky had friends without terminal diseases with whom he goofed off, but when it came to the heady stuff, he went to his kin: Talia from Melbourne and Sid from Toronto. Though they had never met in person, they were tight. At first it was the disease, but the truth was, there were a few kids with progeria who were assholes. Talia and Sid shared more than the disease. They were caught up in what inventor and futurist Ray Kurzweil called "The Singularity."

The Singularity posits that computers, nanotechnology, robotics, artificial intelligence, and, most importantly, genetics would increase exponentially in what Kurzweil called "the law of accelerating returns." In layman's terms, it's the point where progress is so rapid that it grows beyond humanity's ability to comprehend it. Kurzweil looked at humanity in terms of six epochs. According to his theory, four epochs had already taken place: physics and chemistry, biology and DNA, brains, and technology. That left two epochs: the merger of human technology with human intelligence and then, for the knockout punch, the occurrence of Singularity. In other words, "the universe wakes up." Ricky, Talia and Sid couldn't get enough of the idea that the universe might wake up. Their obvious interest in the evolution of genetics and nanotechnology was something the three felt they needed to focus on. They were well aware of the time constraints placed on them. Ricky had just turned fifteen, defying the odds that said the life expectancy for kids with progeria was thirteen. The same went for Talia, who was thirteen and a half. Sid was coming up on thirteen and, though he felt healthy, that magic number stuck in his head like a bad song.

Out of the three, Ricky had been the one with the most media exposure. His disease was fascinating to others. Maybe not more than what a Kardashian was wearing but on the radar of popular culture thanks to the likes of Ellen, Oprah, and local news. Somewhere in an office at a local TV station was a white board with a list of diseases on it noting which would make a good human-interest story. It was fine with Ricky. He used himself as a fundraiser for research and at times found the coverage useful in meeting people, from Robert Plant (Ricky was a huge Zep-head) to Dr. Francis S. Collins, director of the National Institutes of Health.

So what was the agenda for Ricky, Talia and Sid as they sat facing each other via laptop? Charo. Specifically, Charo's third cousin twice-removed, the esteemed HGPS molecular biologist and futurist whose writings greatly contributed to the Singularity canon, Dr. Emile Baeza. As it turned out, Ricky's parents received a phone call from someone, a Philomena or something, who was organizing a charity event for children born with progeria to be hosted on an island in the North Atlantic. When Ricky's parents told him about this, he filed it under his "Axis of Bullshit," where celebrity and cause came together.

"But then, my Dad told me that Charo was one of the invited celebrities," Ricky said to Talia and Sid via Skype.

"Ho-lee shit," Sid said.

"Seriously? Charo's cousin?" Talia asked. They knew all about Dr. Baeza. When they did due diligence on a prospective researcher, Ricky, Talia, and Sid went deep.

"Believe that shit?" Sid asked.

"That's what I thought," Ricky said.

"I told my dad that the only way we'd show up is if Charo's cousin was in attendance. Of course, along with Charo, who might be a D-level celebrity, but how can you turn down the request from such a sick child?"

"Would they even go for that?" Talia asked.

"According to this Philomena's assistant, he would make it happen."

"Dr. Emile Baeza," Talia said. "He might need a vacation."

"It's a bit of a longshot, yes?" Sid wondered.

"Isn't that the story of our lives, longshots?" Ricky added.

All three nodded in unison.

*   *   *

Percy felt that familiar dizziness that came with opening up a vein. He watched the blood drip from his wrist into the tall IKEA glassware (Irdknovist), thinking Rupert was upping the size in glasses he used to collect Percy's blood. It was still better than the old-fashioned neck sucking which, for Percy, was too up-close-and-personal. It was his suggestion that Rupert take Percy's blood in reserves rather than one fell swoop, thus Rupert traveled with a portable freezer stocked with Percy's blood. It was time to replenish the stock. Percy told himself it was a privilege to give his blood to the man in person. An intern usually did it.

"So, as I was saying, I think you give her far too much power," Percy said, sucking on an orange slice. Rupert was vaguely aware of what Percy was speaking about. The blood. It was so, so very good to look at. "Don't you think?" he heard Percy ask.

"Hmm?" Rupert mumbled.

"Look, I know how busy a man you are, Mr. Jagger," Percy said, clearing his throat. "And I'm grateful for this meeting, for I have some very real concerns as to Dory's role in the success of St. Ledo."

Taking the time. Who was he kidding? Percy didn't even make it on to his schedule. It was by chance that Rupert had run into Percy in the bathroom that Rupert thought was secured. It was Rupert's afternoon hunger that made this meeting even possible. And now he had to listen to Percy's blathering. The price of hunger.

"I think it's in your best interest to take a look at the creative and weigh in on it before Dory sends it off to be produced," Percy said.

"I have complete confidence in Dory's decision-making skills." Rupert was being honest. For a zombie, she had her shit together.

"Be that as it may, the truth of the matter is that we are still keeping the lid tight on the St. Ledo opening," Percy said.

"All that my new business associate needs to know about this is that she is getting half of the resort funded by her new partnership with Jagger & Associates. Percy, I've kept you on board because I can rely on you to get things done. That Topo or I haven't killed you yet is a testimony to your good work. I'm confused as to why you would want to throw that all away."

He could care less. The cup was nearly full. Percy was ABO blood type which, for vampires, was the equivalent of a 1874 Chateau Ausone. If not for that, he would've been disposed of like the other heifers (humans). Okay, he was a good errand boy. Give him that.

"I just think," Percy began, "that over the years I've developed a sense of what pleases you. I feel my opinion on matters has helped guide you in your decision making..."

Rupert reached forward and gave Percy's wrist a tight squeeze.

"...I, uh, well, not that I actually have any influence over you. It's more that I feel I serve you well and wish to, to, to upgrade my standing, er, position?"

Rupert gave Percy's wrist a final wring then let go of it, taking the glass. He held it up to the light. "Exceptional," he said. "The campaign will go according to Dory's wishes," he continued, still admiring the fresh yield. "But I do have a special project that I want your involvement in."

Percy tried to perk up at this news but couldn't help feeling once again like the child being placated with a lolly.

"An enterprising travel agent is interested in creating a charity event on the island. I would like you to manage this project as it will be high-profile and good for the resort."

"I'd be delighted to," Percy said, crestfallen.

"Good," Rupert said, bringing the glass to his lips. He took a languorous sip. Percy took this to mean that the meeting was over and stood up then headed for the door.

"One last thing," Rupert said.

"Yes?"

"Should Dory suddenly become privy to Jagger & Associates's extracurricular intent with the opening of St. Ledo, I would be very unamused."

"Of course," Percy said.

"You do have divine blood," Rupert said. "It would be such a waste."

*   *   *

Desmond, the former mobile-barista-cart employee of St. Agrippina, had once enjoyed his promotion to beverage service manager for the resort, a position Dory thought he was more than qualified to hold. But now, with the addition of a second resort, his job had gone from governable to outright chaotic revolution. It took some getting used to, having underlings to execute his desires such as making the foam on lattes look like palm trees or keeping tabs on the supply of almond milk, a beverage that had lately come to eclipse soy milk. Soon enough the realities of the job hit Desmond like a category-five hurricane. Inventory, dealing with suppliers, mechanical issues, employee issues, timesheets, reams of invoices—it was a murder of paperwork. Then there was trying to walk that line of being everybody's pal and boss which was at first arduous; however, that feeling lasted about a week. Desmond snapped to. He was the man and, so long as you did your job with a smile because you're living in paradise and maintained a healthy sense of detached irony, then the rest was cake.

Desmond had a team of twenty-three employees under his tutelage, nearly a third undead. At first Dory was reluctant to hire their kind, Desmond among them, as she wanted a clean slate after the Zombie Land Rush & Barbecue. That diminished as the qualified applicants trended toward undead. After all, employment opportunities were few for those with as well as without a pulse.

On occasion, to feel as if he hadn't completely lost his soul to the management level, Desmond would take out an espresso cart and pull a shift working the grounds that surrounded the hotel. Some thought it subterfuge, management hanging with the little people. Desmond didn't care. It got him out of the office. He was in the midst of making Dory a quad-shot Americano with sugar-free vanilla and almond milk when she broached the subject of undead guests. The resort had slowly let them return, but after serious vetting, such as, have you killed an innocent human being in the last thirty days and if so, under what circumstances. There was also undeadregistration. com, an intelligence-quotient rating site that all undead guests were required to take. Owned by the resort, undeadregistration.com was created by Kyle and Cate.

* * *

BRANDING NAMES FOR THE RESORT
SCREENING PROCESS WEBSITE

1. dipshit.com
2. areufuckingkiddingme.com
3. whatwouldalbertsay.com
4. undeadmensa.com
5. moroninc.com
6. cruciallystupid.com
7. painfullyillequippedtoexist.com
8. cretinousbraineater.com
9. westborobaptistchurchentranceexam.com
10. vacantvacation.com
11. bagofhammers.com
12. cromag.com
13. undeadregistration.com

Dory, not at all amused by the creative team's efforts, nonetheless had relied on them to come up with something inoffensive and marketable, as if such a thing existed in the universe. Kyle had purchased the URL for undeadregistration.com (the safe and obvious choice, but it was fun to come up with the other names), the website had been created and launched—and then they had showed it to Dory, who, by that time, was so knee-deep in construction of St. Ledo that she had let them off with a sad shake of the head, something Kyle was well acquainted with.

"What would you say if I told you that I'm considering letting an undead convention come to the new resort?" Dory asked, as she watched Desmond make her drink.

"Y'mean beyond 'Look what happened last time'?" Desmond asked. "Something about repeating history not learned comes to mind. A phalanx of zombies could be trouble and now I feel like a John Bircher for saying such a thing."

"I know, I know," Dory said. "But we're set up to separate the socially acceptable from the 'brains, brains' crowd via an entrance quiz."

"I saw the website," Desmond said. "Letting Kyle have creative control once again reminds of the famous George Santayana quote."

"Both Kyle and Cate had a hand in that," Dory said. "He's infected her."

"I assume it's a sizeable convention with an equally sizeable dollar amount?" Desmond asked, filling her cup with steaming water.

"Enough to inlay the front desk counter with gold," Dory said.

"What kind of convention? And don't say Shriners. Have you seen one of our kind in one of those miniature cars? Looks like half a mannequin with wheels. You want your almond milk steamed?"

"Sure. No, not Shriners," Dory said. "Could be worse. "It's an Undead Grateful Dead convention."

"There's a joke about the undead listening to the Dead but it's too much effort to connect the dots," Desmond said. "I'll tell you one thing—the place is going to reek of pot and patchouli."

"I've heard maybe three songs by them in my life, but I know all about the fan base so I'm expecting a mellow event," Dory said.

Desmond poured the steamed almond milk into the shape of a cannabis leaf and handed it to Dory. "I bet those undead taste like pot brownies."

"I wouldn't know," Dory said.

"Girl, you need to live a little. It can't all be about kingdom expansion."

"I already lived. It's overrated. I'm sticking with fresh meat."

* * *

Production of the "Temple" ad campaign came together quickly, as did most advertising those days. Kyle wanted to bring in a photographer to shoot the still-life scenes and the locations, but there

wasn't any time; he'd have to go with stock imagery. Kyle, being
of the old school in which you actually put a personal touch into
the execution of the advertising, hated using stock. It used to be
a fear of someone else using the same shot you chose, but more
it was because of the inundation of imagery that had swollen the
stock industry to a level of banality that account people and crappy
creative directors loved. Art directors became Photoshop profes-
sionals, a job once delegated to designers, but now designers were
art directors and art directors did their own design, often poorly.
Concept versus execution smashed up into a single ball of noxious
gas that spewed out branding and messaging and whatever else
young, unschooled creatives could come up with.

Cate's world of copywriting had taken a few hits as well. The
art of long-copy ads had become extinct. When an ordinary citizen
could be exposed to anywhere from three hundred to a thousand
images and messages in a single day it became easy to be dismissive
of anything that took longer than three seconds to digest. Instead,
copywriting was reduced to simple calls to action. What used to be
considered the tripe of the headline-generating world had become
rote. Still, there was the occasion to execute a witticism for a magazine ad or TV, though it was expected to be a catchphrase that
would "go viral" and spread globally. From "Just do it" to "Can you
hear me now?" to "I'm lovin' it," these were the bread and butter
of copywriters. Careers were made on a few simple words placed
together. For the "Temple" campaign, Cate fared better than Kyle
by having the luxury of crafting a few headlines longer than three
words, something Kyle assured he could pull off by himself. Most
art directors fancied themselves copywriters, too. It was seldom true.

Two intense days were spent in the little studio above the deli,
putting together what would be the new ad campaign for the St.
Ledo resort. It was a time for ad creatives to get in the zone. Caffeine
and focus and a sense of urgency akin to repairing someone's
cerebral cortex kicked into gear. Sylvia checked in, bringing deli
sandwiches and espresso by the gallon, knowing to keep watch
from a distance—if she saw anything south of great, she'd say so.
So far there had been no change of direction handed down from
Mount Olympus, aka the client; Percy hadn't stopped by, which
saved him from the awkward scenario of having a laptop shoved

up his ass. Dory had trust in her creative team despite the website naming list they had submitted and kept herself busy with construction overages.

When the work was finished, it was reviewed the old-fashioned way: pinned to a wall, a ritual Kyle would never part with. Eating chopped-liver sandwiches, except for Sylvia, who made short work of a stacked kippered salmon and cream cheese on pumpernickel, the three looked over the work. Now was the time to pick things apart, to challenge the work to suck in any way possible.

"In the temple of five stars, you will rediscover an old friend. Yourself," Sylvia read aloud. The headline had been written by hand on parchment that lay over a photograph of a man standing on a wooden dock that stretched across blue waters, the image adorned by a smashed Audemars Piguet watch on a white linen napkin, a sterling silver demitasse cup (with rising steam), a jacaranda orchid. Swatches of a vintage map of the island seeped through the tableau, which was encased in a hand-carved shadow box (that was a serious Flickr search).

The other ads riffed on the same theme.

"Okay," Sylvia said, nodding her head. "These are almost free of suckage."

"Well, shit, death by faint praise," Kyle said.

"No, but it's advertising, so there's the inherent stink of rotten fish regardless," Sylvia said.

Cate and Kyle nodded. It was similar to being told the earth was round.

"Let's get the files loaded up," Sylvia said. "Well done, kids."

*   *   *

"Charo?" Philomena repeated to Rolf. "CHARO? *You invited Charo to an A-list charity event?*"

"Philomena, please. People are staring," Rolf said.

They were seated at a table in the courtyard of the Fig & Olive on Melrose Place, sharing a fig Gorgonzola tartlet.

"Keep my voice down? KEEP MY VOICE DOWN?"

Rolf looked around the courtyard. Ryan Seacrest glared at them. Rolf smirked back. Fuck that Ryan Seacrest.

"How? Why? I don't even know how to respond to that." Philomena said.

"I thought you just did," Rolf said.

"Honey, this isn't the way to make friends in this town."

"I thought it would add the right touch of panache to the proceedings. I was thinking some of the guests would find it... refreshing. She has a certain Q-score for the zeitgeist of the times. You said it was important to not inundate the event with the usual suspects. I thought it was a nice zag where others might zig. Better than William Shatner."

Philomena had her mouth closed, her tongue running across her capped porcelains. Not a bad speech, this kid. He might even be right. Charo. Cuchi cuchi. She did play a vicious flamenco guitar. She imagined Harrison Ford delighting in her performance as he entered the lobby where Charo would be prominently displayed.

"I've already got the buyoff of three progeria families," Rolf said. "Apparently they're big Charo fans."

"It's the disease talking," Philomena said. "Poor dears. It's like the cancer kids and the cast of 90210—just another Venn diagram of the needy and the ne'er do well."

"Who else do we have lined up?" Philomena asked.

Rolf felt a wave of relief. His well-honed script-pitching skills were paying off. "Let's see, Will and Jada..."

"Jaden and Willow?" interrupted Philomena.

"Of course," Rolf said. "Khloe Kardashian, Heidi Klum, the Affleck/Garners, Blake Shelton, Herb Alpert. I'm working on Bono and P. Diddy."

"Herb Alpert..." Philomena drifted. "I love him."

Of course she did and that's why Rolf went after him. *And here she questioned Charo. Jesus.*

"That's a good start. I have a call in to Miley's people. And Leo and posse. I'd love to get Clooney. We got Affleck, how about Matt?" Philomena asked.

"I dunno 'bout that. He's got the water thing to parched Africans," Rolf said.

"Where are we with the other sick kids?" Philomena asked.

"I've got contacts in the Phillippines, Serbia. I even found a family in Nova Scotia."

"What's so special about that?" Philomena said.

"I dunno. When's the last time you had anything to do with Nova Scotia?"

Philomena nodded. "I'm starting to get that feeling of something magical," she said. "Alchemic, extemporaneous. Capricious."

Philomena spent the next five minutes spitting out words of which she had a vague hint as to their meaning while Rolf picked at the tartlet, which was divine.

CHAPTER 5

"I JUST GOT THE CALL. WE'RE ON," Magnolia said, setting her smartphone on the oak table that wobbled, had always wobbled, and would never be corrected from wobbling.

"That's fantastic!" Marmot said, picking up his mug of mashed root tea to avoid spillage from the wobbly table.

"That was Dory, from the resort. She said we were welcome, although we'd have to be 'vetted'—her term, not mine—but still, we can do an email blast announcing the "Dead for All Eternity" weekend convention. Baby, it's on!" Magnolia rose from her chair and spun around once, letting her dreads swing wide. In her late fifties, with henna tattoos applied to her hands that represented the twelve Hindu levels of consciousness and layers of scarves that adorned her chenille skirt, Magnolia did a Deadhead proud. Her granny spectacles rested on the edge of her nose to put forth that knowing, worldly vibe that said, "Yeah. I've been on the road with the Dead since '69, even when they weren't touring." During that time she had hooked up with Phish caravans and kept herself sustainable by selling beaded necklaces and ice cubes dipped in chloroform—a trick she picked up from a Hunter S. Thompson interview.

She hooked up with her old man, Marmot, in '72 during the "Sunshine Daydream" tour when he set up a stall next to her for trading out bootlegs. Marmot was a graduate of West Point and had planned to make a career in the military working in intelligence, but when he discovered a top-secret program the Marines were running in which subjects were placed in a floating tank of salt water then read detailed reports of genocide while shooting one hundred and ten volts into the participant's testicles, it gave Marmot pause. When he learned that they were creating weaponry designed for chimpanzees implanted with some sort of removable hard drive, that pretty much cinched the deal. It also helped that, at the local off-base watering hole, someone slipped a tab of acid into his beer, which sent Marmot into tripping balls — the last thing he remembered being colorful, smiling bears singing *Box of Rain* to him as they walked a post-apocalyptic landscape. He saw a Grateful Dead bumper sticker the following morning on a passing van as he crawled out of a ditch naked and took it as divine intervention.

A zombie bit Magnolia and Marmot during an impromptu sweat lodge initiation in a small tent made of heavy tarp around a campfire surrounded by buckets of water. The tent was set up behind the stage of a Dead concert in Middlebury, Vermont. Like most people who became undead, the first thing that came to mind was food. They devoured an entire cow on a nearby farm, looking at each other, covered in blood and bits of meat dangling from their mouths, and laughing. It was a trip.

What started as a small gathering of undead Deadheads who got together annually to trade bootlegs, jewelry, strains of hash, and road stories soon grew to a newsletter, a website and, eventually, a convention. There were other Deadhead conventions, but none of them were specifically for the undead. "That's niche marketing," Magnolia had said to Marmot. They were undead Deadheads, but they still acquired some PR chops as the membership grew. They also acquired a bit of money, realizing that there were a lot of undead Deadheads who might have once represented a counterculture but woke up one day working at investment companies or running their own businesses selling car parts for Fiats. There were capitalists among them, but nobody's mellow was harshed, so why not trip the memory fantastic?

Magnolia and Marmot had heard all about the St. Agrippina Land Rush & Barbecue, but through the zombie network had learned that one of their own had taken things over and rebuilt it into a five-star resort. They were looking for a spot that would at once be Mediterranean in feel but with easy access from America's east coast as well as Spain and Portugal—all spots that had seen a rise in Deadhead and undead activity. It was a no-brainer (pun whatever) when they learned about the opening of St. Ledo. It was being run by one of their own! The needs of the undead would be understood.

"This one's gonna be different," Magnolia told Marmot. "It's gonna be a mixtape of cultures and sustainability. (That variation of the word sustainable was used a lot in lieu of words like "Profit.") The Don Henley lyric, "A Deadhead sticker on a Cadillac," had faded as time passed.

*   *   *

St. Bobo's was where the stressed-out met. Xavier (his brother, LeRoi serving the drinks), Thierry, Desmond, Kyle, Cate, Sylvia, and Dory sat around a table, nursing their various alcoholic signatures, gnashing teeth, tapping fingers, expelling air, and brushing back hair in an attempt to keep the fear at bay. Two things were on their collective minds: St. Ledo being a success, and the fight against a gnawing deja vú that whispered "Just like old times" in their ears.

When St. Agrippina first opened, there was an air of crusading commerce that infused them all with a sense of purpose and a measure of pride. Of course, when all hell broke loose and the Zombie Land Rush & Barbecue began with the tearing of flesh and the hail of bullets, those feelings of hospitality-industry largesse gave way to the most basic modes of survival. And now, there they were, on the eve of launching a new resort owned by the same folk who brought you St. Agrippina—mostly the same folk, anyway—with, yet again, an influx of zombies, albeit undead of the more intelligent species, prone to dining on steaks made from grass-fed cow and captured sea criminals such as human traffickers, warlords, their clans, pirates, and gunrunners (though the last category once was home to Oscar Pilson, retired mercenary and casual gunrunner).

Yes, they'd been down this road before, but now, assurances were in place. Besides, who but the undead idle rich could afford such a place? Which was to say, those with the brain capacity for obtaining wealth. Dory knew she was taking a risk with the undead Grateful Dead convention, but these were Deadheads with cash—the twenty-first-century heshers. It was Kyle who felt the proceedings were too reminiscent of St. Agrippina and hadregistered his near panic with Cate earlier in the evening by packing his bag. To Cate's credit, she talked him off the ledge and into a seat at St. Bobo's.

"I mean, am I the only one feeling like Han Solo making a deal with Lando Calrissian?" Kyle said. "We've got a vampire problem on this island. I vote to split."

"Who's Lando Cal… reesun?" Thierry asked.

"A *Star Wars* reference. Let it go," Cate said.

"Amiright? Are we about to make the same mistake twice?" Kyle asked.

"You're talking about opening the resort? Or letting the undead Grateful Dead convention happen here?" Dory asked.

"What undead Grateful Dead convention?" Kyle asked.

"We're hosting an undead Grateful Dead convention at the hotel."

"An undead. Grateful Dead. Convention. Do I have that right?"

"You do," Dory said.

"So, once again I find myself on an island overrun with *zombies* and, now, vampires," Kyle said. "And fucking Deadheads. Lord, I hate the Dead. Not undead. I'm talking about *The* Dead."

"Some of us might take offense at your tone," Cate said. "You know I hate that word."

"I love zee Det," Thierry said.

"My tone? Seriously?" Kyle asked. "This is St. Agrippina all over again. Are there catacombs infested with *zombies* waiting to devour guests? Worse, are there nests of vampires waiting for nightfall before they swoop down on unsuspecting guests? Am I going to run through the jungle with an AK-47 and a machete again?"

"You had to use that word again, didn't you?" Cate said.

"Like you didn't get off playing Rambo," Dory said. "Just drink your drink and relax. I can personally vouch for all undead on this island. And I don't know where you got the idea about vampires."

"*Esteeemated Prophet*, my favorite Det song," Thierry said.

"He got it from the guy who runs the deli. Koufax's," Cate said.

"Noam," Dory said with a chuckle. "Lemme guess. You hit on his daughter."

"No," Kyle said in a pitched voice that conveyed his guilt.

"You dick," Cate said, masking the fact that she too found Sari appealing, possibly for the same reason. So she told herself.

"Noam's full of tall tales," Dory said. "He told you about St. Irene."

"Yeah, the fucking vampire slayer," Kyle said.

"Kyle has a point, Dory," Xavier said. "I mean, look, this situation has more than a few similarities to it. If zombies, why not vampires?"

"Jesus, not you too," Cate said. "I'm sick to my ass of hearing the 'Z' word. Anyway, I think we've all seen the expertise Dory has in running things. I think Kyle's freaked out about the campaign not being a success."

"Wouldn't be the first time a creative got nervous in the service over that," Sylvia added, hoisting her vodka martini in the air before taking a sip.

"It's not that. Okay, it's a bit that. But no, that's not the big deal here. I'm starting to see some patterns emerge, and it's giving me the heebie jeebies."

"Like what?" Dory said, her patience with Kyle on short supply.

"Like what? How about this? I'm out of the hospital for a second time to be recruited to work on an island resort launch. The island, named after another saint, is run by zo... undead."

Cate smirked a "Thanks, asshole."

"There's now talk of another type of paranormal beings. We have the same cast of characters. I'm working with Cate again. We have a favorite watering hole, you have a new 'silent' partner whom we know nothing about. Bet he's a vampire. I could go on. This shit writes itself. I'm telling you, I'm ready to get me a crucifix and beat it to the mainland... Sylvia can give us updates on our pending success..."

"Or failure," Sylvia added. "And thanks for leaving me behind."

"That, too," Kyle said. "Something different needs to happen here. We need to interrupt the space-time continuum, like rewinding the clock and killing Hitler or giving Alex Trebek a cleft palate or something. We gotta roll a huge boulder into this stream and divert the repetition of history, or we'll find ourselves laying landmines and dropping bombs to Glen Campbell."

"What?" LeRoi asked his brother.

"I'll tell you later. It was epic. Like *Apocalypse Now* but with *Rhinestone Cowboy*," Xavier said.

Dory threw her arms up in the air. "I dunno what to tell you, Kyle. Other than I think you need to take something for the PTSD. This is a whole new ballgame. I'm running things now, and I think I've done a pretty fuckin' good job of not repeating past failures, and this so called 'silent partner' of mine is nothing more than an investor."

"Is he undead?" Kyle asked.

"Nope," Dory said.

"A vampire? A werewolf? An alien? Does he dabble in the occult? Did he vote Romney?"

Come to think of it, Dory had never had an encounter with Rupert Jagger in the daylight hours. Pretty sure he was a Republican.

"He's a developer looking for a tax shelter," Dory said, the word "vampire" buzzing around her head. "Run-of-the-mill rich guy." *Surely they had onsite construction meetings? Power lunches? Check-ins?*

"Did you check him out thoroughly?" Kyle asked.

"Well, I did Google him." Angrier, she contined, "What the fuck do you think I did? Just have him write a check without getting to know the man, without doing background?"

"With Percy?" Kyle asked.

All eyes were on Dory. She chuckled, tossing back her Macallan. Did they really think she was an amateur? You don't run a successful five-star resort without knowing a few things about the hospitality biz. So what? Percy was her point man. He was a solid guy for a middle management suck-ass. Assurances were made on his behalf—in broad daylight. Sure, he asked a lot of questions, which was good. Only Kyle thought him a toady. So why wasn't Dory being comforted by the sudden realizations about her new partner and his story? And goddammit, she must have had lunch with Rupert—at least breakfast over projections.

"Could it be, Kyle, that maybe, just maybe, you're a bit amped by the campaign launch?" Dory asked.

"Amped? Y'mean, like, 'over the top with my emotions' amped? Or just 'super-excited to be a part of yet another ad campaign' amped?"

"Let's just take a moment," Cate said. "Take it down a notch. LeRoi? Another round?"

"No, I get it," Kyle said. "Dory's playing the batshit card and Cate's throwing me under the bus."

"Jesus H. Christ, I feel like I'm watching an Ibsen play," Sylvia said. "Here's the news, kids. We're all a bit 'amped' because there's beaucoup bucks riding on this. I'd venture this entire bar is full of batshit of another kind. I'm betting it takes Thierry a fifth to get out of bed in the morning. And Dory? I'm gonna go with Xanax. As for you, Kyle, well, we all know your story. Everybody knows your drama. World's full of mood stabilizers of one form or another, so enough with the mental-stability-persecution complex. You're starting to sound like Liza Minnelli, and I mean that in the worst version of herself. Here's what Sylvia Woodcock wants—another vodka martini, some olives and marcona almonds, a remake of the third *Godfather*, to not fart during yoga, a butler, a ban on biker iding in cities, and I want to find a more inspiring existence that fulfills me spiritually and monetarily. And for the record, I fucking loathe The Grateful Dead, as well."

"We're expecting full capacity, just like last time," Dory said. "Other than that, I'm not seeing a repeat of St. Aggies. However, this time around we're gonna host a bunch of celebrities for a fundraiser. So you see, we're actually doing good in the world."

At this, Kyle's attitude changed, which was a shock to nobody.

"Like who?" Kyle asked.

"How's Neil Patrick Harris and family sound?"

"Pretty good," Kyle said. "Who else? How about Matthew McConaughey? 'Awright, awright, awright.'"

"How about Jude Law, the Affleck/Garners, Ricky Gervais, Charo?"

Kyle spit out his Moscow mule, a small spritz of it landing on Cate's arm.

"Really?" she asekd.

"I fuckin' love Charo!" Kyle said. "I'd take Charo over the Grateful Dead any day."

"Who's the charity event for?" Xavier asked.

"It's to benefit kids with progeria," Dory said.

"Pro-who?" Kyle asked.

"Progeria. That disease that prematurely ages children. It's very rare."

"I saw that documentary about a kid named Sam or something like that," Cate said. "The kid was overflowing with wisdom. Will he be coming?"

"He died," Dory said.

The bar fell silent.

"That's fucked up," Kyle said.

"Yeah, it is," Sylvia said. "The hand you're dealt."

And, like that, the mood of the room changed to that of a nuanced camaraderie that comes with thanking God for good health.

"Here's to doing good things in the world, then?" Kyle raised his copper mug. Everybody raised their glass. "Lord willin' and the creek don't rise."

"Amen to that," Sylvia added.

Glasses clinked.

"My money's on vampires," Kyle said.

"And we have today's winner for narcissistic sacrilege," Cate said.

* * *

It was a little after three a.m. when the gathering of the stressed broke and went their separate ways, hoping to awaken to success. Sylvia, feeling the buzz from the martinis, decided to clear her head with a stroll down one of the island's many cobblestone streets. There was enough infrastructure to light the streets and odd alleyway and, as Sylvia made her way at a leisurely pace, a door in a dimly lit alley strung with small light bulbs opened, spilling just a snippet of Edith Piaf's *Mon Dieu*. Sylvia stopped, watching the string of lights sway in the gentle breeze.

How perfect. An after-hours club and Edith Piaf. Maybe a nightcap was in order, though she was at least three beyond that.

Standing by the door was a woman who could've passed for a flapper straight out of *The Great Gatsby*, holding a cigarette between her long fingers that bent gracefully at the wrist. She was giggling at something said by somebody inside the doorway. Sylvia, enthralled by the tableau, made her way over to the woman who, upon closer look, had a flawless face that lit up as she turned her gaze to Sylvia.

"Well hello, Brooksy," the woman said. "Don't be a wurp. C'mon in. The hooch is flowing."

Sylvia chuckled, understanding less than half of what the young woman said. "Don't mind if I do," she said, turning into the entrance. A pale and handsome man, George Clooney without the smugness, stepped aside, his teeth gleaming as his smile broadened. Sylvia made sure to brush up against him as she passed. How had this place been off her radar?

The club was right out of Moulin Rouge—not the movie, but the real cabaret—or at least from the old photos. (Sylvia had visited the famous landmark back in 2009 for its 120th birthday. Elton John had been at the piano playing *Rocket Man,* the crowd singing along as they had sipped supposed absinthe which had turned out to be the real thing; Sylvia had tried to make out with the ghost of an imp.) The interior, though reminiscent of her experience, seemed somehow more authentic. Red drapery flanked an Egyptian-style stage. To the right was a giant wooden elephant adorned with flowers and shrubbery as if emerging from a garden. A woman on stage, in a simple low-cut black dress, stood at a bulky gold microphone and moved her hands toward the audience as if to embrace them while she sang. Sylvia, being familiar with pictures of Edith Piaf, was impressed by the resemblance.

Peter Lorre, or at least, to Sylvia, his doppelganger, approached with an arm out, a white linen napkin draped over it. "If you'll follow me, mademoiselle." Sylvia did so, quite certain she had time traveled and silently thanking God for taking her back to this time period. She half expected to see Henri de Toulouse-Lautrec sitting at a table sipping an earthquake (his own concoction of absinthe and cognac) out of a goblet, sketching Edith Piaf—and sure enough, there he was, seated toward the rear, his eyes darting from his pad of paper to the chanteuse.

They arrived at a white-clothed table with a small ornate lamp glowing and what appeared to be a drink waiting for Sylvia. Peter Lorre slid back a chair and motioned for Sylvia to sit, which she did with the dip of her head. "An aperitif, compliments of the house," Peter Lorre said.

Sylvia brought her hands together, as if she were praying to the drink. "You're too kind," she said. Peter Lorre bowed then stepped backward and turned to leave. Sylvia let out a sigh that intimated that she had somehow come home.

The band behind Edith Piaf swung brazenly, the other table lamps seemingly floated as if on a pond. The room was full of couples who sat close to each other as they whispered in the ears of their companions, blew smoke into the club atmosphere and played with the stems of their wine glasses.

A couple looked over their shoulders at Sylvia and nodded. Sylvia raised her aperitif, smiled, and drank. The liquid was warm as it slid down her throat. Her head became weightless as if it would soon rise from her shoulders and float away. Another couple, this time to her left, turned and smiled at Sylvia as well, while out of nowhere a waiter appeared, refilling Sylvia's glass.

"It's gonna be that kind of night, is it?" she asked the young waiter, who flashed his brilliant white teeth. Sylvia lifted her glass and took another sip. Probably because she was drunk now, it seemed to her that everyone in the club had their heads turned in her direction and was smiling, heads nodding. Sylvia took another sip and was startled to feel a hand on her shoulder. It was Edith Piaf.

"Are you feeling well tonight?" Edith asked. "You are blooming like a red, red rose."

"Thank you," Sylvia said, feeling off-kilter but enjoying the sensation. "I've found my new haunt."

"They all say that," Edith said, her French accent going soft on *that*.

Sylvia reached for her glass, her hand bumping up against its side. In the time it took for the glass to fall on the white tablecloth, Edith sank her fangs into Sylvia's carotid artery and began draining the blood out of her. By the time the glass was midway into its descent, Edith had stopped just before draining Sylvia completely. By the time the glass had come to a rest on its side, Sylvia slouched over her chair into Edith's arms.

"This one," Topo Bogomil said from the table next to Sylvia's, "is apparently someone we need."

*   *   *

From Joaquin's drink blog, *Beba!*

"Suco de Vampiro" or "Vampire Juice"
There are several myths where vampires are concerned. What powers they posses, how long they live; can the sun, garlic, silver, and holy water keep them at bay? Sometime in the 1700s, vampires became popular. Not as popular by today's standard, mind you, but popular enough to be a nuisance

to their kind. Serbia and Turkey were the earliest recorded sightings, but if we're going to be honest about the provenance of the species, we'd have to take a look at the fossil records that date back to the Neanderthal breeding with the Cro-Magnon.

How does that affect a bartender? Simple. Bartenders like myself have been serving vampires for centuries. It began around the reign of Julius Caesar, when some clever Roman got the idea of mixing distilled spirits with sugar and whatever other ingredients could be alchemized. What happened? A vampire walked into a bar (sans a priest and a rabbi), which in this instance was a bacchanalia, and ordered a drink mixed with blood. If you ever saw Caligula then you know this was not an unusual request. What the bartender was not aware of was that once blood was mixed with any ingredient, it would bind the bartender to the vampire.

Surprise!

Many of you know this. But for some of the Twilight-era vampires, this is news, like you don't have to be sullen to be a vampire. You're immortal! Enough with the moping around castles, bemoaning your lack of humanity or your fall from grace, as if God is keeping score.

For me it was something as banal as a margarita for a vampire from Fire Island. I was not at all pleased with this development, though you proved to be great tippers, you vampiro. I try not to judge you and your animalistic ways. I just concentrate on the vivid creations I bestow upon you not out of a sense of duty but out of my desire to one day mix the perfect drink and embrace the eternal epiphany that will be my reward.

One final note. You vampire owe me a debt of gratitude for inventing a cocktail that stuns your prey into obedience and eliminates the myth that you somehow entrance humankind with your powers. In the end, it is always, always the drink.

Suco de Vampiro
1 part absinthe
2 parts tree resin-infused wine
Shavings from Schinus molle (pepper tree)
1 part AB negative

Put shavings in bottom of glass, add wine, blood, then absinthe. Shake. Pour into aperitif glass made from the finest sands in the Asiatic. Imbibe!

*   *   *

"I think it sounds really interesting," James Franco said to his non-show-business friend Ritchie as they ate chili cheese dogs outside Oki Dog. "I've done some reading on this disease. Something like one in eight million live births? Imagine how the universe looks to one of those kids with it?" Ritchie nodded, his mouth full of a kosher dog and a gooey blend of chili and cheese. "I mean, I heard about Neil Young's kids both being born with cerebral palsy and the odds of that... I mean, what's the larger message here? I mean on the one hand, you have cancer, and the millions of children affected by that, and you think, that's where all the money and attention needs to go because of the numbers. But then you think, why should the numbers matter if you can help even one person?"

James took a bite of his dog, watching the cars on Fairfax Avenue pass by, their windshields deflecting the sun for brief moments. James was about to begin work on Aleksandr Solzhenitsyn's *One Day in the Life of Ivan Denisovich, The Musical*. It was one of the many plates he had spinning. Finding time to jet off to some remote island, even if it was for a good cause, seemed implausible, schedule-wise. It didn't matter to James. The idea of a rare disease intersecting with Hollywood whorish feel-good was only heightened by the fact that Charo's brother Dr. Emile Baeza, the preeminent biologist and Singularity believer, would be in attendance. James had been schooled in the theory by none other than Ray Kurzweil himself and was a staunch believer in its tenets.

"How could I not go?" James said to Ritchie. "You've got a little, a little chili, yeah, on the side of your mouth, that's it. You're good."

Ritchie smiled.

CHAPTER 6

IT WAS MIDAFTERNOON ON THE DAY of the campaign launch. Cate and Kyle were hanging out in their studio, eating Monte Cristos and washing them back with bottles of Viking Sterkur, a lager imported from Iceland. Cate had her seventies classic-rock mix playing; they were in the midst of Alice Cooper's *No More Mr. Nice Guy*. They expected Sylvia to be there and had sent several texts, but there was no response. Kyle figured she was too hung over, which, in his mind, made her a great account person. That it was the day of the launch made it even better. Dory would be checking in with the numbers as soon as she got them from Expedia, Orbitz, KAYAK, Hotwire, Bookings.com, Travelocity, and other booking sites.

Dory was using two cell phones, a landline, and her laptop to field the various calls regarding the undead Grateful Dead convention, the "Charity to Benefit Children Living with HGPS" (a slogan thought up by a writer for the hit sitcom *I'm Telling You, Darlene!*) and all the major things that go FUBAR when opening a resort. She loved it. She had just gotten off the phone with Topo, mostly flirting whilst getting or giving no new information about how things were going. Things were going. Wait and see. When Topo politely rebuked Dory's offer for a lunch meeting, she felt hurt only momentarily, for Topo added that he knew a great little wine bar off the beaten path where they could go over the day's numbers.

Noam and Sari were in the middle of baking New York-style cherry cheesecake as a celebratory/consolation dessert for "the ad people." They'd spent good money on Koufax's with takeout and meetings. Free cheesecake seemed a fair trade. Noam wondered if Sari had taken an interest in Cate. That poor schmuck Kyle had no inkling as to Sari's sexual preference, and Noam thought Cate too much for Kyle to handle. But he worried about Sari getting hurt, as would any parent. Noam assumed Sari could recognize when someone was interested in her and, by what Noam had witnessed, Cate looked interested. Who knew? Noam had just learned about "pansexuality," a term his daughter had introduced, to which he simply replied, "Whatever it takes." He meant it. Noam's daughter's sexuality was never an issue for him so long as she could find someone who could make her smile.

But nobody was more nerve-wracked than Rupert Jagger. If the numbers were small, he would be cast in a silver-lined cement sarcophagus and sunk to the bottom of the ocean.

* * *

To Huntz Reubenfeld, it felt good to be a king. He'd attained such a high ranking of nobility selling Elizabethan-style collars to millions of dog owners the world over. Huntz had seen the potential, with the right marketing, to take E-collars to the next level, which was world domination. His wife owned sixteen dogs: Pomeranians, Corgis, and several neurotic Border Collies. There were other breeds, but Huntz lost track and submitted to the fact that no matter where he sat in his twenty-five-thousand-square-foot manse in Champaign, Illinois, he would be covered in dog hair. In eighteen months he had purchased a small Danish company, rebranded it Reubenfeld Collars, set up direct sales channels, and opened an offshore account to toss the wheelbarrows full of money into. That was ten years ago.

With his kids grown and living their lives in abstract artistic endeavors made possible by generous grants from the Reubenfeld Foundation, Huntz and his wife, Mimi, spent time travelling the world in search of unique experiences beyond the usual, five-star-hotel marathon through Europe. It was really Huntz who felt a hunger for something new. Mimi was perfectly happy to spend the rest of her life indulging in room service.

It was Mimi who spotted the St. Ledo ad in *Vanity Fair* while getting a mani-pedi and saw that the island met all of her and her husband's requirements: exotic locale, high-end, and new. The ad, with its smashed Audemars Piguet (which Mimi recognized—she'd run through all of the watch brands as anniversary gifts) made her feel St. Ledo might offer a bit of whimsy along with nine-hundred-thread-count sheets.

That night over fried-egg sandwiches, which Huntz and Mimi dined on sitting at a small table carved from Carpathian elm overlooking the replica of the Hidcote Manor garden, Mimi brought up the new resort find. One of the Border Collies, Daisy, sat facing them as they ate wearing the size 10 clear plastic model E-collar, small grunting noises emitting from her throat.

"Daisy, what is it?" Huntz asked, half expecting a response beyond a bark.

"She wants some of your sandwich. Daisy, no!" Mimi said. Daisy tilted her head, which mashed up against the collar.

"I have the perfect getaway for us," Mimi said.

"Does it involve a spa where they try to drown you in mud and your own filth?" Huntz asked.

"I think you'll love it," Mimi ignored. "It's in the middle of the North Atlantic, on a new island—St. Ledo."

"How can an island be new?" Huntz asked. "And what's with the saint business? I bet it's chock full of ancient Roman Catholic churches that people with ancestry dating back to the Inquisitions attend. I can already see their eyes rolling at the mention of our last name."

"I checked their website," Mimi said. "It's an island known for olives and wine, and includes a Brooklyn-style deli. Right? In the middle of the ocean." She opened the issue of *Vanity Fair* (featuring Hollywood's best assistant directors), the ad page folded over, and paraphrased. "Buildings dating back to the seventeenth century... cobblestone streets dotted with shops new and old... cuisine from Greenland, Nova Scotia... Portugal... the Western Sahara. St. Ledo was named after the patron saint of happiness and good hygiene."

"Can't go. I have psoriasis on my toes," Huntz said. "Isn't that right, Daisy? Daddy's got some kind of infection from stepping in dog hair and now he can't go to a resort named after a saint who watched over Roman Catholic hygiene."

Mimi sighed. Huntz knew that sigh and understood that the decision had been made.

"Is this really where you wanna go?" Huntz asked.

"It's new," Mimi said. "Let's be adventurous."

"Daisy, she wants adventure. And you want the rest of this egg sandwich. Don't you, you sociopathic dog?"

Huntz tossed the remainder of his egg sandwich on the imported paving stones. "I could use a small vacay."

"Then it's settled," Mimi said. They watched as Daisy struggled to get at the egg sandwich, inching it away from her mouth as the E-collar scraped it across the pavement.

"We could be here all day," Huntz said.

* * *

Though the room was pitch black, Sylvia could still make out the details as if she were wearing night-vision goggles with color correction. It was mid-century modern, sparsely filled with what looked like Herman Miller furnishings. The George Nelson-designed clock read 2:40, but whether it was a.m. or p.m. was impossible to discern as there were no windows. Her hangover was immense. The kind you swore you'd never have again.

"It seems the transformation time grows shorter as the centuries progress," a voice from the middle of the room spoke. How could Sylvia have missed the detail of a person standing ten feet in front of her?

"Forty percent," the voice said.

A light glow emanated from the upper edges of the ceiling. Though it was a subtle light, it still hurt Sylvia's eyes. Standing before her was a well-manicured man in his later fifties, maybe. He was dressed in Victorian attire, his slim build narrowing down to his shoes, which shone like mirrors.

"Can we call the whole steampunk thing dead and move on with the rest of our lives?" Sylvia said, grabbing her forehead.

The man smiled.

"I give. Where am I?" Sylvia asked.

"You're in my house on the south end of the island," the man said.

"Did we..."

"No. We did not. Though I wouldn't rule it out," the man said.

"How pervy of you," Sylvia said. "Christ, what'd I drink?"

"Think about it for a moment," the man said.

Sylvia put her sluggish memory into gear. It wasn't without pain. She remembered the woman by the door in the alley. The maître d'. The elephant. Edith Piaf... Edith Piaf? Looking up at Edith Piaf's chin?

"What in fuck's name is going here?" Sylvia asked. "I got roofied by an Edith Piaf impersonator? How many levels of fuckery is that? Tell me I didn't get cornholed by Django Reinhardt."

The man smiled again, that smile that said he was quite taken with her.

"That was no impersonator," the man said.

"Well, whatever you're calling impersonators these days..."

"You're dead," interrupted the man.

Sylvia slapped her hand down on the leather armrest of the chair she was sitting in. "Obviously," she said. "I need a gallon of water and some Tylenol."

"They all find it impossible to comprehend," the man said.

"So how 'bout calling me a cab," Sylvia said, as she began to rise out of her chair, causing the pain in her already throbbing skull to shoot around her brain like a headband of electricity. She sat back down.

"I'm afraid I can't do that," the man said.

Sylvia had grown tired of this man of few words. "Can't do what? Call a fucking cab? Where's my phone? I'll call. Dammit, when will I learn?"

"I can't call you a cab, because if you were to step outside to get into it, you'd burst into flames and be ashes in the wind before your hand touched the door handle."

Oh, this supernatural bullshit. Sylvia pinched the bridge of her nose, wondering just how many more years of wisdom she would need to acquire in order to listen to the better part of her that said things like "Don't fuck him" and "Don't take the gig" and, most importantly,

"Don't drink that." Naturally she'd burst into flames. She was doing business with zombies, so why would suddenly bursting into flames be so farfetched? When it had become apparent that her new bosses were undead, at first it was a bit of a surprise, but, then, she needed the work and they seemed like good people. She'd had jobs with worse individuals than brain-eaters. DDB? FCB? Yeah, those agencies were chock full of delightful individuals who dined on your brain in another fashion, by degrees. The man said she was dead, yet here she was feeling quite alive with a monstrous hangover.

"You telling me I'm a zombie now?" Sylvia asked. "'Cause that would make my whole week."

"A zombie? No. You are something with infinitely greater power. You are part of a species that is robust with a salacious appetite and a gift that goes on eternally."

"Good god, you wax eloquently," Sylvia said. "Choate? Phillips Exeter?"

The man looked down at his dazzling shoes with the smile he'd been giving her since they met.

"So, I'm hung over in some strange man's house and just been told that I'm something even better than a zombie," Sylvia said. "What could be better than rotting flesh that won't stay dead? A Republican strategist? Tell me. I'm Mary Matalin, aren't I?"

"You're a vampire," the man said. "Your maker was Edith Piaf. You should feel honored to have such talented and gracious blood flowing through you."

"Well, I guess, in the hierarchy of paranormal existence, you could do worse than being a vampire. Does this come with a 401(k)? Profit sharing? A biting bonus?"

"You are marvelous," the man said. "New Yorkers are so urbane. There's no room for panic or doubt, just the facts and what of it. You make such suitable vampires. One tires of the Southern gothic, languid, postmodern, pensive vampire who spent eternity questioning their existence and fall from grace as if, once they were turned, they acquired a burning faith in being one of God's fallen angels."

"I'm with you there, Chief," Sylvia said. "Being a vampire looks like a hoot. How about that Tylenol?"

"I've got something better," the man said, pulling out a glass vial from his tailored suit coat. The liquid in it was dark and viscous.

"I didn't peg you as a hair-of-the-dog kind of man," Sylvia said.

Before the last word came out of Sylvia's mouth, the man was inches away from her, holding her chin in his hand, tilting back her head. "Drink," he said. The liquid went down like Nyquil without the faux cherry flavor. In fact, it was the most delicious drink Sylvia had ever tasted. She wanted more—something the man sensed.

"There's more," the man said. "There will always be more, even if it is harder to get these days."

Sylvia felt as if she had downed a couple of five-hour energy drinks. She could hear the hum of the room's lighting, the sound of dust collecting, and a distinct heartbeat. In the corner of the room, crumpled in a heap, lay a naked man.

"I've taken the liberty of stunning him," the man said. "But he's all yours."

Rapid-fire questions pricked Sylvia's mind. *Who was this man? Why was there a naked guy in the corner of the room? What did he mean, stunned? Can I have some more drink? Why do I smell it on him? Why do I crave this naked man lying in a corner of the room, making me feel like I haven't eaten all day and someone just slipped a tenderloin in front of me?*

"Don't think. React," the man said.

And that was all Sylvia needed to hear. She leapt at the man, biting into his neck and feeling that same liquid pulse down her throat. It reminded her of doing coke in a bathroom at some club, only infinitely more satisfying. Plus, no trance music. She couldn't get enough and began tearing the man's neck apart with her teeth. She felt a powerful grip on her shoulder and was yanked backwards. Blood covered her face and splattered over her Jenni Kayne blouse. She was panting, squatting on the ground, feral.

"Who the fuck are you?" she asked, exasperated to the point of convulsion.

"I'm Rupert Jagger," the man said. "And I've got grand designs for you."

*　*　*

Dr. Emile Baeza sat back in his chair, rereading the latest email on his laptop. He was in his office in a research lab located in the Medical Research Council (MRC) on the Cambridge Biomedical Campus in

England. The email was from Ricky Sheflet, concerning Dr. Baeza's visit to St. Ledo. Dr. Baeza knew of Ricky but had never met him. He knew about the children with HGPS, as it was his field of study. But nobody had ever approached Dr. Baeza about his understanding of the Singularity as it applied to his work in deciphering the mutations in a human body that caused HGPS. Though he had never published his thoughts on the Singularity, he had included it in lectures. As it turned out, Ricky had seen the lectures, which were available on YouTube.

The first email of Ricky's was actually forwarded to him from Rolf Nesbitt, a travel agent who specialized in "high-end luxury experiences." It mentioned his cousin, Maria ("Charo" never stuck with him) and a resort where children with HGPS would meet him. That is, if he agreed to visit, something his sister recommended as she would be booked at St. Ledo for what she termed retirement-sized money. His sister worked hard, Emile knew this. And he understood that hers was a profession that had a descending ladder that could be cruel to a celebrity. He didn't want to see his sister pop up on late-night cable to promote a floor wax or dessert topping. Besides, it was an opportunity to get together with some of the HGPS kids, to meet the disease again in person. He'd had a couple of brief encounters as a researcher, never as just a guy named Emile.

He glanced over at a picture on his desk taken when he was nine years old, standing next to his cousin, Maria, who was holding a flamenco guitar, her grin broad. He had his arm around his cousin. They were close growing up in Murcia, Spain. They had drifted apart as Maria became involved with show business and he became lost in biology textbooks. They kept in touch through the years, but it was spotty at best. It would be good to see her again.

* * *

"Good news," Dory said, as she entered Koufax's, waving to Sari, who was ringing up a customer, and came over to the table where Kyle and Cate sat. "The numbers are starting to come in and it's looking like another sales boom. We're at eighty-five percent bookings and it's sunset the first day of the launch. Are you kidding me?

And that's just East Coast numbers. That, my friends, is very, very good news." She plopped down next to Cate and looked at the remains of a roasted chicken. Dory couldn't help but lick her chops at the sight of chicken remains. Kyle saw them and remembered that, even though he was boning a zombie, they were still zombies.

"That's how we do that," Cate said, looking at Kyle, who was finishing his thought about undead sex.

"Hmm? Yeah," Kyle said, snapping out of it. "Thas' what I'm talkin' about."

"Where's Sylvia? Maybe the news'll actually make her experience some version of happiness," Dory said. "Because we are selling—OUT!"

"We thought she was with you," Cate said, moving her head to the song her subconscious was playing. Kyle picked up on this.

"What's wrong with your head? Are you seizing?" he asked.

"'It's, it's, a ballroom blitz,'" Cate sung, tapping her fingers on the Formica table. "'Ohhhh yyyeeeaaahhh.'"

"Still stuck in the seventies, are we?" Kyle asked.

"This is freakin' awesome," Cate said, still tapping her fingers. "We did it again! Celebrate, bitches!"

Dory began to nod her head in sync to Cate's. Kyle did feel good about the news, even if, deep in his gut, he feared the success was yet another element to the repetition of history. He nodded his head in time to the other two, though The Sweet wasn't playing in his head. It was more a funeral dirge. The bell to the door rang and in came Sylvia, looking as if she'd caught up on the sleep she'd been missing the last decade.

"There she is," Cate said, arms outstretched.

Sylvia did the same with her arms, strutting over to the table.

"So you heard the news?" Cate said.

"What news?" Sylvia asked. "I'm just glad to see my lovelies."

This comment tweaked Kyle as he assumed she was high on something because that's what Kyle always thought about people who radiated positive energy, as was Sylvia at the moment.

"We're kicking ass!" Cate said, rising to hug Sylvia, something else out of character for her. Cate was obviously swept up by the news. The newbie.

"We're in the resort business and business is gooood," Dory said, while Sylvia and Cate came in for the clinch.

"Do tell," Sylvia said, her face peeking over Cate's shoulder.

"We're at eighty-five percent bookings," Dory said, sounding like a true business dork. "Eighty-five percent! That's unreal! It's better than the numbers for St. Agrippina!"

Sylvia and Cate unclenched, Sylvia making fists and shaking them next to her head while squeaking out a low "Yaaaaay."

Kyle was not amused. Obviously Sylvia had taken some kind of mood-enhancing drug, his guess being coke, which was just outside the proper protocol for an account person. Drunk was one thing; being wasted on the hard drugs was very late-eighties, which was bad form.

"I can't tell you how happy this makes me," Sylvia said.

"Y'mean it doesn't totally suck ass," Kyle said.

"Listen to the shlump over here," Sylvia said. "Get happy. You guys did it again."

Okay, she was definitely wasted, this much Kyle was sure of. The other thing that had made itself apparent was his sudden attraction to Sylvia as a woman. With her severe blonde hair, curvy body, and newfound vitality of a high school cheerleader, Kyle found himself feeling just this side of aroused. Was it just her energy or did her breasts always strain the buttons of her blouses? And that mouth— someone just spoke his name.

"What?" Kyle said.

"I said we should hit up St. Bobo's and get this party started," Cate said, giving him a where's-your-head look.

"Absolutely," Kyle said, hoping his face wasn't turning red, his lust betrayed.

"Where have you been?" Dory asked Sylvia. "And what have you done to yourself? You look fabulous."

"I took a spa day," Sylvia said.

"You look like an airbrushed version of Princess Diana," Dory said. "Amiright, Cate?"

"You do," Cate said. "Are you getting some on the side?"

"Now you sound like Kyle," Sylvia said.

Kyle snickered, studying Sylvia's face. They were right. She had an almost sheen to her skin. She glowed. She looked like a hair model in a slo-mo TV spot. Her smile was iridescent, just like... just like the zombies in his life, with their perfect enamels to offset the deterioration. Had Sylvia been bitten? Was she now among the undead? Kyle scanned her, this time sans the crude fantasy. He couldn't make out any chunks of missing flesh. Maybe her ass? Kyle leaned to his right to get a look.

"Meal's on your plate, Dirk Diggler," Sari said, coming up to the table, her hands holding a small dishtowel.

Kyle snapped back to his original position. "What?"

"I assume from all of the commotion the news is good?" Sari asked.

"This island is gonna be crawling with tourists," Dory said. "All of them toting their Merrill Accolades American Express cards."

"I'm buying the first round," Sylvia said.

"Why don't you join us?" Cate said to Sari. "Your dad, too."

Cate and Sari regarded each other a bit longer than would be the norm between two people who didn't have interest in each other beyond friendship. Kyle noticed this and now his mind was a ball of confusion. Zombies, lesbians—lesbian zombies—and Sylvia shaking her ass that seemed untouched by zombie teeth.

"Let's drink," Kyle said. "Let's drink *now*."

"Should we invite Percy? He's over in the corner booth," Cate said.

They all looked over at Percy, whose head hung over a bowl of matzah ball soup. He looked like he'd just come off a bender himself, his complexion pale, his hair mussed.

"I think he's had his fun," Sylvia said. "Besides, he's a buzz kill."

*   *   *

Luria stood in an empty walk-in fridge, holding a glass of Pinot, smiling. She'd just gotten off the phone with Xavier who told her that he was swamped with reservations to fly to St. Ledo and that there were a number of A-list guests making the bookings—well, actually, someone called "Philomena" handled the actual booking. Nonetheless, Xavier was in high-stress mode but elated.

"I'm going to tap into some rich blood," Luria had said. "Literally."

She'd begun to run down the guest manifest in her mind, asking herself who best would represent a blood drive? She searched the various celebrity charity websites. Bono had the RED thing. Damon had water. Denzel had the Boys & Girls club, Ben Stiller had ALS. Who? Politics? Al Gore had climate. Jimmy Carter had his own foundation, as did Bill Clinton. Uma Thurman! No, she had the thing about charity for welfare babies. It seemed as if the moment someone had their fifteen minutes, they were attached to a good cause.

Luria studied the manifest, and there it was, standing out like a pimple on Kate Moss's face—Charo. Who didn't love Charo? She was the perfect blend of kitsch and pop culture. Luria made several calls, finally getting hold of Charo's manager who thought the idea of her representing a blood drive would fit in well with her support of Muscular Dystrophy and PETA, specifically saying no to bullfighting.

Luria took another sip of her wine, her body getting the shivers, not because of the temperature of the roo, but because of the stars lining up in her galaxy. Plus, she'd get to meet Charo.

CHAPTER 7

THE OPENING OF A NEW LUXURY RESORT in an unknown location spread through the upper crust like Koch Brothers money at a Tea Party fundraiser. It had been a little over twenty-four hours and already personal assistants were getting their collective assess chewed out about lining up a suite. The Undead Grateful Dead convention was selling out, with Whoopi Goldberg signed on as the Master of Ceremony. The St. Ledo bookings also boosted business for St. Agrippina, though with more C-list clientele such as Mike Lookinland (Bobby Brady).

Dory wasn't the only one reveling in the good news.

Rupert Jagger was indeed pleased to see that his investment just might pay off after all. His very existence was counting on it. On the eve before the ad campaign broke, Rupert and Topo had received a visitor who came bearing a well-worn sermon. Usually it would've been a short directive, such as "Collect more blood" or, Rupert's favorite, "Collect more blood, now." This time, however, Rupert and Topo would have to suffer through yet another reminder of where they came from and what they represented and what was at stake besides their immortal selves.

The sermon, delivered by Neno, the first fallen angel as depicted in the seventh book of the Enoch Doctrine, had been meant as a scold delivered to those whose failings would prove cataclysmic. Neno was cast out of Heaven for having sex with mortal women. Many, many mortal women, hence the nickname of the Enoch Doctrine, "The Coitus Codex." Enoch, it had been argued, was the first vampire. This was disputed by the Neanderthal skulls found with bone fangs attached to the maxilla and mandible. Thus, you had the Hatfields and McCoys of the vampiric dynasty.

The lecture in its original form is unknown. Throughout the ages, many sects of vampire had rewritten and codiciled the hell out of it, right up until 1741, when the vampire preacher Jonathan Edwards took the remains and fashioned it into a sermon known as "Sinners in the Hands of an Angry God *v.2*" Version one refers to God. Version two, Enoch. A third version exists as well, to appease those who considered vampires to be born out of the Mousterian stone tool culture (Neanderthals—they just wouldn't go away).

Jonathan Edwards, a philosophical theologian, was also a vampire with rapacious appetites, having brought the populace of Northampton, Massachusetts to near extinction. His rewrite of the Enoch Doctrine (The Coitus Codex) brought him fame and fresh blood. He faked his death from smallpox inoculation in 1758 and currently served as the Deputy Director of the Central Intelligence Agency illuminati, a position he had held since Kingman Douglass in 1946. If you've ever wondered who pulled the strings behind the Cuban Missile Crisis and the Patriot Act (among many other CIA activities), Johnny Edwards is your guy.

Neno was winding down the sermon, which he gave while reclined in an Eames lounge chair in Rupert's home, Rupert and Topo standing before him, hands clasped behind backs.

"The wrath of Enoch is like great waters that are dammed for the present. They increase more and more and rise higher and higher, 'til an outlet is given. And the longer the stream is stopped, the more rapid and mighty is its course, when once it is let loose. It is true, that judgment against your evil works has not been executed hitherto. The floods of Enoch's vengeance have been withheld. But your guilt in the meantime is constantly increasing, and you are every day treasuring up more wrath. The waters are constantly rising and waxing more and more mighty. And there is nothing but the mere pleasure of Enoch that holds the waters back, that are unwilling to be stopped, and press hard to go forward."

Neno smiled as if the words provided great comfort to him. "Questions? Concerns?" he asked.

"There was no need for you to..."

"Obviously others felt differently than you," Neno interrupted. "Next?"

"We are humbled by..."

"Humbled?" Neno this time interrupted Topo. "You are not yet worthy of being humbled. Many before you have served in greater capacity before being allowed the position of being humbled. What else?"

"I don't understand..."

"And that is why I am sitting before you," Neno interrupted Topo. "Because of your lack of understanding? Is that all?"

"It's just that..."

"Just that you fear the wrath of..."

"Oh, for fuck's sake," Rupert interrupted Neno, who in turn shot his hand out, crushing Rupert's body through the wall of his living room and a cedar tree before it came to rest against a sculpture garden boulder outside.

"As you were saying?" Neno asked.

"Nothing," Rupert's rasp of a voice called.

Topo smiled and did his best to crumple up into a molecule.

"Then I think my work is done here. Get the blood," Neno said. "Anything further you wish to add?"

Topo lowered his head, squinting, waiting for the next diatribe or worse.

* * *

"I'm not sure what you're getting at, buddy," Oscar Pilson said to Kyle over the phone. While the contingent of ad folk toasted their success at St. Bobo's, Kyle holed up in a bathroom stall so he could talk to Oscar with relative privacy.

"This is St. Agrippina all over again, I'm certain of it," Kyle said. "So whaddaya think? Help me blow the place up?"

Oscar gave a throaty chuckle. That Kyle, crazy as ever. "So you're saying that the new resort, St. Ledo, is opening its doors and recruiting rich people to feed on, this time by vampires. That you and Cate created an ad campaign that's going gangbusters, and you find yourself once again responsible for the fate of hundreds of unsuspecting tourists. You're right—we've been down this road before. I'll be there end of day with enough C-4 to blow the whole island back to biblical times."

"Awesome," Kyle said.

"Not," Oscar said. "Listen, are you taking your meds? Is this another breakdown? Maybe you should come hang with us for a couple of weeks. Fish for tarpon, get drunk."

"Why does everyone assume it's a lack of meds?"

"Son, when you go off them I start getting phone calls like this one."

"I'm stable. Okay, I'm drinking a bit, but Cate has me exercising and eating healthy. Well, more like she has plans for me to do those things. I'm taking ten thousand IUs of vitamin D. I could do with more sex."

"Couldn't we all?"

"Tell me what part of this story doesn't ring true to you," Kyle said. "And don't say you don't believe in vampires. Not after you went up against zombies and became the proud owner of a paralyzed talking Chihuahua."

"Partially paralyzed, and you're catching me at a moment of weakness. Me and J..." Oscar caught himself. He was the only one who knew Woman's name, besides Dog, who kept a tight lip as far as his name was concerned. "Woman and I were talking about how we could use a little extracurricular activity of the paramilitary kind. But you're talking about taking out Dory's investment. She's a friend, man. Doesn't seem right, lighting it up. What if you're wrong?"

Kyle hadn't considered that part of it. He looked at the etching of a talking penis on the bathroom stall door. It had a word balloon above it that said, *Hodor*. Would Dory still go through with it if she knew that things were about to seriously go south—again? Could he convince her? He needed concrete proof. He needed a vampire.

"What if we left the hotel untouched and blew the docks and air strip?" Kyle proposed.

"That'd be bad for business, too," Oscar said. "But fun nonetheless."

"Right?"

"Here's what I want from you. Get me actionable intel, and we'll help with the bang bang."

"You need to see a vampire," Kyle said, sounding defeated.

"Bingo."

"I guess if I could show both you and Dory, that'd be enough evidence to shut this place down."

"You got it, chief."

"How the hell do you catch a vampire?" Kyle whined.

"You kidding? Turn on your TV or read a book. It's vampire mania. Watch a few episodes of *True Blood* or read an Anne Rice novel."

"There's *Twilight*."

"Are you serious about this or not?"

"*True Blood*. Anne Rice."

"Also, listen to a lot of Black Sab."

"Can do."

"That's a good boy. Get me the hard proof, Kyle, because I'm itching to blow shit up but if I've learned anything from Desert Storm it's that you gotta have due diligence, capish?"

"I'm reading you five by five," Kyle said.

Oscar smiled. That Kyle, crazy kid.

*   *   *

One of the many gifts of being a vampire was the power to make a silent appearance. Topo did so in Dory's office, watching her work. It was a little after two a.m. and Topo could smell the vodka coming off her dead skin. He admired her tenacity—drinking with friends then back to work. Topo had sat at the back of St. Bobo's, watching them celebrate the success of the hotel resort bookings. It gave him relief, this news. But watching the assembled toast each other, Topo couldn't help but feel alone in the world. He would've enjoyed their company. Sylvia would understand as she was of his kind now, but the others might get spooked. He thought they were mixing with the undead of another species; maybe he underestimated their tolerance for all things otherworldly.

Dory sat at her laptop and hummed *Ballroom Blitz* as she typed at ninety-five words per minute. The clicking of the keys was soothing to Topo, though he didn't know if it was the actual sound or the fact that her brain was moving so quickly that it made him feel secure, almost protected from the task at hand. Would she forgive him for using her? Would she relate to the idea of a mass feeding, like her kind had attempted to orchestrate a year ago? He knew Dory's history, how she went against her own people to gain control of St. Agrippina. And, knowing what he did to her boss, Jackson Farraday, with his ridiculous white seersucker suit and longwinded bon mots, he couldn't blame her. And how different was it for him, taking orders from a man who dressed in similar affectation, and the sermon and the oaths and the blood rites and on and on? It wasn't enough to just be a simple vampire; no, you had to serve somebody. Meet the new boss, same as the old boss. Topo grinned, wondering if any other song lyrics might apply to his situation.

What if he went against Rupert? It would certainly mean his own demise. Perhaps it was time? The march of time had been worn down to a trudge. Topo no longer cared what humanity had in store next. In his mind, electricity was an exciting turn of events, but then it drew a straight line to nuclear energy and the bomb, and it had horrified Topo that a race could be so willing to self-destruct. He knew that part of his attraction to Dory was her longevity. Though, she needed to keep time at arm's length; the maintenance these undead had to endure was draining. For Topo, it was simply the blood. Dory had none. Could he turn her? Could he tap into the life force that kept her ambulatory? Could she turn him? The existential meditations on the life of the undead amused Topo. It would make for good conversation with Dory. But first, business.

"By the pricking of my thumbs, something wicked this way comes."

"*JESUS!*" Dory spat, pushing herself away from her desk, startled.

"Didn't mean to frighten you," Topo said. "My apologies."

"Topo," Dory said, "you sure know how to make an entrance."

Topo wanted to explain that he'd been watching her for some time but thought it a bit unnerving. He did warm to her saying his name, though. "I'm a fool for theatrics," he said.

"The Shakespeare betrays you," Dory said. "What brings you around this time of night?"

"I was out taking a stroll and saw your office light on?"

Dory scoffed. "You're here, might as well get comfortable." She motioned to a chair on the other side of her desk.

Topo grinned, glad that she hadn't pursued the line of questioning. He took a seat, lazily folding one leg over the other, allowing his foot to sway.

"You seem busy, as usual," Topo said.

"I'm about to get busier. The resort is booking up faster than I thought."

"Good news, then."

"Very good news," Dory said, not tiring of the phrase.

"My employer is no doubt sharing your sentiments."

"I imagine so," Dory said. "I haven't spoke with him directly, but we have exchanged texts. He seemed pleased. Hard to tell with him."

"Yes, he's quite difficult to read, Rupert Jagger is," Topo said, letting the rapid movement of his foot betray his feelings. He took note and calmed himself.

"Looks like it's win-win then," Dory said.

"A rising tide lifts all boats."

"Yes, it does," Dory said with a wry grin. She enjoyed the flirtation. "Shakespeare and aphorisms. You're quite the learned man, Topo Bogomil."

"I've had time to study."

"So, are you here to seduce me or check on the numbers?"

Topo's foot shook again. He hoped she couldn't see it from her vantage point behind the desk.

"And if I answered, 'Both'?" Topo asked.

Dory rose from her chair and made her way around her desk, keeping her eyes on Topo's as she slid herself across the edge and nestled up against Topo's bent knee. It was similar to a feeding, Topo thought, his head reeling. Dory leaned forward, spreading her legs apart, causing her skirt to strain.

"If you answered 'both,'" she said in a whisper, "then I'd tell you the numbers are good and that you have one chance, so you'd better take it."

* * *

There are more than three hundred Grateful Dead tribute bands but only one with members of the undead community. They called themselves Terrapin Space Station No. 2317, taking the name from the eponymous Grateful Dead song and the number from the supposed total number of shows The Dead performed. They'd traveled over several continents, bringing the music of Jerry and company to the masses ever since August 13, 1995, when 25,000 people attended a memorial for Jerry Garcia on the polo fields of Golden Gate Park. Two undead friends, Drew Ternbull and Rocky Sanchez, were so moved by the proceedings that they decided to carry on with the music of the Dead. Neither had any music talent, but as they recruited more members, all undead with musical ability, they soon learned the guitar and percussion.

Magnolia and Marmot first heard Terrapin Space Station No. 2317 (shortened to Terrapin Space Station as there was some dispute about the actual number of shows played and, besides, the numbers just didn't roll off the tongue easily) at DarkStarCon. When they went backstage to meet the band and learned of their undead status, they made sure to book the band yearly. Yes, there were three hundred touring tribute bands, but to Magnolia and Marmot, Terrapin Space Station filled them with, in the words of Marmot, "...an ethereal consciousness that formed a spiral staircase rainbow that ascended the heavens, tickled God's chin then exploded into a multicolored mushroom cloud that rose like a tie-dyed erection, humanity pouring out of it and coloring the fields of earth with a lush, green wonder grass." So you could imagine Marmot's excitement over sharing a plane ride with the band and its entourage.

* * *

Sylvia knew instinctually that the sun would rise in an hour. Also, she had lost her gold Haurex watch somewhere between becoming a vampire and getting drunk with her cohorts, so it was nice to have acquired the built-in daylight timer. Sylvia was down by the docks, watching an old fisherman curse as he untangled his fishing net, the brunt of his foul-mouthed assault being shouldered by his blonde Labrador, Musket. She decided the best thing for the dog would be to put the fisherman down and get a new name, perhaps. The high of her previous feeding had long since been vanquished, replaced for a time by alcohol. But she was sober now and hungry.

When the jolt of energy from drinking blood had been replaced by the mellow buzz of the drinks Joaquin provided her (with a wink and a nod), Sylvia came back to her irreverent self, which seemed to give Kyle tremendous relief. She had meant to pull Kyle aside and break the news that his account person was both a vampire and a battle-hardened advertising account manager but decided he seemed a bit too squirrely for the news, much more so after coming out of the bar restroom. Was he on something, she wondered? What ad creative wasn't, in some form? She'd break the news to both Kyle and Cate. They shouldn't be shocked, especially Cate. In fact, it would probably bring them closer, united as undead sisters. As for her new vampire masters, well, who the hell were they kidding with their benevolent subjugation, as if she were an intern to their cause? Idiots. She had no plans to help with their "feeding"; in fact, one of her first duties as a newly anointed vampire was to warn Dory about Rupert and company's scheme to use St. Ledo as a high-end pig trough. "That's a good boy, Musket," she whispered, then thrust herself upon the fisherman. Musket didn't move an inch. After she fed off the fisherman Sylvia rose from her hunched position. Maybe she'd take the dog in as her pet. Didn't vampires have daylight watchers or something like that, that she'd seen in a movie? She could surely get someone to walk the dog during the day.

*   *   *

From Joaquin's drink blog, *Beba!*

"**دليل مصاص دماء جديدة لمليه الشرب**" or "**A New Vampire's Guide to Drinking**" (courtesy of Morocco).
Do you find yourself keeping company with nighttime hours? Are your reflexes faster than that of a Mongoose toying with a Cobra? Do you have a complete disregard for mirrors? And your hearing, is it heightened to a new decibel range allowing you to eavesdrop on the conversations of ants? Do you find yourself consumed with intense cravings for blood? Viva mutatio! You are a vampire! You are officially a member of an elite club

(though the last century might have proven otherwise with the admission of Tom DeLay, Henry Ford, Eddie Van Halen, and Joey Bishop) whose members are no slouches when it comes to perseverance and preservation.

As you may already be aware, blood has become a fixation, like Imelda Marcos and shoes, but with more insatiability, which is saying something since Imelda owned upwards of 3,000 pair of shoes (with a particular weakness for Pierre Cardin heels). Like all God's creatures and their never-ending quest for sustenance, you seek out blood as a means of survival and because, when mixed correctly, it makes for a delightful aperitif to lift your spirits when you happen upon a train of thought regarding the absence of your soul (the jury's still out on that one).

And that, my new friend, is why along with certain rules you are instructed to follow; you are also privy to a copy of **A New Vampire's Guide to Drinking.** *I should omit the word "copy," as we stopped printing them in the early 2000s and became a blog.*

The first drink mixed with blood to initiate you is a simple recipe based on the effervescent Moscow mule. The history of this drink is nothing original. Borne out of necessity, bartenders needed to find a way to offload lesser beverages (ginger beer). Along came John Martin, who purchased Smirnoff vodka from the Russian ex-pat Rudolph Kunett (vampire), Jack Morgan, owner of the Cock 'n' Bull on Hollywood's Sunset Strip, and Morgan's head bartender, Wes Price. This was around 1941. It's not clear who decided to serve the drink in a copper mug. No matter, it lent a certain mannish elegance to the drink. As the drink caught on, bartenders suddenly became aware of the Russian roots of Smirnoff and refused to serve the ever-popular drink. This point of contention I agree with, not out of a sense of solidarity for the working class who toiled to make the then-considered communist vodka, but because, as a brand, Smirnoff is somewhere between rubbing alcohol and bile. The boycott lasted until Walter Winchell famously put it: "The Moscow mule is US made, so don't be political when you're thirsty. Three are enough, however, to make you wanna fight pro-Communists."

So it goes.

I have chosen to keep the original name for this particular mixture, as it is universally understood that it is a top seller among your kind. Mortals order it as well; they just can't taste the AB negative. Such Charlatans when it comes to imbibing.

The Moscow Mule

1 1/4 oz. Absolut Crystal, Magnum Grey Goose,
   OVAL or for the more modest among you, Reyka,
   Belvedere or Bainbridge Legacy
1 oz. blood (choose type as you see fit)
3 oz. ginger beer
1 tsp. sugar syrup
1/4 oz. lime juice
1 sprig mint
1 slice lime

And for the toast: "Megir þú lifa öllum aldir í lífi
þínu" which is Icelandic for the roughly translated:
"May you live all the centuries of your life."

CHAPTER 8

MORNING FOR KYLE BEGAN A LITTLE AFTER NOON, the yellowish light of day cutting through the embroidered white curtains drawn across the window over his bed.

"Honey. I did a bad thing, again," he said, eyes closed tightly. He let his right hand slide over the bed sheet in search of Cate. When it came up empty, Kyle assumed she was in the bathroom. "Hon? Could you come here and kill me? Maybe bring some Tylenol, too?" There was no response. Kyle rose with considerable effort and dragged himself off to the bathroom, where the door was open. She must've gone downstairs for grease, Kyle thought, because she was awesome. Half an hour later, when Cate was not as awesome, Kyle got himself dressed, grabbed his laptop, and headed downstairs for an egg sandwich, bacon, and a couple gallons of coffee.

Koufax's was abuzz with activity, as it was the lunch hour. Kyle's hopes of a booth and some fresh grease were dashed until he saw Cate sitting, chatting up Sari, who was holding a red dishrag. She always seemed to have sort of rag in her hand. Kyle assumed she was a graduate of the "time to lean, time to clean" school of the culinary arts. The two chuckled, sharing a moment of humor. And then Sari brushed a strand of hair out of Cate's eyes. They looked as if there was nobody else in the room.

If Kyle were like most jealous men, he'd be marching over to pre-coitus interruptus, but seeing how it was Kyle, it gave him an instant erection. There was no denying it: Something was going on between them and, in Kyle's eyes, it was hot. He did register a small pang of betrayal, but not so much as to interrupt the fantasy of girl-on-girl with boy watching—or even better, boy participating. That's when Cate turned her head and made contact with Kyle's eyes. If she had any blood in her, Kyle supposed her face would be rending itself red. Kyle smiled with a head nod and made his way over, titillated and grateful for the seat that would allow him to enjoy his grease.

"Ladies," Kyle said, bypassing Sari and sliding into the booth seat opposite Cate.

"He rises," Cate said.

"From the dead?" Kyle asked.

"Har," Cate said.

"How could you two have let me do this to myself?" Kyle said, grabbing a menu from the holder on the table.

"Riiiight," Sari said, doing her best to insert herself into the small talk without a look of incrimination. "You, my friend, were hammered."

"We're ad people. It's what we do," Kyle said. "So what rascalism are you womenses up to?"

"Cate tells me you think we're going to be overrun by vampires," Sari said.

"Lesbian vampires, I'm hoping," Kyle said.

"Why lesbian?" Cate said.

"It's in the air," Kyle said. "Can't you just smell it?" He was having fun, now. "Sometimes, after a rough night of drinking, I'll wake up in the morning and can just feel the Melissa Etheridge in the air in that sort of Ellen kinda way. Know what I mean?"

The two women gave Kyle slightly opened-mouthed looks. They felt like teens caught lying about ditching class and hiding out in one of their houses because the parents both worked and they could get stoned while listening to Zeppelin's *Physical Graffitti*.

"Does it work the other way?" Cate asked. "Sari, have you ever woken up to the smell of Elton John or RuPaul?"

"Most mornings, I wake to the smell of my cat's ass, which is nestled somewhere under my chin."

"There's a joke about waking to the smell of pussy, but I'm not gonna touch it," Kyle said.

"Ouch," Cate said. "Too harsh."

"Jesus, Kyle. Even for you," Sari said.

"Too much?" Kyle asked.

"Ya think?" Cate asked.

"Aaaand exit Sari," Sari said, turning to leave.

"Hey, could I get an egg sandwich, bacon, and coffee, purty please?" Kyle begged, putting his hands together in mock benevolence.

"Sure, sewer mouth," Sari said, snapping her rag at Cate's elbow before she left. Kyle slid his laptop in front of him and opened it, his eyes looking at Cate's, his grin shit-eating.

"What?" Cate said.

"Nothing. Dirty bird."

"What are you talking about?"

"Me? Nuthin'."

"What's with the laptop? Writing a novel?" Cate asked, more than ready to redirect the conversation.

"Art directors don't write novels," Kyle said.

"They don't do any work the morning after a campaign breaks either," Cate said.

"I'm doing research."

"On what?"

"Vampire hunting."

Cate shook her head, even allowing for a single *tsk*.

"Don't *tsk* me. When the blood starts getting sucked out around here, I'm gonna be your best friend. I'm gonna be the only thing between you and immortality."

Cate gave him a smirk.

"A different, more vicious kind of immortality," Kyle corrected.

"Because what could be more vicious than eating human brains?" Cate slid out of the booth. "I'm heading back to the studio. There's still work to be done. Where the fuck is Sylvia? Another spa day?"

"Sleeping it off, I imagine."

"Anyway, toodles," Cate said, leaning in for a kiss. Kyle sniffed her face. "What are you doing?"

"Smelling for kitty," Kyle said.

"Keep dreaming," Cate said, pecking him on the lips and wondering how he could be so nonchalant about what he saw.

"Honey, it's all I'm doing," Kyle said.

* * *

Two hours had passed since Kyle began his web search for ways to kill and/or abduct a vampire. He felt much better after the egg sandwich and bacon. He was on his fourth cup of coffee which had little effect on Kyle as he was ADD in addition to Bipolar II but couldn't be treated for the attention deficit because it clashed with his mood meds. Focused concentration or a stable mood (with occasional peaks and valleys). Kyle found that the web contained too much information when it came to vampires. Never mind the TV shows, movies, and books dedicated to vampirism, the blogs alone numbered in the thousands. He'd come across a similar deluge when he researched zombies since he had been boning one and had found the same information overload. What was it with humanity and its interest in being non-human?

Noam approached the table with a stack of potato latkes, a dollop of sour cream on top.

"For what ails you," Noam said. "Sari told me it was a long night."

Kyle accepted the dish, grateful for more grease but wondering why Noam was being nice to him. He had seemed, at best, nonplussed by Kyle.

Noam sat down in the booth, pushing the plate of latkes in front of Kyle, nodding with a smile. "Family recipe," he said. "Give it a try."

Kyle pushed aside his laptop, grabbed a fork and spiked a latke. It tasted like the best hangover cure on earth, next to a Tommy's triple cheese with extra chili he'd once had while visiting a friend in L.A. You don't forget a burger like that after a night of heavy drinking.

"You like?" Noam asked.

"Omigod, these are amazing," Kyle said, truthfully. "You're a god among men."

"Whenever I had too much Slivovitz there was only one thing to take away the pain. Potato latkes."

"And how," Kyle said, finding himself coming up short on conversation. Noam made him nervous, though he didn't know why, besides the somewhat chilly reception, which Kyle was used to as he worked in advertising, which ranked below working as a lawyer in the polls. It was a surefire conversation-stopper at cocktail parties, akin to stating that you were a pederast with a taste for blood sacrifice.

"Congratulations on the advertising," Noam said. "Sari and I whipped up something special for you guys, but we'll wait until the cobwebs clear to fully enjoy it."

"If it's half as good as these latkes, I'm sure we'll all be thrilled."

"So you've been in this booth for most of the afternoon," Noam said. "More advertising work?"

Kyle was unprepared for a lie, which was rare for a man in his line of work. Noam raised his eyebrows, waiting for an answer.

"Um, yeah, y'know, always more to be done," Kyle finally said.

Noam nodded, his tongue stuck in one cheek. He wasn't buying.

"Okay, I'm, uh, y'know, uh, you kinda freaked me out about the St. Irene of La Guardia story," Kyle said, amazed that he couldn't bullshit this man.

"That?" Noam said. "Pure myth. The stuff of legend you might say. The olive growers like to perpetuate it—all artisans like a rich history, even if it is mostly fabricated."

"Mostly fabricated," Kyle repeated. "That's the part that gets me."

"Well, you know the saying, 'Don't give me the honey and spare me the sting.'"

"Actually I've never heard that one."

Noam smiled. He was liking this kid maybe a little bit.

"This island has a lot of folklore. Some of it springs out of a bit of truth. It's a matter of faith."

Kyle took a bite of latke. It was his turn to wait out the pause.

"What about that story has you feeling uncomfortable?" Noam asked.

"Hmm, well. Monks who poison young women," Kyle said. "Young women who drive wooden stakes through monks. Vampires, protecting the blood of humanity. Vampires."

"What does your Internet say about vampires?" Noam asked.

"What doesn't it say? As you might have heard, vampires have been popular for a long time now."

"Since the writings of *The London Journal* of March 11, 1732, which describes vampyres—with a 'Y'—in Hungary," Noam said.

"Somebody's been reading Wikipedia."

"I find a lot of good recipes on the Internet."

"I bet. So? You're more than familiar with vampires."

"You could say I have a budding interest in the stories. They come from my ancestors' part of the world, you know. Vampire stories have a long and fruitful history of getting children to do their chores. My grandmother seemed to have one for each and every task. God bless the old country and their methods of striking fear into the hearts and minds of children."

"For me it was Bigfoot," Kyle said. "And Hitler. Those two, my mother loved to bring them up when my room was messy."

"You're Yiddishkite?" Noam asked.

"I honestly don't know," Kyle said. "Adopted."

"It must be difficult not knowing your roots. It's a big part of who we are."

"Someday I'll dig into it."

"Tell me, Kyle. It's more than the story. Why the interest in vampires?" Noam said.

Kyle took a hearty bite of latke, allowing himself a moment to think. Did Noam know about Cate? Did he know about St. Agrippina? The coexisting world of the undead? He knew about vampires. Maybe zombies wouldn't be a stretch.

"Let's say I've had experience with the supernatural," Kyle said. "I know, sounds ridiculous. And for the record, I'm on my meds."

Noam stuck out his lower lip as he shrugged his shoulders. "The world's full of things we can't explain."

"True that," Kyle said. "Anyway, the experiences I've had haven't been entirely good ones. In fact, I've kinda developed a bit of PTSD from it. I'd like to avoid having those unpleasant experiences again."

"I see," Noam said.

"Do you? I know I sound like a nutjob, but... there you go."

He was the wrong type for his daughter as well as the wrong sex, but Noam decided he enjoyed Kyle's honesty and willingness to sound foolish.

"How do you plan to avoid these experiences?" Noam asked.

"Well, that's the thing," Kyle said. "I'll need the help of a friend, but first I've gotta show proof that I might be facing more… 'bad experiences.'"

"Proof is always good."

"Yeah. Nobody seems to take things on faith anymore."

Noam smiled. "Maybe I can be of some assistance in getting you the proof you need."

Kyle tapped his fork on a latke. *Who was this Noam Wysocki?*

"Any ideas on how to kill or capture a vampire?" Kyle asked point blank.

"Killing one is well known," Noam said. "Stake to the heart, cut off the head, set on fire, drag into daylight, silver, immersion in holy water." Noam leaned in. "However, if you want to capture a vampire, read Exodus 40:9: *Use the sacred olive oil to dedicate to me the tent and everything in it.*"

Kyle was stunned. Really, *who was this Noam Wysocki? And what's with the bible thumping?*

"The sacred olive oil and bottle I have," Noam said. "It's the tent we need."

"Tent?" Kyle repeated. "Y'mean one of those wool tents with the wooden poles, biblical-like, since we're in bible-quoting land? O should I say Torah-quoting land? Do you have one? And a bottle? How do you cram a vampire into a bottle?"

"Relax," Noam said. "When cornered, a vampire turns to mist. When that happens, we capture it with the bottle containing the sacred oil. As for the tent, have you never heard of REI?"

Kyle leaned back in his seat. "Okay. Sincerely. Who the fuck are you?"

"I think what you mean to ask, is 'Who are we?'"

* * *

"Read me the list since yesterday," Philomena said to Rolf. They were having sushi at Hamasaku on Santa Monica Boulevard. They'd ordered the Sarah Michelle roll (tuna, spicy tuna, avocado, jalapeno), named after Sarah Michelle Gellar, to celebrate her addition to the roster of celebrities attending the HGPS charity on St. Ledo.

"Let's see," Rolf said, scrolling through his iPad mini. "Since yesterday… ah, Sly Stallone, Donnie Wahlberg…"

"No Mark?" interrupted Philomena.

"He's shooting in the Ukraine."

"Y'know their little burger stand, Wahlburgers? It's taking off in Boston. Maybe we could get them to cater one of the days? Sick kids like burgers. What kind of burgers do they have?"

Rolf opened Firefox and went to the Wahlburgers website. "They have a two-thirds-pound hamburger. They do hot dogs, too."

"Of course they do. Enterprising little sons of bitches. Get back to the list."

"Right. Jessica Alba and guest. Did I mention Ryan Seacrest?

"Don't."

"Bret Easton Ellis, Will Ferrell, Megan Fox and Brian whatshisface, Orlando Bloom, Kate Moss, One Direction. Oh, you'll appreciate this—Pippa!"

"No!"

"Yes!"

"Pippa's coming!"

Philomena drifted off for a moment. Rolf really wanted the last of the Sarah Michelle roll but held off until Philomena made gestures of departure.

"When royalty attends, a true celebutante, the younger sister of Catherine, Duchess of Cambridge—honey, sweetheart, we just blew up the universe!"

"I did good?" Rolf asked. He could feel himself slipping into the magnetic force of Philomena's approval. His friends warned him of this. They said to him, "Rolf, you can check out any time you like, but you can never leave," quoting *Hotel California*, knowing Rolf hated the Eagles more than the IRS hated Las Vegas. What did they know? They were cast members on Disneyland attractions.

"Rolfy," Philomena said, taking the last of the Sarah Michelle roll and dipping it in the thick, brown wasabi-and-soy-sauce mixture then popping it into her mouth. "You jid faboolus." Her mouth was full of tuna, reminding Rolf who was the master and who the servant.

*   *   *

Kyle and Cate were on their backs, naked, entranced by the slow-turning ceiling fan above them as they lay among the messy white bed sheets, Kyle sweaty and panting, Cate neither.

"Y'know, you're making me feel like an out-of-shape cocksman here, with your lack of oxygen intake," Kyle said.

"Did you really just call yourself a cocksman?" Cate asked.

"I did. From what I could tell, you're still a friend of the penis."

"Not sure what you mean there, but anyhoo."

Kyle smiled, letting the slight breeze from the ceiling fan cool his body. It was a nice change, looking up at a ceiling fan without having come out an unconscious state, as was the case back on St. Agrippina. Relentlessly so.

"You and Sari," Kyle said. "You seem... chummy."

"We're friends," Cate said. "She's a cool gal."

"Friends with benefits?" Kyle asked.

"Dude. Seriously?" Cate asked, doing her best impression of tired exasperation.

"Should I be jealous?" Kyle said.

"I dunno," Cate said. "Do you even know what it is to be jealous?"

"You don't think I get jealous?"

"You're sure not showing it."

"AH HA!" Kyle said, raising himself on an elbow toward Cate. "You admit there's something I should be jealous of. Go on, deny it. Deny your lesbian ways. Your fondness for the poon. Your..."

"Jesus, I hate that word."

"Lesbian?"

"You know what word," Cate said. "Why do you take the low road when it comes to serious conversations? You're like a child sometimes, unable to face your true emotions so you dress them up in Howard Stern-speak."

"So this is a serious conversation then?"

"You're asking if I'm cheating on you with another person," Cate said. "I'd call that serious."

"Cheating on me, with another *woman*," Kyle said.

"What difference does it make?"

"'Cuz it's hot," Kyle said.

"I think you mean, it's non-threatening in the fourteen-year-old mind of yours because I'm not cheating on you with another cock."

"Listen, I find dildos a form of cheating," Kyle said. "But I suppose you're right. It feels less threatening and more... awesome. I dunno why that is..."

"Because you have the sexual maturity of Hugh Hefner?" interrupted Cate.

"Hey. Don't knock the Hef."

"My point exactly. Why are we even having this conversation when nothing's happened?"

"So you guys didn't grind on each other?" Kyle asked.

Cate sat up on her elbow, facing Kyle.

"Y'know, when I first met you, you were this troubled doofus with a quick wit and a certain amount of innocence, like you'd been chewed up and spit out by life. I went from feeling sorry for you to having empathy to having real feelings for you. I even admired your talent. You had your moments, the immaturity, the ADD, even your embracing the crude. But since we've landed on this island, it's as if all of your qualities have been cranked up to eleven."

Kyle deeply appreciated the *Spinal Tap* reference that Cate, even as she launched into a tirade, managed to slip in.

"And now this talk of vampires and there being a repeat of what happened last year. I get it. You have some PTSD issues regarding what happened. I had to fish you out of another psych ward. Me. Your undead girlfriend. And you came out of that place with one directive: Take it down a notch. You're on your meds. You're getting some exercise. Eating well. It was my fault that I let you have a few drinks, but I felt you needed it, which makes me an enabler, so fuck you, it's on me.

"The only moments when you're yourself are when we're having sex. The rest of the time, I feel us drifting apart, watching you slip deeper into this vampire fixation which I interpret as fear of your mortality, which, coming from an undead person, seems unfair, but I thought we'd worked past that issue, and no, I won't bite you to make things better, you're gonna need to figure this one out on your own, and Sari and I have an attraction to each other which is weird for me because I thought I was straight and then along comes Sari, and you're acting like a douche which is driving me toward bisexuality now, so I don't know whether to shit or wind my watch. Also, I think she might have a very delicious brain. There, I said it."

The ceiling fan's small motor turned the gears in a tranquil hum. The curtains moved slowly with the airflow. Particles danced in the daylight. Cate bore holes through Kyle's eyes, having laid it all out for him to, what? Make a snark-filled retort? Change subjects altogether?

Pee? This was that moment and Kyle knew it but struggled so very hard with the defense mechanism he'd spent decades refining until it was like breathing, the way he could just kill the moment and destroy the future. He could see the fork in the mental health road, and the inner voice that had spent a lifetime telling him to take the easy way out was now saying, "Don't be a dickhead. Take the hard road. The uncomfortable road. Don't fuck this up. Not this time."

"I'm sorry, Cate. I know it hasn't been easy for you, putting up with me."

Good boy. Now try not to get a boner because her breasts look so wonderful in the light of day.

"You're right," Kyle continued. "I've… it's been hard to just believe how good I have it. Y'know? I'm alive. I'm living in another paradise, and it's only because I have you. I love you, Cate Hendricks, and I know saying that puts a heavy load on your shoulders. But…"

How could he possibly bring up the conversation with Noam? He needed to. He needed her to believe that, despite the psych ward, the meds, the general funkiness that is Kyle Brightman, there really, truly was a threat of vampires pulling the same shit that the zombies did on St. Agrippina. But there was no way he could lay that at her feet and expect to keep her. Maybe some things were more important than a relationship? *Riiiight.* As if he were *that* guy. No, he wouldn't tell her about the conversation. Like Oscar, he'd have to present proof to Cate that not only were there vampires among them, but that they were gearing up for another feast of souls.

"But, what?" Cate said.

"But I have my distractions," Kyle said, coming off a tad obtuse.

"I know, hon," Cate said. "And that can be part of your charm, the way your mind wanders all over the place. Let's just take it down a notch. And I love you, too. Hmm?"

Kyle grinned. He grinned because he did the right thing and saved a relationship and because, well, this was one sexy zombie that lay before him. Oh, what a lucky man he was.

*   *   *

Percy hated meeting with the Sons of Gilgamesh in their "secret" lair, a wine cellar beneath a long ago abandoned vineyard located on the south end of the island. The vineyard, once a robust winery that churned out Moscatel, Port and red wines that had been purchased recently by a vampire family and become a reserve blood cellar in the event the raid went south, was temporarily guarded and occupied by The Sons of Gilgamesh. Blood cellars existed the world over: in tombs, caves, biotech freezers, even underneath famous landmarks such as the Chicago Board of Trade and Grauman's Chinese Theatre. Though humanity kept reproducing, it was getting harder to stage raids on a mass scale, though Serbia and the Congo had helped, without getting the world's attention—even though, to the amazement of the older vampires, the more hideous the massacre, the sooner the general public's attention was redirected to other events, such as a new Kanye West release.

Ekur and his brother, Shulgi, vampires whose births dated back to 2094 B.C., were members of the Sons of Gilgamesh. Back in the day, the Sons of Gilgamesh operated out of Mesopotamia and were involved in everything ranging from grain theft to royal graft. Times were hard and fast in Mesopotamia, as it was an ever-evolving culture and there was no end to ordinary people ordaining themselves gods and goddesses. Contract hits and bribery were common, as was ritualistic slaughter. But there was an upside to the place. Mesopotamians threw epic soirees that went on for weeks at a time with food, drink, nakedness, prayer, and games involving blood sport and piercings.

They were miscreants, the Sons of Gilgamesh, making the Hell's Angels, Crips, Bloods, the Cosa Nostra, the various cartels, and the GOP seem like Girl Scouts peddling their toxic but delicious cookies outside the local IGA. Aside from being true reprobates, they were also vampires, which upped the ante considerably. The membership numbered in the thousands. Each SOG club protected vital blood supplies on a global scale. They were also instrumental in the various blood raids that had begun in the Bronze Age and continued all the way up to assaults on a large scale, such as the Massacre of the Latins in Constantinople and Hemp Fest.

A small crew of SOG was on St. Ledo for the weekend raid that Rupert had planned. It was chump change, with only Ekur, Shulgi, and three other members in attendance. Percy was the crew's go-between. They enjoyed messing with him, though they were careful not to get too dangerous, as Percy was Rupert's private supply. They had just finished throwing darts at Percy's bare back, Ekur having sketched a crude portrait of Gulagakal, Goddess of Sanitation, in black Sharpie as a target, when Ekur decided they should hear what Percy had come to tell them.

"Put your shirt on," Ekur said. "Your blood is too tempting, though I cannot believe its source is a rube such as yourself."

Percy grabbed his Oxford and painfully pulled it over his shoulders, dots of red bleeding through the shirt. He was a man worn down by vampires. His once-buttoned-up appearance gave way to a man on a downward spiral. Bloodletting could do that to a guy.

"Next time, we'll draw the face of Ninkhursag on your testicles," Shulgi said.

"So, what news do you have for us that you couldn't have texted?" Ekur said.

"Rupert insisted I deliver the message in person," Percy said, buttoning his shirt.

"Rupert enjoys your persecution, as do we," Ekur said.

"I'm getting that," Percy said, glumly.

"Speak, pig. Or do we need to waterboard you with urine?" Shulgi threatened.

"No need. Rupert thinks the Brotherhood are reforming on the island."

"He's lying," Shulgi said. "Let's coat his cock with honey and bury him up to…"

"Shulgi," Ekur said, effectively silencing Shulgi's sadistic fantasy.

"We destroyed the Brotherhood with the death of Catalina Guarda. What proof have you that they are reforming?" Ekur asked.

"One of our watchers overheard Catalina Guarda's husband telling another how to capture and destroy your kind."

"You mean *our* kind, you blight on immortality," Shulgi said.

"Y'know what? I'm just relaying the message," Percy said, put out. "Why all the hate?"

Before Percy finished saying "hate," Shulgi was on him, his fangs less than an inch from Percy's throat. Ekur sighed. Percy couldn't help himself. It was as if he'e been given a universal directive to piss off everyone he came into contact with. It didn't help that Shulgi was a touch evil incarnate, but still.

"What would Rupert have us do, if in fact this were true?" Ekur asked.

Percy licked his lips, getting the hint that he might want to choose his words carefully. "He would like you to look into it."

"Let's split him open and eat him from the inside out," Shulgi said. "And then shit him out over a rotting corpse."

Ekur ignored the suggestions. "Tell Rupert that we will look into it. If he's right, this could present a problem."

"I'll tell him as soon as I leave here," Percy said, hoping that would secure his release.

"Shulgi. Let him go," Ekur said. Shulgi grazed Percy's throat with one of his fangs. "I think the next time I see you, I'll clog your ass with your own nose."

"Oh, Shulgi," Ekur said, chuckling. "The things you come up with."

CHAPTER 9

"I'VE SEEN SOME INTERESTING PASSENGERS in my day but gotta say, this flight moves into the number-one slot—and that's saying something. I've been on flights with a sprinkling of celebrity faces, star athletes, criminals, circus troupes. I've even been on a flight filled with coma patients, which now moves into the second slot, just above Sarah Palin's extended family. Rock stars doing the mile-high right in their seats. Politicians and their boyfriends. Small farm animals—it's true, 4-H convention. Oh, the conventions. Listen. When you get a group of like-minded individuals and I don't care who they are—computer programmers, accountants, porn stars, whatever—when they all get together, all hell breaks loose. At least with this flight, you've got your smaller groups—manageable even, but I gotta tell you, we should lock up the liquor and keep the Chex Mix flowing, though the Deadheads probably brought their own, and those kids from iCarly? They're on X, I'm sure of it."

Charlene, a flight attendant for West Indies Air, was surveying the passengers and holding court with the other, younger flight attendants she was training. After the initial excitement abated regarding the cadre of celebrities, Fergie, those two guys from *Supernatural*, Trisha Yearwood, Bruce Jenner, Kelly Ripa, Padma

Lakshmi and Erik Estrada—who only Charlene recognized—the attendants kicked into high gear, serving wine spritzers to the first-class passengers.

"Oh, and those children with that weird aging disease like that Brad Pitt movie, *Benjamin* something, they have such a sweetness to them, it's so sad. I'm gonna make sure they get extra Chex Mix and all the Sprite they want. You two can have the Deadheads and the congressmen—and no, they can't upgrade to first. Remind them of that when they get PO'd, and they will. Oh, and those geeky-looking Facebook or Google or whatever guys. You know, the ones trying too hard to impress the Indian cooking lady. Those are yours too. They're a pushover, grateful for any woman who might serve them—and don't take that the wrong way, but it's true. Okay, girls. I think we're ready for battle."

Charlene walked away, leaving the two attendant trainees in the service area of the plane.

"If I ever get that way, would you do me a favor?" one attendant asked.

"Sure, what?"

"Kill me. Hard."

"You got it."

* * *

Sylvia knew her sudden absences were starting to get noticed. That's why she invited Kyle and Cate for a meeting in an imperio, a small one-story building that served as a chapel and a community hub, usually stocked with goods for use by the less fortunate. There were six on St. Ledo, all replicas of imperios found in the Azores. Ornate in architecture with bold colors: pinks and blues and reds on white. The builders' ancestors became vampires in the early 1900s then moved to the island formerly known as Queixa and brought their culture with them. The St. Ledo imperios sat empty, the windows boarded up. The owners gave no explanation because they were vampire safehavens, and you can't run around an island pointing out vampire safehavens to tourists.

Sylvia had been hibernating in an imperio that looked as if it were designed by a Portuguese Versace. She had texted Kyle to meet her there. "It'll say 1918 on the façade. White building, red detail. Think Rick's Café on acid. Key under red vase."

Kyle and Cate found the imperio and entered, the key as promised under a small red vase containing hydrangeas. The interior was pitch black, the windows covered.

"Close the door, it's chilly out there," Sylvia said.

"Somebody put a light on," Kyle said while Cate shut the door.

A lamp turned on, revealing Sylvia sitting at a wooden table in a sparsely furnished room. The walls were whitewashed; exposed beams were overhead. It was monastic.

"Is this part of the B-and-B chain started by Thor Heyerdahl?" Kyle asked. "Where's the spa?"

"Funny. Sit. Both of you. We've got shit to discuss," Sylvia said. Kyle and Cate took a seat on the barely standing wooden chairs.

"What are you doing…"

"No time for questions, hon," interrupted Sylvia. "I'm sitting at a table with an undead person and her boyfriend so this shouldn't come as a shock to either one of you. I'm a vampire."

"I fuckin' knew it!" Kyle shouted. "I mean, I didn't know you were a vampire, but I *KNEW IT*! This is awesome news!"

"Ohmigod, not you too," Cate said, burying her face in her hands. "Why, God? Why?" She lifted her head. "What's with everyone going to cray-cray land?"

"Oh, the zombie's having trouble buying that her co-worker's been turned into a vampire?" Sylvia asked, knowing that word would irritate Cate. "Look." Sylvia popped out her fangs with a small clicking sound, as if they were spring-loaded.

"Oh," Cate said.

"Yeah. Oh," Sylvia said. "Moving on."

"See?" Kyle said. "Told you. This island's crawling with vampires."

"You're right, Kyle. Now shut the fuck up and listen," Sylvia snapped. "Yes, there are vampires lurking about and they have big plans, and yes, Kyle, you were right again—they want to suck all of the blood out of the tourist trade."

Kyle pumped his fist. "For the win."

"So it's happening all over again," Cate said. "What are the odds?"

"Dory bet against the house. The house always wins," Sylvia said. "The newly acquired business partner? Rupert Jagger? Yeah, he's the main vamp running the show. It's like fucking IBM, layers of vamps, all middle management suck-ups, given marching orders to feed a shit-ton of vampires, even collect some blood for cold storage then move on, leaving the island in tatters, like the New Hampshire primary."

"Why'd they make you a vampire?" Cate asked.

"They wanted to recruit more C-level management," Sylvia said. "We did too good a job on the ad campaign, kids. They think I can land UFOs while conducting *La Boheme*. Who the fuck knows, they see vampire potential in me, what's it matter? All that matters is that we gotta find a way to make this not happen."

"God. Dammit," Kyle said. "I like being right. *I LOVE IT!* But dammit, I'm right back where I started. Sonofamotherufckingshit!"

"Here we go," Cate said.

"Damn right, here we go," Kyle said, shooting out of his chair and beginning to pace. "All of you. Doubters! I knew it. I could just feeeeeel it. In my bones. In my heart. There were too many coincidences, too many things falling together just like before on St. Aggies.

"I warned all of you but no, all I got was 'Take it down a notch' and quaff those fucking Moscow mules and blah blah blah. Well now, I've done it again—I've become responsible for the lives of who knows how many people? Hmm? How many are gonna get their blood sucked right out of their throats because I know how to sell a resort? Really? *Really?* Are you fucking kidding me with this?

"Nah, this is, is too much. I'm so out of here, I'm not even gonna pack. No. I'm gonna walk right out that door and head straight to the airport and get on a plane and get my ass back to Seattle and no, I'm not gonna end up in a psych ward again because, this time, I have the right meds, I've been eating well, getting some exercise— maybe drinking a bit much, thanks Cate, for that slip. No, don't say a fucking word because I'm like Fukushima about to blow my wad all over Japan and the rest of the Pacific. I'm gonna shit out Godzilla and destroy cities n' shit. I'm…"

Before Kyle could say another word, Sylvia was up and behind him, her hand covering Kyle's mouth, her other free arm wrapped around his torso, holding him like a child clutching a Teddy Ruxpin.

"You chose to put up with this?" Sylvia asked Cate.

"Can you believe it?" Cate replied.

"I'll let go of your mouth, but if you utter one more sanctimonious word, I'm gonna make you my vampire bitch, and if you've ever met one of my assistants, that's no way to spend eternity. Got it? Nod if you got it."

Kyle immediately nodded. Sylvia removed her hand and released Kyle.

"Your hand smells like pickled herring," Kyle said.

"We need to nip this vampire gang-bang in the bud," Sylvia said, ignoring Kyle's comment and retaking her seat. "Suggestions?"

"I think we do what we did last time," Cate said.

"And what was that?" Sylvia asked.

"Kyle, can we get our hands on some heavy weaponry that shoots silver bullets?"

Kyle cracked a smile, strutted over to a chair, pulled it out slowly, and sat. He clasped his hands behind his head and put his feet up on the table, crossing them as well. "Does the pope shit in the woods? Do bears give Holy Communion? Do politicians swallow?"

"So, yes?" Sylvia asked with considerable annoyance.

"I can go you one better," Kyle said. "I know a guy who knows two things: How to make a Reuben that a rabbi would shoot his right foot to eat, and how to catch and kill vampires."

* * *

To: northatlanticvampire; nosferatullc; SOG; Michelle Bachman; bloodbankofuniverse; coalitionABneg; algul.com; bruxa.com; chupacabrainc.com; baldwinbrosllc; vladimpaler.org; succubusinc; vampryeindustries.com; dracu; fangbrosltd; chloekardashian; 700club; thedonaldllc; denverbroncos; knickelback; hulkhogan; societyo-neg.com; twbachiatday; jwthompson; omnicorp; rogerailes.org; americanredcrossvamp.org;

For immediate release.

STRAP ON THE FEEDBAG, NORTH ATLANTIC DIVISION

St. Ledo island (formerly Queixa)—*The North Atlantic feed is scheduled for St. Ledo (formerly Queixa), latitude: N 43° 4' 50.3723" longitude: W 36° 7' 22.9688", this upcoming weekend (June 20-22). If you're within* *the 1,500 mile radius, then why not stop in for a feed on your way to the States or Iceland, where the next feed is scheduled in late July? Rupert Jagger will be your host and promises a weekend filled with entertainment ranging from the Undead Grateful Dead convention (though not rich in nutrients, a great source for bootlegs), as well as the celebrity charity for children living with progeria. The resort on St. Ledo is projected to be at full capacity, but suites are still available with blackout curtains. While there, feel free to feed on the local population. The Brotherhood of St. Irene of La Guardia has long been obliterated so feel free to take in the many pastoral sights. The aurora borealis is said to particularly stunning this time of year. For more information, contact PERCY MERRIWEATHER at percymerriweather@gmail.com*

* * *

He was back again. Maybe it was because they had sex and something was transferred (STDs weren't an issue with the undead), but she could feel him in the room, lurking.

"Back for more?" Dory asked, sitting at her desk, clicking through projections on her laptop.

"Interesting," Topo said. "Appears I've instilled a vampire sense in you."

"Is that what you kids are calling it nowadays? At someone point in all of this, you should take me out to dinner, and maybe we could try doing it on a more amenable surface, such as my bed."

"I wonder, what would a vampire and a zombie have for dinner?" Topo mused.

"Turf and fluids?" Dory suggested, typing.

Topo grinned. He liked her more with every encounter, to the point where he had begun to imagine them off together, standing out on some balcony somewhere, laughing at a private joke, his hand stroking her black hair, the moon casting its yellowish light across her face. He liked her to the point that he might forgo this business of a massive feed. He would possibly help her keep the island and her resort free from the same fate that befell her other hotel. Could he go against his own? He smirked at the thought. *His own.* One thing Topo Bogomil had never felt was a kinship or camaraderie with his fellow vampire. Coldhearted apex hunters they were and not much else.

It would mean going up against Rupert and his legions, but he knew a few that would turn on a dime to get themselves free of Rupert's management style, which was predicated on fear and intimidation. The zombies would help. Not as if they had any blood to lose. Topo had found this out when, at the moment of climax, he bit into Dory's neck only to find a lack of O negative. She peeled off a squeal of laughter at this as she came. Joke was on him. Trixster. She complained how she'd need a touch-up as his bite took a small chunk out of her neck. From the looks of it, she'd already attended to it. Wasn't that how she operated? Get it done.

"So, are you gonna stare at me all night or shall we adjourn to the carpet?" Dory asked, her eyes still maddeningly focused on her laptop screen.

"You really put everything into this place," Topo said.

Dory clicked her tongue. "Is this where you tell me I work too much and don't spend enough time being part of 'us'? Because I think we're waaaay too early in the game for that talk."

"I agree," Topo said. "We're not at that point… yet."

Dory kept typing, a wide grin splashed across her face. Topo felt dizzy at the mention of a future with Dory, as if he'd just fed. He'd never put himself out there like that, not even when he was mortal.

"What I meant to say is, you've worked hard to build this," Topo said. "You're a success."

"It's still a story in the making," Dory said. "We'll see how things progress with your boss, who I'm sure has nothing but success on his mind."

"You don't think he wants the same thing as you?" Topo said.

"I think he's a mercurial, macro-thinking bloviator with an ego about the size of this island. He's made no attempt to equate us in our partnership. At first I thought it was sexism, then some sort of class warfare among the undead, but now I think he's someone unaccustomed to being told 'no.' It has been my experience that men of this sort are worth keeping both eyes on. I'm seldom wrong when I go with my gut about people."

"What's your gut say about me?" Topo asked, moving toward Dory.

"You?" Dory stopped her flurry of typing and closed her laptop. He had her full attention now. "I see a man conflicted. A man who has had to make choices not of his doing for too long. An honest man who'd maybe had to do things that went against his loyalty to himself, to the kind of man he should be. I see a deep thinker, even a philosopher. A man with an appreciation for time, but also weary of it. A forever-reluctant vampire—which is a long time to be filled with self-doubt. I see a man on the cusp of something."

Dory rose from her chair, arching her back. Just another workday even if she had just read his soul. "Did I nail it?"

Topo had arrived at that moment he'd so often gone against. He understood what it was to be disenfranchised and yet capable of making decisions that went against the better angels or demons of his nature. But now, the game was different. He had skin in it this time. He might regret this decision later, but fuck it, nobody lives forever.

"What if I told you that Rupert had other ideas about St. Ledo?" Topo said. "That he planned on using the resort much the same way your kind did back on St. Agrippina?"

"Well, if you did, it would confirm what I hoped would happen," Dory said. "That the man I was falling for decided to come clean with me since I already received a text stating the same thing about your boss and his grand designs for my resort."

They smiled at each other. Two right decisions had been made.

"You know I've been down this road before," Dory said. "And since I was dealing with vampires, I took special precautions in the event of history repeating itself. No offense."

"None taken," Topo said. "What precautions are you talking about?"

"A certain metal foundry in Casablanca with a recent order for enough silver bullets to rid the North Atlantic of vampires. Does that bother you?"

"Quite the contrary," Topo said. "I'd expect nothing less."

* * *

Though he felt his usual melancholic self, Noam also felt the need for his daughter to reconnect with her mother, even if it meant talking to a hunk of stone. He still kept up his visits after all these years. His heart still burdened with the theft of a life he saw with Catalina Guarda, Noam brought their daughter along to remember and to tell Sari something that she might have trouble understanding or believing. Which is why he told a few of the others to join him at the gravesite.

Nestled on the side of a hill overlooking the ocean, Catalina Guarda's headstone, carved from one-hundred-year-old limestone, had her name in bold Bembo (as Kyle would identify it) above the family crest, a masonic diamond with an olive branch wound around a spear lying atop an open book that contained the phrase: *Defensor autem sanguis, qui stat pro filiis hominum,* or *Defender of the blood, protector of humanity.* Sari had Google-translated the Latin to discover its meaning and assumed it had to do with the whacked-out story of St. Irene of La Guardia. She had asked her dad about it once.

"Why that?" she'd said.

"Your mother was part of the culture. The olive trees were a part of that."

"Protector of humanity? A spear?"

"Mom was Portuguese. They're a dramatic people."

Noam had brought fresh-cut lavender to place at the headstone, which he kept clean save for a few bits of grass that sprung up—she would've wanted the naturalistic feel. He and Sari stood in front of the headstone. Stratocumulus clouds in long, thick strands drew across a sky that had begun its descent into dusk. A slight breeze off the ocean made for light scarf weather, and Noam had made sure Sari had worn one. Maybe that day more than the others, he looked at his daughter as the motherless child, the little kid missing a big part of her life.

Noam placed the lavender across the top of the headstone, then took a step back and stood in silence. Sari wasn't sure if there was a ritual to this. Sure, she'd been down here with him before, but she wondered if in all those days of visiting maybe her father had developed a routine. Maybe some spoken words? A poem? Some kind of bringing forth what was in his heart.

"Sari, your mom was killed by a vampire. She was a vampire hunter. I still am, though it's been a while, and since you're of our combined bloodline, that makes you a vampire hunter, as well. We suspect vampires are back on the island. We need to hunt them down and kill them," Noam said, as if he were reading Sari instructions on building an IKEA shelf unit.

"Uhhhh..."

"I know, take a moment. It's a lot to lay on a kid," Noam said.

"Yeeeaaaahhh...."

"It's crazy, I know. Life's crazy. There you have it."

"Umm hmmm..."

"I didn't believe it when I met her, either. Whole family, teeming with vampire hunters. Even Uncle Zosa, who by all rights shouldn't have been hunting anything more than lint out of a clothes dryer..."

"Okay. We done here?" Sari interrupted as she turned to leave.

"You don't believe me," Noam said. "Understandable."

"So y'know, most kids, they worry about their parents as they get older, y'know," Sari said. "Their bodies becomes frail. The mind maybe not as sharp as it once was with names and dates and what-not. At first, you say to yourself, 'they're old.' But then things take a turn, such as standing at the gravesite of your mother with your father, who has just told you that the parents you thought you knew happen to be vampire hunters. So okay, that happened, and you now have to start thinking about healthcare coverage and finding a nursing home that works with Alzheimer's patients and, man, it becomes a big deal. A really big deal." Sari turned to her father and brought her hand to rest on his elbow. "It's okay, Pop. We're gonna take care of you. Everything's going to be fine."

Noam smiled. What heart this kid had. Of course she'd think he was losing his mind.

"I lied to you, honey," Noam said, placing his face on Sari's cheek. "I lied to you and now it's time to come clean, to lay the cards on the table. Your mother didn't die of a heart attack per se."

Sari moved her hand from her father's elbow and covered the hand on her face. "It's hard, I know, Mom being gone. You guys were a true partnership. True love. I can't imagine the loss. The pain. It's gonna be okay, Pop. We'll take care of everything." Sari paused. "When you said, 'per se,' what were you referring to?"

"All of the blood was drained out of your mother, so none was able to get to the heart. So, in a sense, it wasn't the vampire who killed your mother but the lack of blood to the heart, thus causing a heart attack."

Off in the distance, three men walked along the hillside. The wind brushed Sari's hair into her eyes. This was worse than she thought.

"Dad, Mom did die from a heart attack. Her family was full of heart attacks. Her arteries, they failed her."

"Exactly," Noam said. "All of those family members had the blood sucked out of them, as well. This was in the small villages in the old country, in Portugal. Santarem, Beja, Faro, up north, Lamego and Guarda. All of them, they gave their lives to protect those around them. Just as we must now protect Queixa."

"Okeedoke," Sari said, feeling the impatience begin to rise in her. "Did we hit the Slivovitz this morning? Maybe clean out the walk-in? Is that it, some Ajax-fume action going on here? You're starting to scare me more than just a bit, Dad."

"I can tell you're getting angry with me. You went from 'Pop' to 'Dad.' Please don't be angry…"

"I'm trying my best here. But you drag me up here to…"

"You have never been dragged to your mother's gravesite."

"You know what I mean—Dad. This crazy talk about vampires and Mom is, at best, completely fucking unsettlling. What did you think would happen here? We come up to Mom's grave, share a few tender remembrances, and then you unload this shit on me and I'm supposed to, what? Tell you it's about time? That I always had a sneaking suspicion? That I'd ask when the hunt begins? Jesus Christ, Dad! Anything else? Am I really your daughter? Is my name really Sari? Are there any vampires in our family?"

"Actually, there are," Noam said.

"*OF COURSE THERE ARE!*" Sari shouted to the sky, arms raised. "How could there not be?" She turned back to her father. "It's not me, is it? You'd tell me, right?"

"Stop this nonsense," Noam said. "It's not you."

"You? Are you a vampire deli owner?"

"We're standing here in the daylight. Don't be foolish."

"Uncle Zosa? Aunt Coria? It's not one of the cousins? Is it Cousin Evora with the lazy eye?"

"*Listen to me!*" Noam shouted. "Stop talking and just listen." Noam blew out a sigh, his cheeks filled with air. He looked around. Sari did the same, noticing the three men who were now closer. One of them wore a brown derby hat. They all appeared to be around her father's age.

"Some of us who defended the blood were turned against their will," Noam said. "One of them, it happened centuries ago. When you turn, you become the property of them. You do as they say against your will. Only a few have been able to break free. Unfortunately, one who was unable went from fierce defender to attacker. His name was Topo Bogomil, and we suspect he is here on this island."

"Where do you come up with these funky names?" Sari asked.

"Have you heard a word I said?" Noam spat.

"To recap," Sari said, "my mother was killed by a vampire as were many of the Guarda family line. Both she and my father, Noam Wysocki, were and remain vampire hunters. St. Ledo…"

"Queixa," interrupted Noam.

"…Queixa is chock full of vampires, and we need to hunt them down and kill them. Also, there's a really powerful vampire on—Queixa—named Topo Bogomil who is centuries old and is here for the waters or to Jet Ski or who the fuck knows. Do I have that right?"

"If Topo Bogomil is on Queixa, that can only mean one thing. He's here to exterminate us all by means of a raid," Noam said.

"Oh."

She didn't seem to be any closer to believing his story, but at least she seemed to have calmed down.

"Sooo, do we close up the deli and go hunting?" she asked.

"No need to close the deli, we'll put Juan on it."

"Juan steals from the till."

"He's poor, let him. Is any of this believable to you?"

"What can I say? Either you're batshit—pun intended—or we're in big trouble. Did you make enough kreplach for the nighttime rush?"

"Okay. I can go with that," Noam said. "It really is a lot to take in."

Just then, the three men were standing beside the grave.

"Did you tell her?" the man with the brown hat said.

"I did," Noam said.

"She buy it?" another man wearing a herringbone coat asked.

"Not really," Noam said. "But she seems game."

"Show her," the hat-wearing man said to the silent third man.

"Show me what?" Sari asked. "Friends of yours, Dad? Vampire-hunting buddies?"

The silent man wearing the black overcoat and gray scarf nodded, then unbuttoned his coat and opened it wide. It looked like a coat Harpo Marx would've worn except, instead of watches, there hung various crucifixes, small bottles filled with water, and various-sized wooden stakes.

"The fuck?" Sari asked.

"Show her," the hat man said. The silent man let go of his jacket lapel and pulled down his scarf. A chunk of skin was missing from his neck, which looked as if it had been chewed off by a large dog. Sari took a step back.

"Show her," the hat man said.

"Y'mean there's more? I dunno if I can take it."

"Watch," Noam said.

The silent man unhooked one of the small clear bottles from inside his coat, pulled the tiny cork from it, raised his other hand palm up, and let a few drops of water from the bottle land in his palm. It immediately began to smoke, the silent man wincing.

"What the fuck!" Sari said. "Stop it. Stop it!"

The silent man rubbed his palm against his coat.

"You can be bitten by a vampire and live," the hat man said. "But you will spend the rest of your days as a part of that vampire curse."

Sari's mouth was agape.

"To answer your question, no. I haven't made the kreplach for the night crowd," Noam said.

CHAPTER 10

THE BLOND LABRADOR FORMERLY KNOWN as Musket lay outside St. Bobo's sans leash, his face resting on his front paws, completely uninterested in the evening's walking traffic that passed him by. There were occasional pats on the head and a few "Hey boys," but he didn't give an inch. He was thinking how it'd be nice to have a friend and a new name. The vampire who took him away from Trejo, his abusive owner, told him that she would find another name for him that more suited his personality. The dog had mulled over new names ever since. What kind of dog was he? He considered himself laconic, wise, maybe a bit of a misanthrope. Years with Trejo had taught him to be a bit of a nihilist, but even as he sat outside the bar, knowing he belonged to the woman vampire, he could feel the negative energy that filled him dissipate like the fog down by the docks, where Trejo's throat had been ripped out, his blood sucked up.

He'd heard lots of dog names in his life, most of them ill-suited to their animal. He did prefer human names to dog-sounding ones. "Bingo," "Bandit," "Boomer," "Buster,"—he hated all those names, especially when they started with the letter "B." He didn't know why, it was just how they sounded—trite and demeaning, as if the human was letting them know they were not equals, which was bullshit because he'd known plenty of dogs better than their owners, himself included. "Scamp," "Pooky," "Dash," "Rover."

"I fucking hate Rover," he thought as the names ran through his mind.

There was that guy who had headed into the bar about an hour ago. The one who'd stopped, kneeled, and said to him, "I knew a dog once. Never caught his name, though. Just called him 'Dog.'"

Thanks for that one, dipstick.

Several more people went in just after him. None of them cheerful to be going into a bar. Trejo used to feed him beer. It tasted pretty good but gave him diarrhea. *What would he call himself?*

* * *

"His name was Musket, but that's so, I dunno. Fuckin' manly. And reminds me of the Civil War, which always bored me to tears whenever someone spoke of it," Sylvia said to Kyle as they sat at a table in St. Bobo's.

"How about Quint?" Kyle said.

"Y'mean *Jaws* Quint?"

"Yeah."

Sylvia nodded. "Not bad. Le chaim." She raised her glass and took a swig.

"You're Jewish?"

"Seriously? A *Sylvia*?"

"Yeah, but 'Woodcock' isn't very daughter of Abraham."

"It used to be 'Wolodarsky' until my grandparents hit Ellis Island."

"Wolodarsky to Woodcock," Kyle said. "I like Wolodarsky, better."

"What about your name? 'Brightman?' Seems a tad self-satisfied."

"It's…"

"Where is everybody?" Cate interrupted, carrying her Moscow mule from the bar. The copper cup was already chilled over.

"We're talking about names," Sylvia said. "I was asking about Kyle's."

"Good luck with that," Cate said pulling up a chair. "I can't get the name of his parents out of him."

"You were just about to tell me, weren't you?" Sylvia asked Kyle.

"I was going to say…"

"You guys," Sari said, also carrying a Moscow mule, which didn't go unnoticed by Kyle. "You guys, we've got some serious shit to talk about. Where's my dad?"

"I saw him go to the head," Cate said, motioning Sari to sit next to her. "Also something Kyle filled with deep, lesbian sexual signifigance."

"Nah, we've got some serious shit to tell you," Kyle said.

"Really? More serious than vampires?" Sari said.

"What the hell, Cate? You told her?" Kyle said.

"I didn't tell her anything. I came with you."

"Trust me when I say that nobody in this bar has more serious shit to tell than me," Sylvia said. "Including vampires."

"Hold up," Dory shouted from the bar, where LeRoi was setting down her vodka martini. "You guys. There's some serious shit going on that we need to talk about."

In walked Thierry, Xavier, and Desmond, who immediately set upon the bar, barking drink orders to LeRoi and Joaquin.

"Everybody chill the fuck out and go siddown," LeRoi said. "We're just gonna get a bottle and some glasses going here. Joaquin has some shit he wants to talk to y'all about anyway."

Everybody fell silent. Anyone who had a drink sipped it. Dory, Thierry, and Xavier came over from the bar, dragged some chairs from other tables, and took a seat.

"It's too quiet in here," Kyle said. "LeRoi, can we get some tunes?"

"Sounds as if we've all got shit on our mind," Sylvia said.

"Some more than others," Dory said to Sylvia. Could she tell that Sylvia was a vampire now? Was that a special zombie power, spotting other undead creatures?

"Well, I just got some news from Kyle that he got from Noam," Cate said.

"You, too?" Sari said. "'Cause Dad just laid a serious mindfuck on me."

"I doan evin know why I'm heer," Thierry said, his thick French accent making his words just barely understandable.

"That makes two of us," Xavier said. "And I don't care what shit anybody has to tell, I'm up to my eyeballs in flight arrivals, so what's so damned important that we had to meet up?"

Creedence Clearwater Revival's *Bad Moon Rising* came out of the sound system.

"Gimme a fuckin' break," Sylvia said.

"Creedence, nice," Noam said, pointing to some place in the corner of the room where a hidden speaker was as he walked over from the restroom. "Listen kids, we have some serious things to discuss tonight."

"No shit," said everyone else.

Noam raised his hands. "Whoa. We're all a little wound, are we?"

LeRoi came over with two bottles of Thierry's St. Bertold bourbon while Joaquin carried a tray of shot glasses along with a dish of olives and oil.

"Make way," LeRoi said, placing the bottles down on the table. "Now, Joaquin. Tell them what you told me about the kinda drinks you make for some of the locals."

Joaquin shifted his weight between feet.

"Now you're getting quiet on me?" LeRoi asked. "I can't get you to shut up about all the stories about this island—'LeRoi, have I told you about the Saints who could see in the dark with the palms of their hands? LeRoi, do you know about fanged skulls? LeRoi, I was once married to seven women...'"

"LeRoi, what the hell does Joaquin have to tell us?" Xavier interrupted.

"I make drinks for vampiro," Joaquin mumbled.

"How's that?" Kyle said.

Louder now. "I mix drinks for vampiro from original recipes. I write a blog about it."

"BFD, Joaquin. I've been conscripted to hunt and capture vampiro," Kyle said.

"Both of us," Cate added.

"Whoopdee shit. Me and Dad come from a long line of vampire hunters," Sari said.

"She's right," Noam sighed.

"Pfft," Dory said. "I'm sleeping with a vampire."

"For the win!" Kyle said.

"Pipe down," Sylvia said, raising her glass. "Joaquin, I just love the drink you mixed for me."

As if it were rehearsed, and what would probably look like a Busby Berkeley flick from above, everyone pushed themselves back in their chairs, away from the table, like a shockwave. Sylvia took a sip from her drink and smacked her lips then, a beat later, popped out her fangs. Once again, chairs screeched further back.

"No fuckin' way!" Xavier said.

"Way," Sylvia said, retracting her fangs.

"There goes one of my scoops," Kyle said.

"When...? How...? What?" Xavier fumbled.

"S'crazy, huh?" Sylvia said. "But wait. It gets better."

"If you're gonna mention that the island's about to be overrun by vampires who've come for a weekend feast, forget about it, because I just did," Dory said.

"And if you're gonna say there's a Brotherhood sworn by blood oath to protect the citizens of this island from vampires, nevermind, because two of the members are sitting amongst you," Sari said.

"And if any of you are thinking that this is St. Agrippina, part two, move on, 'cuz it is AND it's time to call in the marines—which I already did. BAM!" Kyle said, his hand slapping the table.

"You know what every marine needs?" Dory asked. "That's right, ammo made out of pure silver. Whoops. That just happened."

"Shit. If this is gonna be that kind of party, I'm gonna stick my dick in the mashed potatoes!" Kyle said.

"ENOUGH!" Cate shouted, knocking her chair over as she shot up out of it. "WHAT THE FUCK IS WRONG WITH YOU PEOPLE? HUH? We're looking at a vampire invasion and all we got are one-up-smanship taken to a level of dudebro-speak you wouldn't find at a frat party at Arizona State! Jesus H. And now we got defenders of blood? Silver bullets? Marines? And our very own vampire?"

"Don't forget about Joaquin's vampire cocktails," LeRoi said. "He uses human blood."

"That's fucked up," Kyle said. "How does it taste?"

"I get no complaints," Joaquin said.

"I'm going to eat both your brains in about ten seconds," Cate said. "Y'know, usually Kyle would be the one losing his shit here, but seeing how it's me, I'll ask the million-dollar question. What the fuck are we gonna do?"

Again the group fell silent, the only sound being alcohol swallowed. Alice Cooper's No More Mr. Nice Guy played.

"We have two choices," Kyle said. "Cut and run or stay and start spraying the treeline with silver bullets. I've already got Oscar and company on their way here, and when he shows his face, shit gets blowed up but good."

"I got skin in the game," Dory said. "Gotta protect the investment."

"Oh, Got. Not agane," Thierry said. "I'm in dee same boat as Dor-ee."

"It turns out it's my birthright and a score to settle," Sari said. "I'm sure I speak for my dad, as well."

Noam smiled, his arms crossed.

"Hoo wah!" Desmond said.

"That's right. This guy turns into Rambo. It's awesome," Kyle said.

"I'm down for whatever," LeRoi said, Joaquin nodding in agreement.

"Well aren't we all the Magnificent Seven," Sylvia said. "First, before we go any further, you guys should know I'm on your side, so don't plug me with anything silver or wooden, agreed?"

"'Course nots" and "no shits" mumbled.

"Good," Sylvia said, "because I've got the inside dope here…"

"You're not the only one," Dory said.

"That's right, you're banging one," Kyle said.

"What's his name?" Sylvia said.

"Topo Bogomil," Dory said.

Sari looked at her father, who had already closed his eyes at the mention of that name. He sighed heavily, shaking his head and mumbling the Shemah prayer under his breath.

"You know him?" Sylvia said to Noam.

"Yeah, he does," Sari said. "And he's dangerous. Very freakin' dangerous."

"That may be," Dory said, "but he's on our side. I can promise you that."

"Topo Bogomil did not survive the centuries by being noble," Noam said. "He is a student of Machiavelli, literally. He cannot be trusted."

"Obviously there's some history between you and him. But this is a guy worn down to the nub. I can give you my word. He's with us."

"I would like to meet with the newly transformed Topo," Noam said.

"No problem," Dory said.

"Fine. Anyway," Sylvia said, "though I'm a newbie vamp, I gotta tell you, we're pretty lethal."

"Been on the hunt already?" Sari asked.

"Let's just say any guy who beats a dog deserves what's coming to him," Sylvia said.

"Quint," Kyle whispered.

"This Oscar friend of yours, he's a vampire hunter of some sort?" Sylvia asked Kyle.

"He's the kinda guy who introduces people, living or not, to a world of hurt," Kyle said. "He turned me, Cate, Thierry, Xavier, and Desmond into zombie-killing machines. Especially Desmond, who gets all Robert Duvall-smell-of-napalm-in-the-morning with an AK."

"Obviously they didn't kill all the zombies," Dory said.

"Of course not," Kyle added. "Just the bad ones. Remember, I'm shacked up with one. She's a good one. A great one. Aren't you honey, you little dirty bird..."

"Really?" Cate asked. "Now?"

"I know the ways to catch and kill vampires," Noam said. "And Sylvia is right, these are no zombies. They are true apex predators and they have an arsenal of powers that reduce us mortal beings to field mice."

"The odds are not in our favor," Sylvia said.

"It's like my friend Oscar Pilson would put it," Kyle said, raising his glass. He paused, waiting for the others to raise theirs. "Nobody lives forever. Le chaim."

Everybody drank. None of them felt heroic.

* * *

Ricky Sheflet, Talia, and Sid were in Ricky's hotel room, eating breakfast, while Ricky's mother, Lois, unpacked bottles of aspirin, statins, and anticoagulants as well as boxes of calorie-dense snacks. There was a knock at the door, which Lois answered. In walked a man of smallish build, holding a Panama hat.

"Dr. Baeza!" Ricky said, recognizing the doctor from all the web searching he'd done on his favorite molecular biologist.

"Mr. Sheflet, it's a pleasure," Dr. Baeza said. "Please. Call me Emile. These must be your cohorts, Talia and Sid?"

"Hey," Sid said.

"I'm Talia."

"He probably guessed that by the dress," Sid said.

"As if there couldn't be a transgendered progeria kid," Talia said.

"We're an enlightened group," Ricky said.

"Please, sit," Lori said, motioning Dr. Baeza to the table.

"Oh, I don't want to disturb your breakfast. I just wanted to say hello."

"We've got plenty of Ensure," Ricky said.

"Well, how can I refuse?"

Dr. Baeza took a seat at the small birchwood table. Sid passed him a can of Ensure, which Dr. Baeza took and opened like a pro. "Salud," he said. They all drank.

"I mean this in all seriousness, we're big fans of your cousin," Ricky said. "I know it sounds weird, and this is coming from a huge Led Zeppelin fan, but when I put on *Malaguena*, I mean, she just shreds it. Jimmy Page would blush. I know there's the whole cuchi-cuchi thing with Dean Martin and the play on dialect and accent disguised as innuendo, but good god, when she plays *Caliente*, it's like she has four sets of hands and they're all creating something incredible."

Dr. Baeza leaned backwards as if he'd opened a hot oven door. He'd heard many accolades regarding his cousin, most of the sexual variety, but very few regarding her expertise as a flamenco guitarist. It was greatly appreciated.

"She is a magnificent talent on the guitar," Dr. Baeza concurred.

"She really is," Ricky said. "So you can imagine my consciousness imploding when I learned you two were related because not only am I, are *we*, big Charo fans, we are also fans of your work in molecular biology and your thoughts on the Singularity. And that's why we're here, Emile."

Ricky took a deep breath. It was a lot to expel. Dr. Baeza remained silent, feeling there was more to come.

"Often one hears of great minds coming together to talk about the universe and possibly solve one particle of understanding in that universe. For us, we enjoy the conversation, but, given the time frame we exist in, we're more interested in the hard science of what is and what could be."

"Emile," Sid said. "We don't want to volley conjecture. We want to leave this island knowing something about our condition that will give us real faith in what we can do in our lifetime and beyond."

"In the law of accelerating returns," Talia said. "We want to wade into the deep waters where human technology merges with human intelligence."

Ricky leaned forward, looking directly into Dr. Baeza's eyes.

"We want to be there when the universe wakes up."

For the first time in a decade, Dr. Emile Baeza felt in over his head. What amazing thinkers, these kids. There had been studies done on HPGS kids regarding IQ. In the end, it turned out that when you have a stopwatch that went to fifteen years, you tended toward sucking up everything around you. It was a heavy load they were laying on the doctor, and he didn't want to disappoint them with the "we're currently researching" line. But he couldn't tell them that there existed a cure, though, in truth, clinical trials using cancer drugs had improved weight gain, hearing, and flexibility of blood vessels. It was something but not the magic bullet they were in search of.

"You should see the expression on your face, dude," Sid said.

"You posit some remarkable benchmarks," Dr. Baeza said.

"We do," Ricky said. "I think we're in search of something that points to a cure, if not for us, then for others. We know about the various clinical trials, but..."

"Wouldn't it be great to freeze time so we could find a cure?" Talia said.

Dr. Baeza smiled. It had been on his mind lately that all the people doing the research probably wouldn't last long enough to find a cure. He had often wished the very same thing, to freeze time, so that he could carry on with his work to completion.

"So let's discuss being there when the universe wakes up—most importantly, defining what 'being there' truly means," Dr. Baeza said. "Particularly if that means simply being corporeal." That was the first time Dr. Baeza had spoken of his thoery on keeping conciousness alive after the body dies. He'd be labeled a quack if anybody heard his ideas. Anybody but these kids.

* * *

"Hold still, you big baby," Ryan Seacrest's publicist said as Luria removed the catheter from his vein. Ryan sighed, lying on the red velvet-covered gurney, tweeting on his smartphone that he'd landed in paradise and all it'd cost him was a pint of blood—but that it was for a good cause.

Luria couldn't help but feel a little starstruck at whom she'd taken blood from. First, there was Charo, who was gracious and witty.

Then Jonah Hill, who was quiet. Then there was Charlize Theron, who was even more beautiful in person. And then there was Pierce Brosnan, who, like Charlize, was stunning in person—his charm beyond reproach.

"All done," Luria said, smiling. "That didn't take long, now did it?"

"Hmm?" Ryan Seacrest sat up, eyes still on his phone. "You're welcome."

"He meant to thank you for the opportunity," his publicist said.

"Right," Ryan Seacrest said, looking up from his phone. "For a good cause."

"No, thank *you*," Luria said, taping a cotton ball to Ryan Seacrest's forearm. "Cookie or OJ?"

"Is the cookie gluten-free?" the publicist asked.

"Uh... dunno," Luria said. "OJ then?"

"Is it not from concentrate without pulp?"

Luria gave the publicist a hard, cold stare.

"The orange juice will be fine."

Several sanctioned photographers stood off to the side, taking dozens of pictures of celebrities donating blood. Luria wished she'd paid attention to her hair that morning, but the thought evaporated at the first blood draw. It wasn't going to solve the problem of a blood shortage at the hospital, but it would make a nice dent. Sometimes, while Luria slept, she dreamt of rapelling down into a dark tunnel, her headlamp running over stacks of full pint blood bags. They lined the walls of the tunnel, which seemed bottomless. She interpreted the dream as her endless pursuit to obtain blood, finding herself down a dark hole with more blood than she knew what to do with. She'd had the dream repeatedly, never considering it more than a mere metaphor for her struggles.

Matthew Broderick and Sarah Jessica Parker approached the gurney.

"Is this the vampire blood intake?" Matthew Broderick asked. He was even more adorable in person.

*   *   *

The ride was bumpy aboard Xavier's Grumman G-64, the first plane he'd flown for St. Agrippina back when he labored under the guise of the Rastafarian, Jimmy Dank. It felt familiar and exactly like getting

on a bike again, since his management of West Indies Air had transformed him from pilot to desk jockey. Oscar, Woman, and Dog were
aboard, as were several thousand rounds of silver bullets courtesy of
an armory diguised as a rug merchant in the middle of downtown
Casablanca. Oscar sat in the co-pilot's chair, a slight grin on his face, a
Perrier in his hand. Xavier never saw Oscar look so well. Tanned, clean-
shaven, no bags under the eyes—even his camo gear looked pressed.

"Y'know, last time you flew this bird, you were dropping bombs
on a cruise ship while blasting Glen Campbell," Oscar said into the
headgear intercom.

"Good times," Xavier said. "Good times."

"Can't help but wonder if we'll need the same air support this
time around."

"I don' think we have time to make silver bombs," Xavier said.
"Unless you know a guy, which for you wouldn't be a stretch. You
did turn Dory on to the armory in Casablanca. Guess that was a
heads-up, huh?"

"Between Kyle's phone calls and emails and Dory, I'd say things
were gonna get hairy soon."

"So history really does repeat itself," Xavier said.

"What else was there to learn from Iraq if not that?" Oscar asked.

"We've got the bullets. What about the guns?" Xavier asked.

"Oh, I've got a spectacular array of firepower headed to St. Ledo
as we speak," Oscar said. "I still had the stash on St. Agrippina, plus
I got a shipment coming in from Prince Edward Island."

"What the hell is Prince Edward Island doing with a stash of
weaponry?"

"That'd be the last place you'd expect to find it."

"Copy that. So what's our strategy?"

"Well, the way I see it. We raid their nests by day, send them back
to hell with silver bullets by night. Either way, this is gonna get
more in the shit than the Zombie Land Rush & Barbecue. We might
want to prepare for some actual casualties."

"Or newly minted vampires," Xavier said.

"What shall we then say to these things?" Oscar asked. "If God be
for us, who can be against us?"

"You got religion with the new haircut."

"How's this: 'Shrimp may attack dragons in shallow water'?"

"Yeah, so you've been writing religious fortune cookies. No wonder you look so good."

*   *   *

Sylvia had arranged the meeting, which was to be held in a bright red plaster treatro just outside of town, in the middle of an olive orchard. Since it would be daylight, Noam felt he had some advantage over the situation. The truth was he had no idea what to say or what might transpire. Sari had insisted on coming, but knowing his daughter's propensity for drama, he demanded to go alone. Noam didn't often demand things, so Sari took it to heart. He was about to come face to face with the man responsible for his wife's death—perhaps indirectly, but that was a matter of context. And in this context, Noam carried a wooden stake inside his wool trench coat next to the silver chain and cruficix.

Noam arrived at the bright red treatro, the color of it not amusing in any sense of irony that vampires might possess. He was told that Sylvia and Topo Bogomil would be waiting inside. Sylvia also gave the heads-up that, because it was during a rest cycle, their powers would be diminished. Noam wasn't sure it was imparting knowledge or offering a chance at revenge. Like everything else about the meeting, Noam wasn't sure if he'd try to kill the vampire as soon as he lay eyes upon him, or hear him out because, buried deep in his hatred for Topo, there was one sliver of doubt as to Topo's role in Catalina's death.

Noam was told to knock once, which he did. From behind the door, Sylvia told him to enter. Noam moved swiftly, shutting the door behind him and leaning up against it. His eyes were adjusting to an already pitch black room, his hand against his overcoat feeling the stake underneath it.

"Give it a few seconds," Sylvia said. A match was struck then lit a candle sitting atop a wooden table. There he was. Looking every bit the ageless vampire as he had decades ago and, before that, centuries. He remained so still in his chair that Noam thought him a wax figure. Sylvia stood over the candle. "Have a seat."

Noam stood for a few moments, eyes not blinking, the rage in him flooding his soul, making his hand curl up into a fist. He kept his other hand on the overcoat, the stake underneath embolding him.

"Please, Noam. Sit," Sylvia said. Noam blinked, then pulled out a chair on the opposite side of the table, keeping his coat open but close to his body as he sat. There was a moment's pause.

"If you've come to kill me, I won't stop you," Topo said.

Noam reached into his coat and pulled out the wooden stake, which he placed on the table. He reached his hand into his breast pocket and took out the silver crucifix on a chain and placed it on the tabletop as well. He kept his eyes on Topo. This was it. His chance at retaliation. Would it be his chance at peace? Would he feel his wife's complete departure from him once he sank the stake into the vampire's dead heart? Sylvia seemed to be holding her breath or at least simulated the act.

"I won't stop you, brother," Topo said.

"You're not my brother," Noam said. "You stopped being a brother to us all centuries ago. I never knew the Topo Bogomil who was mortal, only the one who killed my wife. The monster that you are. The vampire."

"I did not kill Catalina, but I didn't stop it from happening," Topo said.

"*Fun vaytn nart men laytn, fun neont zikh aleyn,*" Noam said. "It's Yiddish. *At a distance you fool others, close at hand just yourself.* It was Neno's fangs that took my wife's blood. But it was you who stood by and watched. You could've done something, *brother.* You could've stopped him from taking her life, but you stood there and watched it happen. Why? I've asked myself this question until I grew weary of it, but still I kept asking. I arrived at many answers: Fear, servitude, indifference, the nature of a vampire—to destroy mortals?"

"You would've been right on all accounts," Topo said.

"And that's what makes me the most sad. All of the reasons I thought of, just banal reasoning. Common emotions."

"Did you expect something more?"

"Love?"

Topo was startled by the word. For the first time, his composure let him down.

"I don't understand," Topo said.

"You had many chances to put an end to her, yet you didn't," Noam said. "You felt something for Catalina, even as she put your kind in the ground permanently. I saw it. We all did. You admired her. She made you feel in touch with something that left you all those years ago. Your humanity."

Topo's eyes filled with a faint reddish mist. Noam decided that his words had done more to hurt Topo than any piece of wood could have. Hopefully.

"I was at the service of Neno," Topo whispered. "I was as power-less as a child. I had been reckless in my pursuit of loyalty. A loyal vampire. So rare a creature. I am sorry, Noam Wysocki. I am sorry I did nothing to protect the one human being who ever meant some-thing to both of us."

The two men sat silently, mourning. Sylvia felt she needed to say something, anything, that would move this situation forward, but she could only join them in the sadness of the story.

Topo reached for the wooden stake and offered it to Noam. "Please," he said. "Please."

The door burst open, slamming against the wall, a ray of light slicing across Topo's face, setting it aflame instantly.

"*SARI, NO!*" Noam shouted as he dove out of his chair and knocked Topo out of the light, into a dark corner of the room. "*SHUT THE DOOR!*"

"*GET OUT OF THE WAY!*" Sari screamed. She had a bow and silver-tipped arrow pointed at Topo.

"*SARI!*"

It was too late. Sari released the arrow, sending it in a smooth trajectory into Topo's Achilles tendon. He howled. In the next mil-lisecond, Sylvia was up and had shut the door, shoving Sari up against the wall. Topo's foot and face were on fire, the acrid smoke filling the room quickly. Noam used the tail of his coat to stamp out Topo's face while Sylvia set upon the arrow, whipping it out of Topo's tendon. The flames died down, the smoke-covered room back to its darkness.

"Put that thing down before you do real damage," Sylvia said.

Sari was crying now, huge heaving gut busting gasps of air. Another candle was lit. It showed Noam uncovering Topo's smol-dering face. The sunlight had cut a diagonal line that went between Topo's eyes, ending up at his ear.

"Daddy," Sari said.

Noam left Topo and rushed over to his crying daughter, enveloping her with his arms. She cried hard, her animal-like wail muffled by her father's chest.

Sylvia went over to Topo. "I'll be fine," he said. "Tend to her."

Sylvia was pissed but held it together as she patted Sari on the back.

"Why did you save him!?" Sari said, her face red, mucus strings running down her mouth.

"He was not the cause of your mother's death," Noam said.

"But you said he was! He is! We hafta kill him!"

"Shhh," Noam said, stroking his daughter's hair. "I was wrong."

"What do you mean wrong?"

"I... Things were not as they seemed. She's gone, and there is only one person truly responsible for it. And he is the man we will hunt down."

Sari lifted her head and looked at her father.

"I shot the wrong vampire?"

"Where did you get a bow and arrow, and since when did you study archery?" Noam asked.

"I saw the silver-tipped arrow in an antique shop," Sari said. "Came with the bow. Y'know, a set."

"Well, hon, for a first try, it wasn't too bad," Sylvia said, feeling herself calm down.

"Not good enough," Sari looked at Topo.

"She's right," Topo said. "I should be removed from the earth. Noam Wysocki's daughter has a brave soul. You should let her carry out her task."

"I believe you," Noam said. "I should let her finish you off. But you're not the true cause. I don't think I can ever forgive you standing by, no matter what spell you were under. But you can be a powerful ally. We're going to need that to defeat them, brother."

* * *

Since water was like Kryptonite to vampires, there was considerable pushback regarding the raid. Why not open a resort on the mainland? Portugal had a beautiful coastliine. They could finish off most of Iceland. Besides, there had been an attempt on an island by undead a year before—everyone knew how that went. And now, they were being hosted by the same person who ran that raid. Granted, it was zombies. They might have evolved in the last millenia, but the stigma of slow-moving, brain-eating, boring conversationailsts remained. It was acknowledged in the vampire world that Rupert Jagger had a history of putting together ravishing baccanals of blood harvesting—who could forget the Promise Keepers raid outside Houston last year? And the *Huffington Post* cruise in the Baltics? They made Arianna one of their own, and she proved to be a worthy acquisition. The number of pro-blood donation columns that appeared in *HuffPo* had risen dramatically. But then, raiding a Red Cross donation site was easy pickings and often a rote affair. Besides, they too had recruited vampires to keep watch over the supply.

So, with much griping about the location, about the method of transportation—by ship, housed in Maersk containers filled with dirt and rats—and about Rupert doing business with someone whose history of both raids and resort management were a bit sketchy, regardless of the occupancy rates, the plan moved forward. Vampires, like everything else on earth that fed, often bitched about the food and/or the service. However, in the end? It was like a Walmart cafeteria—they came in droves. The first container ship docked in St. Ledo's, which was a feat unto itself seeing as there was no crane to take the containters off the ship, which meant the vampires had to be transported by barge. The logistics alone kept Percy on edge as Rupert had put him along with some SOG in charge of that operation.

It was slow going, but steady. The containers sat out in the open in an abandoned farm sixty miles outside of Oliveira, which, by vampire speed, was a two-minute trip. Then there were the aristocracy vampires who booked suites in the resort, having brought along their own blackout curtains, which their dutiful mortal valets hung, mortals who also provided them with the occasional hotel staffer on which to dine. The aristocrat vampires enjoyed a good nocturnal party and assembled in various suites to drink one of Joaquin's recipes and schmooze—possibly with some celebs such as Kevin Dillon, who was in the suite next door.

When the noise level got too loud, Kevin Dillon decided to let the neighbors know. The vampires were thrilled, as they were big fans of *Entourage,* and quickly welcomed him into the party with an enticing, thick red drink, delivered by the Grand Duchess of Finland, Ingeborg Eriksdottir of Norway (turned in 1353) who bore an uncanny resemblance to Kate Upton. Having a famous mortal mingling among them was akin to dog paddling around a group of great whites while wearing meat swim trunks. It was nearing dawn when one of the vamps finally took Kevin Dillon down.

"Should we turn him?" the hungry vampire asked. "Let's. I loved him as 'Bunny' in *Platoon,*" said another. And so it was.

Things were getting off to a great start for the aristocratic vampires who called the front desk asking for rooms of other celebrities, which were given, as one of the front desk people was a vampire. "Sofia Coppola's mine, though," the front desk vampire said. "*Lost in Translation* was epic." As for the lesser, common vampires in the barley field outside of town, they snacked on pigs, cows, rats, and, in a few instances, farmhands passing through on their way to pick olives before sunrise.

Things were also looking good for Magnolia and Marmot. The numbers for the Undead Grateful Dead convention were at capacity. They had imported enough brains to feed them all (harvested from Joseph Kony's Lord's Resistance Army), and the list of vendors was at the top of the Grateful Dead industry. Master of Ceremonies Whoopi Goldberg had been ensconced in one of the best suites the hotel offered. She was pumped to get her hands on some authentic Dead merch and dine on LRA brain. Terrapin Space Station No. 2317 had put together a set list that ran to nine hours.

Philomena and Rolf made the rounds, and that's when Rolf met Desmond. Sparks were instantaneous. Desmond volunteered his services to Rolf in any way possible. They boned within two hours of their first meeting, in a little-used break room in the basement. "You, most certainly are not undead in any traditional sense of the word," Rolf had told Desmond, who replied, "Once you go undead, et cetera."

Philomena, for her part, did what she did best and gladhanded the celebrities, even the ones she loathed, which was pretty much everyone except Bill Murray. She'd yet to meet with the HGPS kids but had planned to lunch with them in her suite, along with Charo, who, much to Philomena's disappointment, had absolutely no accent other than a flat Southern Californian one.

They always disappointed her, celebrities. If it wasn't their height or bad complexion, it was often their boorish behavior, behavior that, over the years, she had herself acquired. Self-hatred was alive and well in Philomena.

CHAPTER 11

"I CAN'T FUCKIN' BELIEVE WE'RE ABOUT to do this again," Kyle said to Oscar as they came in for a bear hug on the dock next to the Grumman. "Just like I can't believe you're holding a Perrier bottle."

"Booze ain't the only thing to go by the wayside," Oscar said.

"No more Oxy?" Kyle asked.

"Sold the inventory to Sean Hannity's maid. I'm done with that shit," Oscar said.

"At least as long as I'm around," Woman said, emerging from the plane, holding Dog.

"What's up, bitch?" Dog said. "Seen any good flicks lately?"

"When I was in the psych ward, TMC was runing a foreign film marathon," Kyle said. "Bunuel, Fellini, Kurosawa, Ophuls."

"No Bergman?" Dog asked. "I call bullshit on that."

"Well, when we finish killing vampires, we can watch *The Seventh Seal*."

"Attaboy," Dog said.

"On that subject, just what in hell have you gotten yourself into?" Woman asked. She placed Dog into the harness that buckled up around his dead lower haunches, the wheels of the harness making that familiar squeak.

"To be perfectly honest, I almost met you guys with a suitcase in hand," Kyle said. "I mean, really, do we need this again? What's at stake, pun intended, besides saving the lives of innocent bystanders?—rich innocent bystanders, which I'm less inclined to give a shit about. If vampires want the one percent's blood, I say have at it."

"What's Cate's take on it?" Woman asked.

"If she had a beating heart, it'd be bleeding," Kyle said. "You can guess where Dory falls out on this, too. I dunno, this time around, things feel different as in not funny, y'know? Zombies are kinda funny. Vampires are just creepy motherfuckers."

"You thought St. Agrippina's was funny?" Woman asked.

"Well, yeah, kinda," Kyle said. "Zombies? That's funny, no?"

"No," Woman said. "That was dangerous. You could've been killed. One of us could've gotten a bite taken out of us."

"It was a little funny, blowin' the heads off zombies," Oscar said.

"See? Splattering brain—funny," Kyle said.

"I didn't think it was funny, either," Xavier said. "And I agree. This time around, there's some freaky bloodsucking shit going on. But I'm in with Dory. I've got an investment to protect."

"I say we get back on the plane and head over to your island, drink some Dark 'n' Stormies, and wait out the bloodlettiing," Kyle said to Woman. "Seriously, I'm ready to grab Cate and get on this plane right now. Today."

"Kid's got a point," Dog said. "It's hard enough bein' a zombie dog. But a zombie vampire partially paralyzed talking Chihuahua? That I don't need."

Oscar looked at Woman. He hunched his shoulders.

"Oh, what?" Woman said. "You're dyin' for the action just like I am."

"Vampires *are* creepy, hon. What if one of us gets bitten? We both love our vitamin D," Oscar said.

"Jesus, did you forget your testicles?" Woman said. "We have a moral imperative here to save lives, just like we did on St. Aggies. Pure and simple. I'm ready to hump it into the jungle with my bolt action and start taking out vamps this very night. Remember, WHEN IN DOUBT…"

"EMPTY THE MAGAZINE!" Oscar shouted back, as programmed.

Kyle had Oscar for a second. But the Marine sound-off pretty much killed his chances for getting off the island carrying his own blood supply. Oscar was pumped now, his chest jutted out along with his jaw. Kyle's friends were willing to go into the breach once again. Why didn't he share their fervor? He, too, caught the Rambo wave back on St. Aggies when they were wasting zombies. They all did. And here, again, was the same situation. Why didn't he respond to the call to arms? All he could think about was getting off the island. He made the motions of getting into it, but he wasn't a true believer. He wasn't sure about Cate, either. He had hoped Xavier felt the same: get the hell out before things got blown to shit. But no, Xavier was gonna stand his ground and protect his runway. Woman was looking at Kyle as if she could read his thoughts. It unnerved Kyle enough to look away, out toward the ocean.

"What's it gonna be, Kyle?" Woman asked.

Kyle watched the white tips come and go in an infinite loop. The breeze made his shirt flap now and then. *How? How could this be happening again?* Another thought crossed his mind. *Groundhog Day.* If he was living it again, maybe he could predict certain outcomes. Get a leg up on the vampires with a little history in fighting the undead. Seeing into the future. Just like the movie *Groundhog Day,* except no annoying nasally voice of Andie MacDowell. Life was already strange; what if he really could predict events? That's how they told the weather and fought other wars. He would be living in *Groundhog Day.* Great fuckin' movie. Bill Murray. Brian Doyle-Murray. Chris Elliott. Some great lines. "Ned... Ryerson? Needle Nose Ned? Ned the Head? The song? *I Got You Babe.* Classic. A real...

"Kyle!" Woman shouted.

"Hmm?"

"What's it gonna be?"

Kyle nodded for a moment, then smiled. He knew how to come at this.

"'...'Cause you got me, and babe I got you...'," Kyle sang. "'Babe. I got you, babe.' C'mon, everyone! 'Babe. I got you, babe.'"

"Fuck," Oscar said. "They got a psych ward on the island?"

* * *

Rupert stood before Neno who was drinking blood from a golden chalice because Neno was big on affectation and claimed the golden chalice once belonged to Jesus Christ, which Rupert knew to be bullshit because, in *Indiana Jones, The Last Crusade*, it was the simple wood-carved cup that proved to be the one Jesus Christ drank from because he was a carpenter, not a fucking goldsmith. God, the effort Neno put into being all that was staggering, even to Rupert, himself a mid-level drama queen.

"Percy must be severely tapped out by now," Rupert said, referring to Neno's drink.

"I keep him just at the point of expiration," Neno said, as if it were something only a few knew how to do.

"Of course," Rupert said.

"Where is Topo?" Neno asked. "He should've been with you to give your progress report to me."

Progress report. What was this? Third grade for vampires?

"I'm not sure of Topo's whereabouts, but I can assure you it's in the service of your wishes," Rupert said. Topo could be off somewhere draining a couple from Boca for all Rupert knew.

"Of course," Neno said. "So? What news have you?"

Now we're channeling Shakespeare. Rupert had known Shakespeare. He didn't talk like that and found great humor in writing in that manner of language. "The fools," he'd often say. "As if any of us actually spoke like that."

"Vampires are arriving as we speak," Rupert said. "By container ship, by jet. It's rumored that a submarine has been leased from the Korean government. Vampire occupancy for the upper echelon is nearly complete. This raid is already a success before it's begun."

"Your modesty is astounding," Neno said. "Has any blood been officially drained and collected?"

"Not yet," Rupert said.

"Then we are nowhere near success."

"Of course not. I'm getting ahead of myself. It's just that things are proceeding smoothly. It reminded me of the GOP convention held in St. Paul in '08. The yield was high as was the conversion rate. Forgive my trespass."

"Forgive my trespass," is what Shakespeare used to say to Rupert after a night of drinking, topped off with pissing himself. "Forgive my trespass, Rupert." Then he'd cackle like a fiend as urine pooled in his velveteen boots.

"And the Brotherhood? What of them?" Neno asked.

Crap. Rupert had hoped to keep Neno in the dark about that. Percy? One of the SOG? They served under him. Why would they rat Rupert out to Neno about this?

"Yes, the Brotherhood," Rupert said. "There has been the slight rumor…"

"I'm told that they are being reformed, that our plans have become known to mortals," Neno said.

"It's merely conjecture," Rupert said. "They died with Catalina Guarda, as you know firsthand."

"Catalina Guarda…" Neno pondered silently. Rupert endured the pause. "What of her family? Do they not have a cross to bear?"

I dunno? Why don't you ask Jesus since you stole His cup, Rupert thought to himself. "They are mortal and of little concern to us. The Brotherhood are in the wind."

"Not unless they have help," Neno said.

"Help?" Rupert said.

"Who is not present for this meeting?" Neno asked.

"Topo Bogomil is a trusted servant of…"

"That's what the Brotherhood once said of him. We all know how that turned out."

Rupert remained silent.

"I want Topo brought before me."

Rupert nodded. "Is there anything else?"

"There usually is," Neno said. "And that is why I rule."

*   *   *

They met at Ruvane Acevedo's mancave. They were all that remained on the island: ten of the Brotherhood. They sat around Ruvane's custom-made poker table, the Brotherhood coat of arms woven into the black velvet with a red stripe running lengthwise. The table had black leather armrests with stainless steel cupholders. There had been many twenty-four-hour games played at this table. And now, ten members of the Brotherhood of St. Irene of La Guardia occupied playing spaces, sipping Thierry's bourbon, plotting revenge.

"That's incredible," Ruvane said. "You had him right there. You could've finished him off."

"Stupid is what it was," Herculano Torres said.

"He wasn't the one," Noam said.

"So what? One less vampire in the world the better," Herculano said.

"It was Noam's choice," Ruvane said. "We must respect it."

"Topo Bogomil has rejoined us," Noam said.

"How can you be sure?" Filipa Nocas said.

"I saw the regret on his face," Noam said. "I believe he has kept a small part of himself in grief just as I have. He is one of us, maybe not in the flesh but in the soul."

"Vampiro have no souls," Herculano spat.

"Now is not the time for debate," Ruvane said. "Topo is a valuable resource now, and we will need his help in the fight." The Select-O-Matic jukebox that sat in the corner of the mancave shifted from The Band's *The Weight* to Derek and the Dominoes' *Layla*.

"What of the Brotherhood on the mainland?" Filipa said. "Can we count on their help?"

"Somewhat," Ruvane said. "Remember, they are old men and women now. Just like us."

"Old? *Pfft*," Herculano said. He held up his arms and flexed his still-considerable pecs through his powder-blue cardigan, giving each one a kiss.

"But they still know the ways," Filipa said.

"I cannot wait to get out there and get down to the business of killing vampiro. It gives me ereção! I'm hard as a rock right now!" Tito Duarte said.

"Since I'm sitting next to him, I can vouch for that," Filipa said. "And I'm impressed, Tito."

"If we could focus," Ruvane said. "Not that it's nothing to have an erection these days, we're happy for you, Tito…"

Tito rose out of his chair to show the tent pole in his tweed slacks. "Eh? See that?"

"Sit down, you old fool," Herculano said.

"Why? You got to show off," Tito said. "This is what I got."

"Tito, please," Ruvane pleaded. "We've serious business to discuss."

Tito sat down, winking at Filipa.

"As I was saying earlier. We have help from the mainland, from as far away as the UK, and even two members from Norway," Ruvane said. "But I still feel that we are woefully inadequate in numbers."

"There might be a solution to that," Sari said. Though she had a seat at the table, she was still the recipient of a few sideways glances.

"Go on," Ruvane said.

"You might recall what happened on St. Agrippina with an undead problem of another kind?"

"You're referring to the zombie invasion," Ruvane said. "That was not our business."

"True," Sari said. "But several of the people who fought and won the island from the zombies are here, and they are willing to fight the undead again. They're not large in numbers, but from what I can tell, they're crazy when it comes to the killing of undead. There are even zombies on our side—that would make them impervious to the vampires since they have no blood."

"Zombies fighting vampires," Herculano said. "Sounds like a bad movie."

"It does, Herculano. But they have their reasons for fighting, as do we. And they come heavily armed with silver bullets and the heavy weaponry to fire them," Sari said.

"What of tradition?" Filipa said. "We have our ways of killing them. We don't need guns."

"I disagree," Noam said. "I still abide with the traditions of killing vampires, but if we can get some help in the form of a weapon that fires hundreds of silver bullets a second, I say we welcome it."

"You're both right," Ruvane said. "Be it wooden stake, fire, beheading, daylight, holy water, sacred oil in the tent, *and* machine guns firing silver bullets, by any means necessary, we must kill the vampiro."

"Then let's get our friends together and whup some vampire ass," Sari said.

"I like her. She's got huevos," Tito said.

"You keep your distance, you dog in heat," Noam said.

* * *

The cruise ship that was used for St. Agrippina and subsequently bombed belonged to a third-rate cruise line that refused to send another one, even though the damage was blamed on a gas leak. Dory thought that, in the kingdom of cruise lines, a gas leak would be a no-brainer. But there were rumors about the true nature of the ship's destruction, and thus the cruise line denied Dory's request for service to St. Ledo. Instead, she handed it off to Philomena, who insisted she had connections and could deliver a cruise ship full of guests.

Before becoming the high-powered travel agent that she was, Philomena had been in the boat-buying business. That was, boats on a medium scale and coming mostly from Russia. In August 1974, Philomena bid on a cruise ship dubbed *Laika* after the Soviet space dog that was the first living being to orbit Earth. Some questioned the "luck" of naming a cruise ship after a dog that was either euthanized with poisoned dog treats or oxygen starvation, depending on which KGB-authorized story you chose to believe. However, Laika was a national hero. The name had some serious branding to it.

It didn't matter, as the ship was renamed *Aquarius* and did time as a floating casino docked outside of Hong Kong. The take from running a casino ship was pretty good, but Philomena thought there would be a better revenue stream by converting Aquarius to a cruise ship, which she did in 1989. By then the ship had been renamed *Enchanted Paladin* and spent time in the Gulf of Mexico, making trips to Belize and Honduras. When Philomena's travel agency became the preeminent cruise-ship-booking shop of the Hollywood elite, the ship was once again renamed *Greta Garbo*.

It was the *Greta Garbo* that docked at St. Ledo and set free the first wave of tourists to spread across the resort and the island like an onset of Ebola, slashing its way through air-conditioned suites and cobblestone streets. The vampire community that had assembled began to seethe with anticipation of a massive feed. They would be unleashed on the unsuspecting mortals at Neno's command, which, like most things about Neno, set Rupert's fangs on edge. Neno, who sat in his suite, sipping moronic Percy's blood out of his ridiculous Jesus chalice, ordering the underlings around. Neno, the centuries-old Liberace of vampires. Neno, the idiot king of darkenss.

Rupert had been entertaining the idea of a coup since the last raid, in Indiana, when the Colts won Super Bowl XLI and had a parade in downtown Indianapolis. He kept it to himself, not having a cohort to scheme with. He'd thought that Topo might want to be in on it, but Rupert decided that Topo was more a loner than a planner. So

Rupert served Neno and now found himself in his coffin, unable to sleep and getting updates from his mortal slaves. He had to give it up for Dory's marketing plan—it was bringing in the fresh blood. It was looking like another notch in Neno's belt.

West Indies Air was also offloading its share of tourists, rich and famous. There were even red-eye flights for the vampires, unbeknownst to Xavier but suspected by the flight crew who were unable to hand out a single bag of pretzels or Chex Mix. The island had begun to fill up. The resort buzzed with activity. Undead Deadheads in tie-dyed shirts and Ferragamo loafers were rubbing elbows with the likes of celebrities of various rankings. Hedge-funders and orthopedic surgeons and search-engine-optimization specialists and the offspring of coal and shipping magnates, even a Kennedy (thrice-removed second cousin and entourage) were in attendance.

All at once, St. Bobo's and the various boutiques and eateries that lined the streets of Oliveira were overrun with people of all xenophobic origins. Koufax's had a line out the door, both Sari and Noam trying to keep up with orders while thinking about the task ahead of them. When would they find the time?

The tidal wave of tourists overwhelmed many of the business owners, who deputized local teens right on the streets as new employees and directed them to get in the back, get an apron, and start taking orders. Noam was part of that hiring practice. It was too late to turn back the vacationing horde. Kyle and company and the Brotherhood couldn't prevent that. They barely had time to formu-late a plan of resistance beyond nighttime recon. It was clearly time to transform the ideas into action.

* * *

Dusk had settled in St. Ledo. Neno had yet to unleash the vampires on the mortals. But that didn't stop a few stray SOG from sampling the wares. First up: Lucrecia and Phillip and their Shih Tzu, Marcus Aurelius. They had gone for a stroll along the beach, capris pants and Nine West sandals, Phillip holding a half-emptied bottle of Dom to pass between them. Two SOG stood off near a gathering of mangroves, bickering about who would get the dog for dessert.

They decided to make it a blood-draining contest since the couple seemed to weigh the same.

"Pardon me," Ekur said, bowing. "I was wondering what your blood type was."

Shulgi appeared out of thin air, a wicked grin as he nodded his greeting.

"Blood type?" Lucrecia said. "Why on Earth would you want to know that?"

"Though I must say, in the witty repartee department, that places pretty high up," Phillip said, lifting the bottle of Dom in salute.

"I think one of you is AB negative," Ekur said. He leaned toward Lucrecia and sniffed. "Yes, AB negative."

"What is this...?"

"O positive," Shulgi said.

"It is a common blood type," Ekur said.

"I assure you, there is nothing common about my wife's blood," Phillip said.

"I am a descendant of Greek royalty, which happens to be in line with Kaiser Wilhelm II. Hardly ordinary," Lucrecia said.

"Maybe it's the dog," Shulgi said, lunging at the dog and sinking his teeth into its furry little neck. Marcus Aurelius briefly yelped before submitting.

"That was fucking dessert," Ekur said to the horrified couple. "Shulgi is one impatient son of a bitch."

Shulgi rose, his mouth smeared with dog blood. "I like to switch things up now and then. Breaks the monotony of being a vampire. Like having pancakes for dinner." With that, Ekur and Shulgi attacked Phillip and Lucrecia, nearly beheading both with their rabid thirst.

Next up: two pastry chefs sharing a smoke behind the resort kitchen door. Ninhursag had been hanging out in the alley behind the resort, watching various kitchen and wait staff come out for a smoke. Ninhursag was hungry but was also enjoying the smorgasbord that paraded before him. He was also waiting for lower-level kitchen help, a busser perhaps, someone who wouldn't be missed immediately. The back door opened, letting out the noise of the buzzing kitchen, and a goth girl walked out, carrying her pack of Marlboro Lights. She waited for the door to shut, lifted her face to the stars, lit her cigarette, and took a long drag. Ninhursag watched her expel the blue smoke into the atmosphere. He was intrigued by her heavy eyeliner, pale face, and deep black hair tied back, exposing her many facial piercings. His guess was that she operated behind the scenes.

Ninhursag walked out of the shadows, over to the goth girl, and asked for a smoke. She gave him the once-over. As he was dressed in what looked like a fifteenth-century biker uniform, the goth girl was immediately taken.

"You like working here?" Ninhursag asked.

"It's a job. It got me out of New York," Goth Girl said.

"You didn't like living in the city?"

"I didn't like the outstanding warrant."

"Criminal element you are, then?"

"I believe in the free-market system," Goth Girl said, taking another drag and exhaling. "If it's in the market, it must be free."

"It seems that life wasn't cut out for you," Ninhursag said. "It sounds like the outstanding warrant was for an arrest?"

"Unpaid parking tickets, actually," Goth Girl said.

"Ahh," Ninhursag said.

They smoked in silence for a few moments.

"Seems I'm always outnumbered, always outgunned," Goth Girl said.

"It can get tiresome, survival," Ninhursag said. "What's your name?"

"Nebula."

"Interstellar dust. Fascinating."

"*Guardians of the Galaxy*," Nebula said, with a shrug. "Sci-fi geek. What's your name?"

"Ninhursag."

"What's that? Norwegian?"

"Sumerian."

"Oh," Nebula said.

"Nebula. What if I told you that there is a way to be truly at the top of the food chain? That survival was actually exciting? That the hunt was eternal?"

"What're you? A Scientologist?" Nebula said.

"Close. Vampire," Ninhursag said.

"Oh, yeah?" Nebula flicked her cigarette into the alley then pulled down the collar of her white kitchen uniform. "Have at it, 'cuz I'm ready for something different," she said in a mocking tone. Her eyes went wide for a moment, then relaxed into a heroin gaze as Ninhursag drained her almost to the point of extinction, just enough to turn her.

And lastly: Keith Richards. Or what would be called on YouTube, "I'm fucking Keith Richards, man." The Rolling Stones guitarist/singer/songwriter/pirate was sitting in his balcony hot tub with triplets, all heirs to the throne of the Republic of Latvia (which would require a coin toss at some point), telling tales of life on the road and talking about who made the best Batman. They were pretty much in agreement that, though they enjoyed George Clooney's work, particularly in *Syriana* and *The Descendants*, he was by far the worst Batman. They were mostly in agreement about Joel Schumacher being the worst director on Earth, though Keith did have a soft spot for *Falling Down* with Michael Douglas.

"What about *The Lost Boys*," someone off-camera asked.

"Bring us more bubbly, wouldya', mate?" Keith asked.

"I thought *The Lost Boys* was able to capture the loneliness of vampiredom," the off-camera voice said. A moment later, a man looking like a fifteenth-century biker entered the frame and put one leg up on the hot tub. "Kiefer Sutherland did a good job as the forlorn vampire leader, David, I thought."

"Thas wunnerful, mate…"

The biker, in a blur of motion, tore into the necks of the triplets, blood spraying all over Keith Richards, the hot tub quickly turning red. When the vampire finished with the last triplet, he rose and stood before the nonplussed Rolling Stone, his mouth dripping blood, fangs jutting out.

"You've made one hell of a mess 'ere," Keith Richards said. "But you best be moving along before 'ousekeeping comes along."

"You show no fear?" the vampire asked.

"None," Keith Richards said.

"Why is that?"

"Why, mate? Because I'm fucking Keith Richards, man."

The vampire stood perfectly still, the only sound being the bubbles of the hot tub churning. And then, the vampire was gone. Keith Richards took a sip from a bottle of Henri Jayer Richebourg Grand Cru and sighed heavily. That was all the kid in the suite next door captured with his iPhone. He had it loaded up to YouTube within the hour. It went viral and began racking up hits by the millions. Percy, who had been trolling YouTube looking for foot-fetish videos from his laptop, found the footage (foot fetish being a tag for *Gimme Shelter*) and quickly sent the link to Rupert, who saw an opportunity.

* * *

"It's beginning," Topo said to the assembled, who now had to make do with the backroom of Koufax's Deli as St. Bobo's was overflowing with tourists. "You saw the YouTube video?"

"What are you doing on YouTube?" Dory asked.

"It's a communication tool among vampires."

"I watch it for the articles," Kyle said.

"What?" Cate asked.

"He's referring to the number of teenage girls making twerking videos," Xavier said. "He was making a joke about reading *Playboy* for the articles only."

"And you know about the twerking how?" Kyle asked.

"Okay, pervs, let's get back to the task at hand," Sylvia said. "Seems there are a few rogue vampires on the loose, and the night is young."

"How do we know it's not the start of something big?" Cate asked.

"The island would be full of people running and screaming," Topo said. "It's time to start taking defensive measures."

"Lock 'n' load!" Desmond said.

"Let's take it down a notch," Kyle said. It felt good to say it to someone else for a change.

"Here's the plan," Woman said. "The Brotherhood will cover the resort lobby. Oscar, Desmond, Kyle, Cate, and myself will take the dock. Xavier, you take LeRoi and Joaquin to cover the tarmac. Topo, Sylvia, and Dory—you're guerillas. Run 'n' gun."

"Hold on," Oscar said. "I'll take Desmond and run 'n' gun."

"Why?" Woman asked.

"Have you met Shiva the Destroyer?" Oscar asked, motioning to Desmond. "I wanna cut this boy loose with a 50mm caliber gun and a backpack full of silver ammo. Between the two of us, we can uphold the scorched-earth policy pretty well."

"Fine," Woman said. "Topo and Dory, you can also help out in the lobby. Look, even though we're divvying up, it's still gonna get confusing out there. We're not hunting zombies. This prey has air superiority and speed. We've gotta stay sharp."

"Very fucking sharp," Dog said.

"They do have those things," Noam said. "But they also have several weaknesses."

"And that we can exploit the hell out of," Sylvia said. "I'm a newbie, but I'm still in the vamp pipeline. I assume by now they know about Topo's defection. Hopefully I can relay some vamp movement."

"Is anyone else getting a boner about this?" Kyle asked.

"I've got Bethlehem steel right now," Desmond said.

"Oscar? Lead us in prayer?" Kyle asked, knowing that the former Marine had a delectable array of prayers for combat.

"Bow heads," Oscar said. "We call on you, Yul Brynner, Steve McQueen, Charles Bronson, James Coburn, Robert Vaughn, Brad Dexter, and Horst Buchholz, patron saints of defensive measures and ungodly destruction…"

"The Magnificent Seven," Kyle whispered in awe.

"We ask that, with your blessing and guidance, you bestow upon us the cache of total annihilation, strategic and tactical genius, and your forged-from-the-sacred-fires-of-doom weaponry of death unto us so that we may, in service of search and destroy, dispatch profligate undead of a bloodsucking nature to the bowels of hell. In the words of Eleanor Roosevelt, 'We are of the cleanest bodies, the filthiest minds, the highest morale, and the lowest morals of any group of animals I have ever seen. Thank God for the United States Marine Corps,' and, in this instance, the faithful civilians serving among us. May God bless us and show no mercy on the lifeless, soulless beasts we seek to terminate with extreme prejudice. Amen."

Nothing but unwavering trust in military success in that room.

*　*　*

Luria stood in the walk-in fridge in the basement of the hospital, looking over the pints of blood stacked on metal shelving. For kicks, she had each pint labeled, thus there were pieces of masking tape with "Ben Affleck," "Joe Namath," "Lady Gaga," "Babs," and the like written in black Sharpie affixed to the plastic bags. Percy had made good on his promise to allow the blood donations to happen, and all of the celebrity guests were happy to comply except for John Mayer, who, it turned out, was a zombie. Charo had been a gracious host, making chitchat with the celebs as they lay prone on the red velvet gurney. That idiot woman, Philomena, made things complicated with her demands for getting the paparazzi to photograph the stars at certain angles, but Luria assumed that's how things went for these kinds of events. She even had a chance to meet with Ricky and his friends and was blown away by their positivity and charm.

Luria allowed herself to feel good in the moment, that she was making a difference, that she might actually save a life.

"You should feel very proud," a voice behind her said, startling her. She turned to face a man she'd seen every now and then at the hospital. An administrator perhaps? Someone she'd offended with her requests, no doubt.

"There's still a lot of work to be done, but thanks," Luria said, taking a moment to read the name on his hospital ID badge: MR. GLENN BECK (NOT HIM).

"At your service," Glenn said. "We've all admired the work you've done for this hospital."

"Then you must be new," Luria said. "I don't get invited to many of the fundraising events or mixers. Call it bad blood between me and management."

"Bad blood is better than no blood at all," Glenn said. Luria had no idea what that meant. Nonetheless, she smiled.

"I've seen you around. Your face is familiar…" Luria trailed off.

"I'm here most nights," Glenn said. "I prefer to work when the hospital is quiet."

"Burning the midnight oil administrating," Luria said.

"Something like that," Glenn said.

Luria stuck out her hand. "Well, it was a pleasure to meet you. I've gotta…"

She assumed his cold hand was due to where they were standing. But it was more than cold. It was a hard hand, immobile even. His grip grew stronger. He opened his mouth slightly and out came the fangs.

"I think maybe I'll take things from here," Glenn said. "I'm so very adept at admin stuff as it is."

Like most of the other hospital administrators at St. Hermens, Glenn Beck suffered from ineptitude as well. He sucked out Luria's blood but not enough to kill her. She turned right there on the floor of the walk-in fridge. Glenn was long gone when it happened.

"Nobody puts Luria in a corner," she said, rising off the cold floor.

* * *

"Fucking Keith Richards?" Neno askedd. "Our entire operation's been blown by Keith Richards? I hate the Rolling Stones. I hate being one-upped by an ancient Brit-pop group. I hate that I have to learn about this from the Internet. I hate that YouTube has become a method of communications for our kind. I hate that you brought it to my attention, even though it's good that you did. I hate that the Sons of Gilgamesh couldn't wait until my order, which means I now have to either destroy them or, at the very least, break some fangs. I'm in a hative mood, Percy. I'm overflowing with hatred."

"Does that mean we should start the raid...?"

"Yes, start the fucking raid. Dammit it all to hell, start the raid, find me Topo and Rupert, and, for fuck's sake, come over here so I can at least get a little snack before I receive more news of incompetence."

Percy could handle Neno's tantrum. He could handle the double-crossing Topo, the demands placed upon him by the SOG and Dory, and now the deboarding of passengers from the cruise ship. He could even handle listening to The Stones being slandered—the one saving grace to Percy's otherwise foolhardy existence, as he was a Stones fan. But what Percy simply could not stand was another round of bloodletting. He was barely able to walk as it was. He felt lightheaded and was sure he was running a fever. He couldn't eat enough to replenish his blood supply. He just wanted to crawl under a table and sleep. And now? Neno wanted to feed like some insouciant little vampire who cared nothing for the people who made his operation run. What if Percy called it a day? He could die now. He was baked. Maybe Neno would turn him. He'd do that just to abuse him into eternity. The thought made Percy's shoulders sink even lower.

"What are you waiting for?" Neno demanded.

"Fuggit," Percy said. "Finish me off. Stick a fork in me. Stick some fangs in me." Percy giggled deliriously. "Suck me dry. Then mash my bones into a fine white powder and let the breeze carry me out to sea."

Neno was impressed. He was pissed still but impressed by Percy's candor. He'd often wondered if there was any courage or pride in Percy beyond being a middle management asswipe. Turns out there was, though it wasn't the best time to show it. But it proved to be enough of a distraction to Neno to spare Percy's life, if not give him a few moments to breathe before trudging back into the fray.

"Perhaps it's time I take a walk around," Neno said. "See the machine in action. Deus ex machina, if you will."

CHAPTER 12

THE COMMAND TO ATTACK HAD BEEN GIVEN by word of mouth, YouTube, Vine, texts, tweets, Facebook messaging, a few creative Instagrams, by phone, and by very low-frequency telepathy (the centuries-old could still bang out a few thoughts, something that had become a lost art over time). Vampires poured out of the shipping containers, from the hold of the cruise ship, and from the jets that had landed. Some who had the talent flew. Others used their legs (3,000 feet per second), while a few had rented cars and drove, opting to take in a few of the sights before finishing off with dinner.

Kyle, Cate, Sylvia, the Brotherhood, Xavier, LeRoi, Desmond, Thierry, Oscar, Woman, Dog, Topo, Dory, and Joaquin split into their respective groups. Like the Zombie Land Rush & Barbecue that took place on St. Agrippina last year, Kyle wanted to give names to each group then hand out nicknames for each participant. "Right. Because it was such a success last time," Cate had said. "Let's just keep it simple and use our names, 'kay sporto?" Kyle ignored the comment, making it known that for the duration of the mission he'd be known as "Johnny Rio." Nobody would comply.

Meanwhile, things were getting under way at the HPGS charity event dinner held in the main conference room of the hotel. Charo was playing her guitar. Ricky, Sid, Talia, and Dr. Baeza sat at a table, politely taking in the event, Ricky anxious to get back to the suite and get some serious exchange of ideas going. The Undead Grateful Dead convention was in full tilt with vendor booths set up, and crowds of well-to-do zombies reliving their Haight-Ashbury days by plunking down six hundred dollars for a Dead bootleg featuring Jerry Garcia telling a sick joke before launching into "Bertha."

> JERRY GARCIA: Hey, people. We got a technical problem we're working on. So, a quick joke—a riddle, maybe. Here it goes. What's the only part of a vegetable you can't eat?

> CROWD: (various vegetables named, mushroom stems being the most proffered).

> JERRY GARCIA: Give up? Okay, man. So, as it turns out, the only part of a vegetable you can't eat is the wheelchair.

> CROWD: (collective moan)

> JERRY GARCIA: What?

All it took was a bell—similar to a prize boxing match—to sound, announcing the start of the melee. The closest thing was a vampire fart, caused by one of seven vamps hidden in the mangroves outside the entrance to the hotel. For the uninitiated, when a vampire farts, it sounds like a foghorn. In fact, exactly like a foghorn. This stopped guests in their tracks as, unlike a normal foghorn, this vampire fart came out at about eighty-five decibels. The jig was up. Scores of vampires swarmed down into the lobby of the hotel, biting into necks and sucking in blood like two-legged ticks.

Topo, recognizing the sound, began ripping off vampire heads while the Brotherhood went into action with silver-tipped stakes.

Dory shouted out an announcement to the lobby guests: "IF YOU'RE NOT A VAMPIRE, DUCK!" She had a Glock 9mm and several speed-loader rounds of ammo and immediately began aiming for vampire heads, which proved difficult as they were a blur as they moved between victims. Still, she managed to land a few decent headshots.

Oscar and Desmond heard the screaming and gunfire and headed for the hotel. As they made their way along a dirt road, driving a small Russian-made Moskvitch 400 they had rented for the night, Oscar hung his weapon of choice, the 50mm machine gun, out the window and picked off vampires headed toward the resort, Desmond shouting, "YOU LIKE THAT? HUH? THAS' RIGHT MOTHERFUCKERS!" Oscar couldn't help but smile at Desmond's thirst for vampire bloodshed.

Xavier, LeRoi, and Joaquin were camped out behind a wall of luggage with assorted machine guns. Xavier gave them a crash course in short, controlled bursts of gunfire then set them loose on the approaching vampires, who saw the carnage the silver bullets were causing and beat a hasty retreat into the bush.

In the suites located on the top floor of the resort, the aristocrat vampires heard the screams and the gunfire and took one of the elevators down to the lobby, sipping blood from martini glasses, feeling very noble in their descent into dinner. The elevator doors parted where they were met by Dory, who, by this time, had two Glocks and shot the vamps before they had a chance to react. After Dory dispatched the vampires, she took a moment to tilt her weapons to the ceiling to empty her clips with a smirk. She had worn leather knee-high boots for the occasion and, like the others, could feel the badassery flow through her with every kill.

Hiding in a closet, James Franco sat cross-legged, reading Pablo Neruda's *Twenty Love Poems and a Song of Despair* with an LED headlamp while his guests, Bansky, Morrissey, Pink and Sting's eldest daughter, lounged around the suite, sipping Pimm's and remarking on the sounds of gunfire. It was Franco's idea to invite guests who went by one name, in honor of Charo, whom he'd always listened to; he thought there might be some kind of interesting mix of psychology and art with people who christened themselves with one name. As it turned out, they were just talented, regular folk, so Franco retreated to the closet to read one of his favorite poets rather than ask them all to leave. He was rereading the line, "I don't love her, that's certain, but perhaps I love her," when he heard the door burst open followed by screeching sounds mixed with screams, furniture being knocked over, and "You're not room service!" shouted. A moment later, the room fell silent. James scratched at his chin hair and continued reading.

Amidst the chaos in the main conference room, Dr. Baeza ushered Ricky, Talia, and Sid out through a side door that led to the kitchen into a service elevator that took them up to the doctor's suite. The kids were frightened by the commotion, but Dr. Baeza felt a sense of calm he'd never known he had during a crisis. He instructed the kids to hide under the beds while he slid a dresser across the door, leaning up against it, listening. A moment later, there was a frantic knock at the door.

"Emile! It's Maria!"

Dr. Baeza quickly pushed the dresser aside and let a shaken Charo into the room. She was clutching her blood-spattered guitar but otherwise looked like she could step out onto a stage at Caesar's.

"What's going on?" she asked, sans accent.

"I don't know," Dr. Baeza said. "Terrorists?"

"I saw things. People being bitten! In the neck! By other people!"

"I'm guessing vampires," Ricky said from beneath the bed.

"Who's that?" Charo asked, clutching her guitar to her considerable bosom.

The kids climbed out from underneath the beds.

"I think it's a vampire invasion," Ricky said.

"You say that like it's an everyday occurrence," Dr. Baeza said.

"If I believe there's a method of thinking that can transform civilization as we know it, I got no problem believing in the undead. In fact, as we were on our way up, I got to thinking about the nature of being undead," Ricky said.

"I dunno if now's a good time for hypothesizing," Talia said. "People are firing guns."

"What about the undead?" Sid asked.

"Just a thought," Ricky said. "About finding a way to continue with the work."

"Interesting," Dr. Baeza said.

* * *

Luria heard the screams emanating from the lobby of the hospital and quickly (in vampire time, which blew her mind temporarily) ran down the stairs and burst through the door. It looked like she had stepped into a Jackson Pollock painting in red, with vampires tearing apart hospital personnel and waiting patients.

Luria got pissed. She grabbed the first vampire to cross her path and bit into his neck, instinctively sucking the blood out of the bloated vamp. It tasted like honey but the sudden intake proved too much and she immediately puked out the blood onto the linoleum floor. It was a lot of blood that came out of her. In Luria's estimation, at least four pints. The lightbulb in her head burst. She ran into one of the operating rooms and grabbed hold of an empty blood bag. She ran back out to the lobby, grabbed another vampire, bled him, then heaved into the blood bag, the blood quickly overflowing.

"Holy fuck!" she exclaimed.

* * *

Kyle, Cate, and Woman, along with Dog, who sat comfortably in a backpack strapped to Woman, took up positions at the dock and began picking off vampires. One had grabbed Kyle from behind, but Cate was ready and put one in the vampire's forehead. "You're welcome, Johnny Rio," she shouted. Woman was unleashing a current of gunfire when she felt a sudden weight on her back.

"You gotta be fuckin' kidding me!" Dog shouted.

Reflexively, Woman unsheathed her silver Buck fixed-blade knife and twisted to the left, ramming the blade through the attacking vampire's ear and forcing it to release Dog's neck from its fangs. Being that Dog was a zombie, there was no blood but instead a mixture of formaldehyde and resin that leaked out of two puncture holes on the side of Dog's neck.

"There's no fucking way I'm turning vamp," Dog said.

"Doubt it," Woman said. "No blood."

But no sooner had she said that than Dog began to shake violently. A moment later, his canines grew out almost a full inch.

"Jesus Christ," Woman whispered.

"What?" Dog said, unaware of the transformation. Woman motioned to her own teeth. Dog licked his chops. "I'm undead twice. Twice. Unbelievable."

"How do you feel?"

"Duck," Dog said. Woman did so, just in time for a vampire to crash into Dog, who grabbed hold of the vampire's neck and shook it until the vampire's head was severed completely. Dog was now perched atop Woman's shoulder, his hind legs having demolished the wheelchair. Before Woman could respond, Dog launched himself from her shoulder and flew into the mass of vampires running down the dock. Dog was a blur of blond hair, ping-ponging off one vampire to the next, beheading each along the way.

"What the fuck's that?" Kyle shouted.

"Dog," Cate whispered to herself. She considered the idea of a zombie dog-turned-vampire and watched as the Chihuahua cut heads like a weed whacker. She stood up from behind the light post she was using as cover.

"CATE!" Kyle shouted.

A vampire swooped down on Cate, her teeth sinking deep into Cate's neck and getting only a mouthful of chemicals. The vampire released Cate and flew off in search of blood. Cate's body vibrated in a blur for a few seconds then settled. She smiled at Kyle, her fangs coming from underneath her top lip. She blew Kyle a kiss and jetted into the air. Kyle looked at Woman, who in turn gave a beats-me shrug and resumed firing. As Kyle and Woman resumed their attack, they couldn't help but be amazed at the amount of destruction Cate and Dog were inflicting on the flow of vampires.

In the hotel lobby, Dory, Sylvia, and Topo were joined by Oscar and Desmond, who saw the conference room doors smashed open and ran toward them, clearing a path with 50mm silver bullets. There was already a large amount of human carnage lying on the floor, and the blood made things slippery. Two vampires attacked Oscar, who jammed his machine gun into the mouth of one vampire and ripped a hole through its head as the other vampire accidently bit into the barrel of Oscar's machine gun.

Oscar, with one fluid motion, whipped a hand grenade from his side camo-pants pocket and jammed it into the vampire's mouth as its fangs came away from the machine gun. *"FIRE IN THE HOLE!"* he shouted, hitting the floor. A moment later there was a midair explosion that sent pouring down over Oscar. *"THAT'S WHAT I CALL A BAPTISM BY BLOOD!"*

The conference room resembled a butcher's chopping block, body parts strewn about on tables and the floor. They were too late to save many mortals but just in time to spray the room with silver bullets, which they did with great efficiency. Vampire bodies exploded in midair and on the ground.

"*BACK TO HELL, BITCHES!*" Desmond screamed.

Oscar couldn't get enough of Desmond's glee. Topo raided the break room behind the front desk, where several vampires were passing around a teenaged boy close to being completely drained of blood. "Cowards," Topo muttered as he rounded the table, ripping off heads.

The Brotherhood had a tent set up outside the lobby entrance and were dragging vampires into it to be demolished and stacked like cordwood. It wasn't terribly efficient but did seem to lend an air of tradition, much like drunken Thanksgiving family fights. They were low on holy oil, but the Brotherhood continued to carry on with the old ways despite their arms being tired from all the staking. Noam and Sari had opted for cutting-edge vampire-killing technologies, Sari carrying a 9mm submachine gun, Noam equipped with a MAC 10 for each hand. They used the tent as a reloading station, stepping outside to spray silver bullets across the surrounding manicured lawns of the resort lobby entrance, mowing down the vampires who made it past the dock.

It was Dory who first noticed the dead celebrities lying about, feeling a tinge of sadness over seeing the cast of *The Real Housewives of Beverly Hills* in a heap of drained flesh. "Kyle, when you get a chance, you gotta come to the lobby and check out the celebrity carnage, over," she said into her walkie-talkie.

"On my way. Over," Kyle said.

"We're good here. Go," Woman said. It was true. Between Cate and Dog, the only thing left for Woman to do was mop up the few stragglers who had made it past the newly minted zombie vampire-killing machines.

It seemed to the group that they were taking their toll on the vampires. The hold of the cruise ship had been drained. The conference room was emptied. There had been a goodly number of mortal survivors, who walked around in a zombie-like state (Kyle's term) and were ushered by zombie hotel personnel to the rooms on the lower floors of the hotel. Oscar radioed everyone to assemble in front of the hotel. Fifteen minutes later, the group, covered in what they hoped was vampire blood alone, gathered in a circle.

"Okay, first things first," Kyle said. "Have the rest of you met Cate and Dog, the twice-undead twins?"

Cate and Dog both flashed their fangs, causing the rest of the group to point their weaponry at them.

"Hold on, you trigger-happy motherfucks," Kyle said. "Lower your weapons. Desmond, get the crazy out of your eyes. Lower 'em."

"It's cool," Cate said. "We're not out for blood."

"What the hell happened to you?" Xavier asked.

"We got bit," Dog said.

"But you're bloodless," Dory said.

"Surprised the shit out of them, too," Cate said. "I dunno what you'd call it, but we've got vampire powers without the bloodthirst."

"Just so we're clear, you're still on a brains diet?" Kyle said.

"Don't be an asshole," Cate said. "And yes."

"And they are killing machines," Woman said. "Really, Oscar. You should see them in action. It'd bring tears to your eyes."

"Nice," Oscar said.

"Well, eet wen well, yays?" Thierry said.

"Too well," Topo said.

"We passed by the Undead Grateful Dead convention on the way back form the airstrip," LeRoi said. "The band was still playing. *Sugaree*, I think.

"That makes sense," Dory said. "Not a lot of blood to be had there."

"What about the town?" Sari asked. "Would they attack Oliveira?"

"That wasn't part of the plan," Sylvia said. "But since things didn't turn out the way they'd hoped, it might be a good idea to check it out."

"God knows we can use a drink," Kyle said.

"We're being too sure of ourselves," Topo said.

"Whaddaya mean?" Kyle asked. "We did scorched earth here. Look around you. A couple of machine guns firing silver bullets? Game over, man. Game over."

"There was no sign of Rupert," Topo said. "And I didn't count very many SOGs."

"SO whosawhatsit?" Kyle asked.

"Sons of Gilgamesh," Noam said. "An ancient order of vampire."

"You guys and your orders," Kyle said. "I say we head over to the order of St. Bobo's and have Joaquin mix us some drinks."

"Topo's right," Oscar said. "We came in from the olive orchards where the shipping containers were. It didn't feel like we got 'em all, judging from the size of the containers. We need to secure the perimeter and that includes Oliveira."

"Hey, did you guys see any dead celebrities? I saw Ryan Seacrest's head," Kyle said.

"Mr. ADD, we're in the middle of something here," Cate said.

"We're headed to town," Kyle said. "I heard Oscar. Doesn't mean we can't get a couple of selfies with some recently drained Kardashians."

"Is he always like this?" Topo asked.

"Honey, it gets worse," Sylvia said.

*   *   *

"Well, that was, without a doubt, *the* worst charity event I've hosted to date," Philomena said to Rolf as they sat in the empty hotel lounge, nursing Old Fashioneds, surrounded by blood and bone. "And let me tell you, I've had some less than perfect events. The 10k run for Chronic Exhaustion? Bad. The Tori Spelling jobs fair gala for television writers? Worse. But this? A vampire invasion? Doll, forget about it."

"It's not a total write-off," Rolf said, leaning forward. "I met someone."

*   *   *

By the time the group gathered in front of Koufax's deli, the feeling of dread was contagious. The town of Oliveira was silent. There were no signs of attack or even struggle, just silent streets, with a light breeze blowing the strings of lights that crosscrossed above the cobblestones.

"We should split up and recon the area," Oscar said. "Keep your dick hard and powder dry. This doesn't smell right."

"Could be everybody called it a night early," Kyle said, his words sounding as unconvincing as his tone.

"Topo? Did you hear anything about this? About an attack on the town, maybe?" Sylvia asked.

"No. Nothing," Topo said.

"Why would he be privy to such information?" Rupert Jagger asked as he emerged from the flower shop entrance. Guns went up into attack mode. Rupert smirked. "Put those silly things down."

"These silly things fire five hundred and seventy silver bullets per minute," Woman said. "I'd hesitate to label them 'silly.'"

"They might cause some harm," Rupert said. "Nothing more." He looked up to the sky. Above them all, like a fog that hung over the city, were hundreds of vampires hovering over them, fangs bared, limbs twitchy. They were at once horrifying and wondrous, the patterns the vampire bodies made as they floated together, motion waves rippling through them as they made adjustments to height.

Kyle threw his gun to the street, the echoing sound of metal clinking against stone.

"Keeerighst," Oscar said. "Where's your balls?"

"Right now, I'd say they're up around my lower intestine," Kyle said.

"The rest of you would do well to follow suit," Rupert said.

Oscar stood his ground, the 50mm gun he held pointed right at Rupert's head.

"Oh, fuck all," Sylvia said. "I hate to agree with this massive douchebag. Do as he says."

"When you pry my cold, dead hands off my weapon," Oscar said.

"Sylvia's right," Woman said, lowering her weapon then letting it fall to the street.

"Hon..." Oscar said with disbelief.

"It's the battle, not the war," Dog said.

Rupert sighed. Everyone dropped their weapons.

"What did you do with the town?" Topo asked.

"The traitor speaks!" Rupert said. "Use your vampire senses. That is, unless you've lost those along with your loyalty. And your face. Good god, man, you're a shambles."

"You always had to take the long way to answer a question," Topo said. "Are they all dead?"

"Not yet," Rupert said. "But soon enough."

"Just how many vamps you got hanging around this island, anyway?" Kyle asked.

"More than those you dispatched at the hotel, obviously," Rupert said. "Or did you think we'd make such a weak showing?"

"Topo was right," Dory said. "It was too easy."

"Yes, Topo was right," Rupert said. "Did you think you'd have a chance with seasoned vampires had I sent them to the hotel? Those vampires you did kill were all newly turned. They lacked the knowledge and the skill in extermination. Ending them shouldn't have proven to be much of a challenge."

"A distraction…" Xavier whispered.

"A distraction," Rupert said. "We needed to keep you occupied to tend to the real task at hand."

"Bleeding Oliveira dry," Dory said.

"I'm surprised you didn't 'crunch the numbers,' Dory. The number of people in attendance at the hotel versus the population of the rest of the island… All of you, so focused on history repeating itself. Trying to prevent another St. Agrippina. So convinced were you that your prowess in killing the undead was equal to the task of dealing with our kind. None of you stopped to think about the other inhabitants. The ones who didn't reserve a suite in your luxury hotel."

While Rupert was explaining how it was, Cate, who'd brought up the rear, faded back behind a clothing store. Then, with her newly acquired vampire skills, she spun out of Oliveira and made her way to the Undead Grateful Dead convention. A few vampires tracked her movements but turned their attention back to the others. Cate assumed she had enough vampire in her to not get pinged.

"What did you do with them?" Topo asked. "You obviously didn't take them in the streets or in their homes."

"Come," Rupert said. "You'll see."

* * *

Nebula stood in front of the door in the hotel suite, legs spread, hands on hips, blood dripping out of her maw. She couldn't explain the events of the last few hours other than that some sort of base animal instinct had taken hold of her and turned her into a predator. She felt nothing but the quench of her deep thirst when she sucked the blood out of the mortals. How many were there? Five? Fifty? She'd lost count, her brain holding but one thought: kill. Dr. Baeza stood in front of Charo, Ricky, Talia, and Sid, not knowing what to do next but willing to give his life for theirs.

"Let's just all calm down," Dr. Baeza said. "We don't want anybody getting hurt here."

Nebula growled in a way that was at once foreign but stimulating—she was a serious animal.

"What's your name?" Dr. Baeza asked.

Nebula's eyes darted back and forth between her prey. Whatever she once was existed no longer.

"I'm Emile," Dr. Baeza said, extending his shaking hand.

Nebula took this as a sign of aggression and reared back on her feet, her torso seeming to telescope in height, her elbows raised, clawed fingers curled, fangs dripping with blood as she opened her mouth to twice the length of a normal human being. She was ready. He would be the first. And then there was a crash. Nebula was flattened by the door. Atop it stood Luria with a backpack full of blood bags.

"Luck's on your side," Luria said. "I was going room to room when I sensed the coming attack. Hold on a sec." She lifted the door and tossed it aside as if it were a napkin. Nebula was a flattened mass of blood, flesh, and bone. Luria located what was left of Nebula's throat and sank her fangs into it, making a sound similar to the end of a milkshake. A moment later, she sat up, her cheeks puffed out, and grabbed a blood bag from the backpack, which she put against her mouth, a small tube disappearing beyond her fangs, and began heaving. Blood shot into the bag with force, filling it instantaneously.

"That's completely gross," Talia said.

"Y'mean completely awesome!" Sid said.

Luria sealed the pint bag and shoved it into her backpack.

"Are we next?" Dr. Baeza asked.

"What? No. Unless one of you is a vampire, which I don't detect," Luria said. "But you are special. Progeria?"

"Party of three," Ricky said, raising his hand.

"Your friends, I saw them in the lobby. They're dead," Luria said. "Sorry. Listen, I've gotta get you guys out of here and to someplace safe. I've got a busy night ahead of me before the sun rises."

"It looks as if you're... blood collecting," Dr. Baeza said.

"I'm with Talia," Charo said. "Gross."

"Where's your accent?" Luria said, shaking her head. "Never mind that. Yes, I'm collecting blood—I'm St. Hermen's hospital's bloodmobile."

"Taking blood that was already taken," Dr. Baeza said, incredulously. "That's fantastic. How can we help?"

"You can't," Luria said. "In fact, you're like chum for a shark. This is a one-woman operation. Let's move out."

"Hold on," Dr. Baeza said. "It's obvious that you're a vampire, but you're putting the needs of mortals ahead of your own. I take it you're immortal?"

"As the day is long," Luria said.

"Imagine that. Immortality. The things you could get done. The race against time would cease to exist."

"Where are you going with this, doctor?" Ricky asked.

"The Singularity posits that human beings would meld with technology," Dr. Baeza said. "But there's nothing mentioned about humanity mixing with ... undead."

"I don't think the minds behind the concept of the Singularity were aware of the paranormal, such as vampires," Ricky said.

"Yeah, but here we are," Sid said.

"And I know exactly where Dr. Baeza's headed," Talia said.

"Someplace with a bar, I hope," Charo said.

"Don't you see?" Talia asked. "We're looking at a way to stop the clock. Buy some time. Figure things out."

Dr. Baeza turned to the kids. "No. This is something I must do. I know it sounds selfish, but the life of a vampire doesn't seem too enchanted. Am I right...?"

"It's Luria. And I don't know, this is my first night. And if we don't get the hell out of here, there's not gonna be any time for debate."

"Bite me," Ricky said.

"S'cuse me?" Luria said.

"I want you to bite me. I want the immortality. I want to remove the sword of Damocles and give me a shot at finding a cure for people like me. I want to help Dr. Baeza with his research."

"Dude," Sid said. "Seriously? You want to suck blood and sleep in a coffin?"

"I want in, too," Talia said.

"You're all crazy," Sid said. "You've seen the movies. Vampires mope around, wishing they'd made another choice instead of being eternally damned. I heard your dick falls off."

"Eww," Charo and Talia said in unison.

"I'm not turning anybody," Luria said. "I didn't have a choice in this, but I damn sure as hell'r gonna make the best of it. Now, let's beat it."

"We're not leaving until you bite us," Ricky said.

"Count me out," Sid said.

"Don't you see? You can stay alive," Talia said to Sid.

"I'm alive right now," Sid said. "And if I had the chance to relive my life, I'd do it exactly the same way. This is who I am. People say we've been screwed over, but I don't see it that way. I've lived a lifetime of experience and thought and ideas in fifteen years. This is who I am and who I'll stay."

The room was quiet. Glances were exchanged.

"I can respect that," Ricky said. "But I want to make a different choice."

"Fuckin' A," Sid said. "I can be your control for your research, then." He smiled.

They all turned to Luria.

"You're going to need help collecting blood," Dr. Baeza said. "And the sun is coming."

*   *   *

Cate arrived at the Undead Grateful Dead convention, formulating a plan to make some converts. She had been unconsciously scratching at the palm of her hand, a long-held habit she had as a human being that she had had to give up when she turned into a zombie, as the scratching would create a hole in her palm. She'd had it fixed three times as it was. But now, as she scratched, no flesh separated. She quickly moved her hands to her sides reflexively then lifted her hand, palm up. There was no hole. No markings whatsoever. She felt her arms then her face. She dug her nails into her forearm and pulled. No flesh came apart in her hand. A man dressed in tan khakis and tie-dye passed Cate, holding a bong made out of a femur with dancing bears etched into it. Cate attacked the man, bringing him down with ease, and sank her fangs to the hilt into the man's neck.

"What the fuck, lady!" the man shouted.

Cate lifted her head, spitting out the pot-tasting formaldehyde. "Give it a minute," Cate said.

"There's zombie law about doing..." His body went into spasms. The bong slipped from his grip. A few more seconds then the shaking left. The man blinked several times, not sure what had happened.

"How do you feel?" Cate asked.

"Wha... Why'd you bite me? I'm already... I... I feel great!" the man said.

"Check this out," Cate said, grabbing the man's hand and biting into it. She tore at him like a rabid dog but came up with an empty mouth. "Tougher than leather."

The man looked at his hand, then at Cate, then back at the hand.

"Check these out," Cate said, snapping her fangs out for display.

"You're a vampire!" the man said.

"Better," Cate said. "And you've just been recruited to my cause. Take a hit off your bong, we've got converts to make."

*   *   *

Neno sat on the purple crushed-velvet throne he had transported to the clearing of the olive grove. He'd always admired the way kings throughout history would sit on a portable throne at the edge of a battle, usually with a drink in hand which, in this case, was Percy's wrist held over the chair's armrest; the remainder of Percy lay prone on the grass. Before him stood thousands of people herded into a huge oval, a circle of vampires surrounding them on the perimeter, with twice the number of vampires suspended in the air above. You could almost smell the death.

A beam of light from a truck crossed Neno. It was a large orange-and-white U-Haul moving truck. It pulled up to the left of Neno and his retinue of vampires. Two of the SOG got out of the truck, unlocked the back, and slid up the metal door to the truck's cargo bay.

"This way, blood sacks," Shulgi said, motioning to the group in the truck.

"Did you get a deal on the truck?" Kyle asked as he hopped down. "Because the nineteen-ninety-five price is total bullshit."

Shulgi bared his fangs.

"I'm guessing no," Kyle said.

More vampires came over to the truck and, together, they ushered Kyle and company to Neno.

"That's him," Topo whispered to Noam. "I'm sorry it couldn't have been someone of more substance."

Noam nodded, pulling Sari close.

The vampires lined everyone up before Neno, who sat with his hands in a praying position against his lips.

"This is a very Auschwitz-styled assembly you have here," Kyle said.

Neno chuckled. "I would know. You have to be Kyle Brightman."

"And you must be what? Upper middle management?" Kyle asked. "I can't tell you vamps from Monsanto with your corporate hierarchy."

"Kyle, shut it," Sylvia said.

"Seriously, look at what we've got here. A steampunk dandy, complete with traveling throne and his phalanx—oh, I'm sorry—his court. Scaring the shit out of all these folk. Way to fuck up an island vibe, King of Sanctimoniousland."

Neno lowered his hands, forming an O with his lips. "Oh, I like him," he said to one of his sidekicks. "I like the show of bravado. The complete disregard for his own safety or that of others."

"He's off his meds," Sylvia said. "I'm certain of it."

"I'm not off my meds—and don't tell me to take it down a notch. I'm just sick of this paranormal, dystopian, apocalyptic, sacred, and holy evil hoo-haw. It's starting to sound like a Black Sabbath song, and I don't mean that in a good way. I mean it in the worst way possible, when they made *Forbidden*, which sucked ass and even the band hated it. You guys should go back and listen to *Paranoid* 'to get an idea of what evil sounds like. Fucking charlatans."

A brief pause.

"Anything else, before they eviscerate us?" Sylvia asked.

"The Sons of Gilgamesh are to badass motorcycle gangs what Liberace was to classical music."

Ekur made a move toward Kyle, but Neno motioned with his hand for him to remain still.

"Okay. It's getting tiresome," Neno said. "Somebody do something to abate this man's ignorance and rage."

Kyle was about to reply when Sylvia got in his face, her finger to her lips. "I mean it," she growled. Kyle's shoulders sank a bit.

"Here they are, as requested," Rupert said, impatiently. If he were to make a move on Neno, the time would be soon.

"Do any of you wish to come forward and ask that the people of Oliveira be released unharmed or maybe trade yourselves for them?" Neno said.

"Neno, this raid hasn't gone to plan as you had hoped," Topo said.

"Hasn't gone to plan? It's going exactly as planned, minus a few inconveniences, nothing worth mentioning," Neno said. "In about ten seconds, we're going to feed on these good citizens and there is not a single thing on Earth any of you can do about it, except watch."

"It doesn't have to go this way," a voice called out. A moment later, Luria rounded the van with a beat-up red truck with Dr. Baeza, Ricky, Talia, and Charo. The truck stopped and everyone tumbled out.

"You're Charo!" Neno said.

"Eees true!" Charo said in her patented thick Spanish accent.

"I admire your work," Neno said, pointing at Topo. "You knew I loved Charo. Topo. Was this your doing? Your way of apologizing for defecting? Never mind. She's here now! Charo, might you regale us with song? Maybe *Dance a Little Bit Closer*? Or *La Mojada*? Anything off *Cuchi-Cuchi* would do."

Kyle looked at Sylvia, mouthing, *What the fuck?* Sylvia shrugged and motioned slowly to her wrist as if she were wearing a watch. Charo, who had never balked at any opportunity to perform, felt a wave of stage fright come over her. Her pulse quickened. She'd never performed for vampires before, at least she didn't think so. There were the *Love Boat* appearances as April Lopez. The whole cast and crew felt off and weird in that coked-out-and-lost kind of way. Like watching an off-Broadway staging of *Cats*.

She didn't have her guitar with her so it'd have to be a capella. She looked around, thinking this was probably the toughest room she'd ever played. "Well," she said, stepping forward, clapping her hands together. "Eye muss tell you, my goose has bumps, bean here with ju all toonigh."

Neno laughed.

"I seeng for ju a song that ees from dee Spaanish folklore. Ju will loof it."

"Not *Cuchi-Cuchi*?" Neno said, crestfallen.

"No. Dees you gone to loof, I promeese."

"Very well, then," Neno said, brightening. It was still Charo, after all. Charo cleared her throat, patted down the gold-sequined dress that hugged her curvaceous body, and took a deep breath.

> *Negras tormentas agitan los aires (Black storms shake the sky)*
> *nubes oscuras nos impiden ver (Dark clouds blind us)*
> *Aunque nos espere el dolor y la muerte (Although pain and death*
>   *await us)*
> *contra el enemigo nos llama el deber. (Duty calls against the enemy)*

Neno closed his eyes, listening to Charo's soothing voice. Just like the records, even if he didn't know what the hell she was singing about. There were few things Neno felt badly about himself, but one was his never having learned to speak Spanish. Sure, Akkadian, Eblaite, Elamite, Phoenician, Semitic, and Sumerian—and, of course, English and a smattering of Russian. No Spanish.

> *El bien más preciado, (The most precious good)*
> *es la libertad, (is freedom)*
> *hay que defenderla, (And we have to defend it)*
> *con fe y valor. (With faith and courage)*

What Neno didn't know was that Charo was singing *A las Barricadas (To the Barricades)*, a Spanish Civil War fight song sung by the anarchists who opposed Francisco Franco's military coup against the Spanish Republic. Charo was many things, one of them being a student of history and a fan of labor unions.

> *Alza la bandera revolucionaria, (Raise the revolutionary flag)*
> *que del triunfo sin cesar nos lleva en pos, (which leads us*
>   *unceasingly to triumph)*
> *Alza la bandera revolucionaria, (Raise the revolutionary flag)*
> *que del triunfo sin cesar nos lleva en pos, (which leads us*
>   *unceasingly to triumph)*
> *En pie el pueblo obrero a la batalla, (Working people march*
>   *onwards to the battle)*
> *hay que derrocar a la reacción (We have to smash the reaction)*

Charo paused, knowing that, within the herd of townsfolk, there were people who understood what she was singing.

> !A las Barricadas! A las Barricadas! (To the Barricades! To
>   the Barricades!)
> por el triunfo de la Confederación, (For the triumph of
>   the Confederation)
> !A las Barricadas! A las Barricadas! (To the Barricades! To
>   the Barricades!)

Luria gave a shout and held up an empty pint bag. "It's time the vampires of this island give back to the community from which it takes!

In a blur of motion, Luria, Dr. Baeza, Ricky, and Talia were on top of Neno's court, sucking blood out of their necks. Luria was the first to heave the blood into a pint bag.

"That is just wrong," Neno said.

Ricky, Dr. Baeza, and Talia followed suit, though their technique had yet to be honed, thus causing some spillage.

"Oh, man," Kyle said. "Luria's got her own vampire gang."

A swarm of vampires descended on Luria and the rest, and all hell broke loose. Vampire descended onto the townsfolk, sending bodies flying as they sucked and tore at the flesh of human beings. Kyle and the rest stepped back, feeling helpless without their weaponry. Neno smiled at Topo, watching for a reaction, which Topo granted, taking flight into the melee, vampire bodies being flung behind him as he savagely tore into vampire flesh.

"Fuck," was all Sylvia said before following suit.

"Not much of a rebellion!" Neno shouted above the din as he sat on his throne, letting go of Percy's wrist. A few SOG moved toward Kyle and the rest, but Neno intervened. "*NOT YET!*" he barked. The SOG backed off. The din of shouts and screams was horrible and provoked a feeling that this was truly the end.

And then the rumble started. You could feel the ground shake.

"*NOW WHAT?*" Kyle shouted.

"Something wicked this way comes," Oscar whispered to himself.

Neno felt the vibrations and rose from his throne with a look of annoyance. "Now what?" he mumbled.

"It's coming from the olive orchards!" Woman shouted. The rumbling developed into roars and shouts of the animalistic kind. Joaquin hugged LeRoi. The rest braced themselves for what they assumed would be another wave of vampires.

They came out of the olive orchards, hundreds of them. Zombies turned vampire led by Cate, her eyes wild, fangs protruding from a mouth that stretched out unnaturally but then there was nothing natural to her appearance or that of the others who followed her.

"Ho-lee shit!" Kyle shouted. "Cate!"

Cate was in full-on apex predator mode, pulling vampires off mortals and tearing their bodies in half. Out of the horde came a group of zombie vampires carrying various assault weapons they had picked up in Oliveira. They headed straight for Kyle and the rest of the group, who smiled in unison.

"Come to Papa," Oscar said, holding out his arms as if receiving a newborn child to cradle. Instead, Oscar was rewarded with his 50mm gun. "*INTO THE BREACH!*" He tilted his gun to the sky, firing into the cloud of vampire.

The rest followed suit, and muzzle flashes lit up faces painted with anger and grit. Vampires began exploding in the sky, their blood raining upon the mass of people who were all running, groping, doing anything to escape a pair of fangs. The zombie vampires, along with the newly armed Kyle, Oscar, and the rest, were starting to even out the balance of bloodshed.

"Hold open your bags!" Luria shouted, doing so herself, collecting the blood from the vampires exploding overhead. Ricky was enjoying himself too much to listen, beheading vampires and throwing bags over the necks to catch the blood. The feeling of being impervious to the ever-running clock of life was a new sensation, and he'd be damned to stop the feeling now.

Topo came out of the fighting, grabbing hold of Noam.

"It's time," he said.

Sari was too busy spraying the sky with silver bullets to notice Topo and her father moving toward Neno, who had his fangs out but remained immobile.

Dog, strapped to Woman's back, was calling shots for her: "Ten o'clock!" and "On the right!" A moment later, he jumped out of Woman's backpack and joined the fray. Xavier, Desmond, LeRoi,

Thierry, and Joaquin stood in a line, looking like thugs out of an old gangster movie, shouting as they unleashed a hail of silver bullets. Desmond bared his teeth, a twig from an olive branch clenched between them. The Brotherhood, Glocks in one hand, silver-tipped stakes in the other, moved among the vampires like International Harvesters as they churned bodies, careful to avoid humans.

Despite all of this, a fair amount of human carnage covered the ground. Though the vampires were evenly matched, they had managed to inflict early damage. Dory saw Topo as they strafed the vampires around Neno, opening up a path. Topo nearly dragged Noam as they made their way toward a distracted Neno.

"Now," Topo said, darting up to Neno and getting him in a hold from behind.

Neno, caught off guard, screamed. His fangs, larger than most vampires', sprang out. Noam advanced, stake in hand. In a moment it would be accomplished, this moment of revenge. Catalina Guarda's death would be avenged.

"Did you really think it would be that easy?" Neno spun, and now it was Topo who was caught in a hold. "She did not die well, Catalina," Neno taunted. "She begged for her life, as all mortals did."

"NOW!" Topo shouted, thrusting his chest forward.

"I can't!" Noam said.

"BOTH OF US!" Topo swanted Noam to go through his body to reach Neno's.

"That's a noble gesture!" Neno shouted. "Go ahead, Noam Wysocki. Let's see if you have what it..."

Neno tensed up, releasing Topo, who turned to see the tip of silver that protruded from Neno's chest. Neno fell to his knees and revealed Percy, his hands still holding on to the wooden stake. Neno tilted his head skyward. His mouth began to stretch; a terrible screeching sound emanating from deep within. His mouth continued to stretch and then something nobody could have predicted occurred. A thick stream of blood shot out of Neno's mouth like a geyser, into the sky. Vampire shapes began to peel off the stream. They sprouted by the dozens, taking flight as they headed toward the crowd of humans.

"Mother of God," Noam whispered.

The sky began to fill with the fresh birth of vampires who, despite the gunfire, darted around at a speed that made the already attacking vampires seem sluggish by comparison.

"*FUUUUUUUUUUUCK!*" Kyle shouted, slamming a fresh cartridge into his AK-47.

Neno's body shook violently as the blood continued to shoot out of his mouth, which had stretched to the size of a car tire, vampires still pouring out of the stream and attacking. It took only a few more moments to realize the battle had turned back in the vampires' favor.

Oscar looked over at Woman and Dog. "Nobody lives forever!" he shouted, as three vampires took him down.

Then came the deep, basso, horn-sounding tone that echoed through the valley, as if the mass of vampire had farted in one coordinated effort. The sound grew in volume, causing everyone—vampire, zombie vampire, and human—to cover their ears. Most sank to the ground in pain. Lightning struck as the sound grew louder. A wind began to howl, smashing airborne vampires to the bloodied dirt and grass. A halo of light came out of the dark storm clouds that had formed over the killing ground. The halo of light, too brilliant to look at for more than a few seconds, slowly descended.

Each individual light source began to take on human form, arms outstretched—only the arms were twice as long as the bodies that formed. In a moment it became apparent that the arms were wings. As they continued their descent, a shockwave hit the bodies below, blasting everyone to the ground. And then the really big ball of light appeared and descended as well.

"That's a really big fuckin' ball of light!" Kyle managed to say, his arms splayed out as his body stuck to the ground.

The ball of light stopped moving, and a figure began to slowly come out of the light source, feet first. The deep horn sound remained and a vocal choir grew in volume. Flowing robes followed the feet as if a fully clothed body were being birthed through the light. Out came wings that unfolded into a mass of white feathers.

"That's a really big fuckin' pair of wings!" Kyle shouted.

Moments later, the rest of the body appeared. It was a woman, hands folded in prayer, her eyes closed. "St. Irene of La Guardia,"

Noam said breathlessly. The woman slowed her descent, opened her eyes, and spoke.

"Turn that fucking noise down," she said.

The deep horn and angelic choir faded to a barely audible wisp of sound.

"What is this holy fuckery I have before me?" the woman asked.

"St. Irene of La Guardia!" Noam shouted.

"No shit, Noam," St. Irene of La Guardia said.

"You're real," Noam said.

"I'm real pissed off."

"That's not a good sign," Kyle murmured.

"What's that, fuckchops?" St. Irene of La Guardia barked.

"Nothing," Kyle said.

"Always a fucking class clown among you. You and your friends, get up."

Kyle and his friends slowly stood. Vampires hissed.

"Oh, shut the fuck up, you plasma pimps," St. Irene of La Guardia said, waving her hand and silencing the vampires. "So who's running the goddamned show here? Hm? What is this clusterfuck of humanity and otherworldliness that we have in this perfectly good little olive orchard which you all thought nothing of destroying?"

Desmond quickly spat out the olive branch he'd clenched with his teeth.

"We're battling the vampire," one of the Brotherhood said.

"Thanks, Captain Obvious," St. Irene of La Guardia said. "Where the fuck's Rupert Jagger?"

From behind the throne, a hand slowly went up.

"Show yourself, dickwad."

"What a mouth on her," Kyle whispered to Oscar, who slowly let out a "shhhhhhh."

"I thought we had an agreement," St. Irene of La Guardia said. "No more raids."

"I know," Rupert said. "I was just following orders."

"Just following orders," St. Irene of La Guardia muttered. "If I got a dime for every asshat who repeated that same line. Are you a Nazi now, Rupert? Hmm? Are you a member of the Shining Path? Hutu majority? The Darfur Liberation Front? The GOP? Just following orders. What part of 'Don't fucking kill any more mortals' did you not understand? Sweet Jesus, must I be surrounded by undead idiots?"

"I was under orders from Neno," Rupert said. "I couldn't break his control over me."

"My sacred ass. Look at fucking Percy. He was a motherfucking bottomless meat sack of blood and yet he found the inner strength to take down Neno. Not in a million years would I have put my money on Percy Merriweather to fuck over the third oldest vampire. But look at him! He grew a pair and did what none of you were able to do. I ought to make this kid a saint right here and now. Christ, what a mess."

Rupert hung his head in shame.

"Where's Luria de Graciosa?"

"I'm here, Your Holiness," Luria shouted from the middle of the field. She still had a vampire head in her grasp.

"Cut out the Holiness BS," St. Irene of La Guardia said. "Join your friends—and drop the fucking head. What is this, *Antiques Roadshow, Vampire Edition*?"

Luria dropped the vampire head and climbed over the bodies to reach Kyle and the others.

"In fact, let's get all of God's little soldiers together. Cate Hendricks? Ricky Sheflet? Charo. Everyone. Gather around. I don't want to have to repeat myself."

From off in the distance, a vampire snarled.

"Seriously?" With the slight flick of St. Irene's finger, a plume of smoke puffed up into the air from the rear of the killing field. A few other vampires shrieked. A few more flicks of the finger and they too evaporated into thin air. The group had assembled, looking at each other in a daze. They didn't know what to think, meeting a real saint, let alone one with such a short fuse who cursed like a drunken politician.

"Look at you," St. Irene of La Guardia said. "You look like Hogan's Heroes."

"I was thinking more like the Magnificent Seven." Kyle couldn't help himself.

"Again with the mouth," St. Irene of La Guardia said.

"I meant in spirit, not literally," Kyle said.

"Really? You're going to argue with a saint over a movie?" Cate said.

"I'm getting an idea why he did two stints in the psych ward," St. Irene of La Guardia said. "You're not in cray-cray land anymore, okay? Listen up. I know that Noam told some of you my story. My thanks to Noam for keeping the name alive. For those of you who don't know, I'm St. Irene of La Guardia, the protectorate of blood. I staked a sonofabitch vampire monk, which sounds like a musical comedy, and now here I am, sworn enemy of the blood-sucker, defender of humanity—and olives. And looky here, I've got both trampled upon. That's what I call efficient. I had struck a deal with Rupert and Neno long ago to lay off the blood raids, and they did for a while. But then the rise of human-on-human killing rose considerably in the last decade, and I found myself elbow deep in blood again, but this time it wasn't on account of vampires. So, what'd they do, those little fucks? They saw I was busy elsewhere and began to stage raids again, assuming I wouldn't notice. Well, surprise, bitches. I noticed. But I had a few folk in my corner. The Brotherhood. Buffy, Van Helsing, the Frog Brothers, Seth Gecko, Vincent Price, Kolchak, Blade..."

"You gotta be kiddin' me," Kyle said. "They're all real?"

"Believe that shit? Yeah, they're all real. And those were the pop-culture bitches. I had some covert folks. Chief Sitting Bull, Jimmy Carter, Mavis Staples—it's a big list. And they all went to bat for humanity. So here I am, back in the vampire game, and I'm severely fucking disappointed by this. I'm talking Peyton Manning against the Seahawks disappointed. And look how many people had to die on this tiny island. For what, Rupert? A fucking human buffet. Luria here had the right idea. She really kept her eye on the ball, while the rest of you went commando. I swear to God, some-times I wanna take humanity and stuff it into a sausage grinder then pack it into pig casings and bury it a hundred feet down."

"We were trying to protect the island from vampires," Noam said.

"We're on the same side," Dory added.

"Maybe," St. Irene of La Guardia said. "But look at this FUBAR situation you got going on here. And what's with the zombie-vam-pire hybrid? Like I don't have enough shit to worry about? Now I got a creature that eats brains AND sucks blood?"

"We're defenders of humanity as well," Cate said. "And we don't have a thirst for blood."

"Said the woman who eats human brains."

"Only the bad guys," Cate murmured.

"And while we're on the subject of faux mercy killing, we now have kids with fatal diseases turned vampire. Can't wait to see what you do with tuberculosis. I feel like I walked into Dr. Mengele's House of Undead Disease-Ridden Husbandry."

"That's my doing," Dr. Baeza said. "I only wanted it for myself, but…"

"But we decided that it was the only way we could help eradicate our disease," interrupted Ricky. "It was a conscious decision. You'll see. It was worth the trade."

St. Irene of La Guardia rubbed her forehead. She knew about making trades. Ever since ascending from mere mortal to saint, it had been a nonstop push against evil. She'd often wondered when it was that saints got a little time off. Ten days in Aruba or some sublevel of cosmic oasis. No. Humanity kept her plenty busy, as did the undead.

"That's the bitch about humanity," St. Irene of La Guardia said. "It's forever a battle among the self-righteous and the selfish and the selfless and the misguided. It's worse than the Middle East. It's a gangbang of ideology, pure evil, and land. There's always 'who wants more land.' And oil. Fucking fossil fuels. When are you all gonna give up the ghost and switch to alternative sources of energy and quit fucking up the planet already? *Ach!* Might as well be trying to sell shrimp to a Hasidic butcher. But yet, here I am, pulling for the mortals, defending the blood, eating a shit-ton of olives—the eternal struggle continues. Do I sound fried? Well, I may be. But nonetheless, as Charo put it best, *A las Barricadas!*"

Charo beamed with pride.

"So, thanks to Luria and company, I've got a simply fanfucking-tastic idea," St. Irene of La Guardia said. "And it's gonna take some elbow grease. First thing, we gotta clean up this sad-as-shit situation and get souls laid to rest properly. So smoke 'em if you got 'em."

"Hoo-wah!" Oscar shouted.

"Oh, one more thing. I've got to meet fucking Keith Richards."

CHAPTER 13

THE REST OF THE NIGHT THE VAMPIRES dug graves, while angels marked them with small stones bearing the names of the deceased, which they already knew because they were angels and "they kept tabs on you fucksticks," as St. Irene of La Guardia put it. The vampires proved to be highly efficient gravediggers, burrowing into the ground with their hands like dogs on speed seeking out a buried bone. The frustrated saint sat on Neno's portable throne, smoking a cigarette she bummed off one of the Brotherhood. Kyle and the rest had taken up residence at the back of the rented U-Haul, exhausted from the fight. Thierry had found a bottle of his bourbon in the truck cab and passed it around. Kyle had been waiting for the right moment to approach the saint. Despite or because of her foul temperament, Kyle felt a certain kinship with the angry saint, who reminded Kyle of some of the residents back at the psych ward. Particularly the ones with Tourette's.

"That was quite an entrance you made," Kyle said, approaching the throne.

"Standard issue," St. Irene of La Guardia said. "You shoulda seen the one I made during the U.S. Civil War. Scared the bejesus out of Lincoln. Knocked him out of his depression for a few minutes, anyhow."

"Woulda loved to see that," Kyle said.

"Looked like a fucking Vegas show number on steroids."

Kyle chuckled. She was something.

"I guess you're proof of God," Kyle said. "With all these angels flying around, backhanding slacker vampires, clouds parting, the horns of heaven blasting. A few atheists got religion tonight."

"You including yourself?" St. Irene of La Guardia asked, taking a drag off the smoke.

"Maybe. I dunno. Could be."

"I'll let you in on a little secret. God doesn't give a shit one way or the other. Same goes for His son, though by the way churches act you'd think Jesus was a Greenpeace activist trolling for signatures to save the fucking whales."

"Seriously?"

"I shit you not. Believe, don't believe. In the end it's a wash. Souls come and go, faith comforts and wanes, the world keeps spinning. This ain't a race or a game. There's no finish line, just attitude adjustments based on morality and whatever that voice inside you mortals makes you do right and wrong. Remember, I was mortal once, so I get it. And now that I'm a saint, I get it even more. I got boatloads of people praying to me on a daily basis and as many detractors. I'm like Earth, we can take the hits. You can sling all kinds of crap at us, we'll go the distance. Nuke each other, tell God to piss off, ruin the climate, kill in the name of religion, it's free will. Believers, non-believers. Y'know what? Just don't be an asshole about life. That's it."

St. Irene of La Guardia took another long drag then blew the smoke into the night sky.

"That's some heavy existential stuff you just laid on me," Kyle said. "Yet, here you are, so some things must be true."

"Since when has the truth outed anything in human history?" St. Irene of La Guardia asked. "Look, kid. Monty Python, Carl Sagan, the Dalai Lama, Van Morrison—all truths. You want me to sit here and tell you what to believe, and I'm telling you right now, sunshine, that ain't the way it works. Truths? How many people believe in vampires or zombies? The truth mutates like Donald Trump's haircut. Here's some truths—you can't always get what you want, but if you try some time, you get what you need."

"You're quoting the Stones to me?" Kyle said.

"They were right. But then they also wrote *Sympathy for the Devil*. Wily pricks."

"You said 'truths,' plural. What else?"

"What else? There is a beyond. Some bad guys get the shit put to them. Bigfoot is too mind-blowing to ever be discovered. We're not alone, but we are often ignored. I could go all night."

"So you're saying we're not alone in the universe?" Kyle asked.

"Maybe someday I'll make an introduction for you. Life's funny that way," St. Irene of La Guardia said. "But, right now, there's bigger fish to fry. We're gonna need a buttload of blood bags."

*   *   *

Given her new life as a vampire, Luria had to take refuge in one of the colorfully painted treatros that luckily had good cell coverage so she could relay the details of what needed to happen that day in preparation for nightfall. Sylvia and Topo were with her as well, all on cell phones, all chattering plans and arrangements. The vampire horde had been marched back to their various sleep chambers, angels hovering about them, throwing the occasional punch to the head for misconduct or just because it was fun to whack a vampire. Dory was back in her office, running the logistics of what would be a fairly large endeavor: getting her hands on as many pint blood bags as possible. Calls were put in to hospitals ranging from the States to the U.K. By boat, plane, and FedEx, the bags would find a way to the island. Dory found a blood-bag manufacturer in Mauritania and made his nut for the year with her order of bags. There was talk of sterilized barrels once used for holding rainwater, but Luria deemed it too iffy.

There was the storage situation to figure out. Philomena had, through her connections in the shipping industry, secured a small fleet of mid-sized ships that transported fish to take on the blood for delivery—which would be on a massive scale, as there would be hundreds of vampires whose bloated bellies would be emptied as per St. Irene of La Guardia's plans. Luria was beside herself with joy at the bounty of blood that would be flooding hospitals locally and across the North Atlantic. There was concern about the human blood the vampires had taken being mixed with their own, but

Luria decided it was worth the risk. "What's the worst that could happen, except for healthier enzymes?" she asked.

Taking blood from vampires for the human race. Luria thought St. Irene of La Guardia would've made a pretty good hospital administrator.

That night the vampire blood drive would begin. As Luria saw it, there would be two ways to take the blood from the vampires: by traditional means and by inducing vomiting in the vampires. Luria knew from personal experience that vampires could easily puke up the blood, and that might actually prove to be a more rapid and efficient method of blood donation. Staging areas would be set up at St. Hermens and elsewhere on the island, including St. Bobos. Kyle, Cate, and the rest would divvy up the locations and help out. Townsfolk volunteered to help with the storage of blood using their refrigerators as well as sticking vampires with needles to extract the blood. It was a small gesture but one that would help the locals feel a sense of victory over the invading vampires who had wrought destruction to families of the fallen, as they stuck vampire arms a few extra times, "looking for the vein."

St. Irene of La Guardia and a few select angels—"the real badasses," led by Michael, who bore an uncanny resemblance to Hugh Jackman—would patrol the various blood donation areas, keeping the peace and killing the occasional vampire for sport. "That's the thing about angels," St. Irene of La Guardia said. "It's a long existence and they gotta get their kicks to keep the game fresh." Nobody argued that point. Dory had arranged for Keith Richards and St. Irene of La Guardia to get together for a drink at St. Bobo's. It went like this:

St. Irene of La Guardia: I'm a big fan of your work, particularly the stuff between *Beggars Banquet* and *Exile on Main Street*. Great stuff. *Some Girls*, too. Great one.

Keith Richards: Yeah, thanks, love. Some good playing.

SIG: Do you have a favorite album?

KR: That I can remember, love? (*chuckles*). Y'know, all my babies, right? How d'ya choose? You have a favorite bible passage?

SIG: (thinks for a moment) Deuteronomy 15:29 has some nice shit to say about charity. Like you said, they're all my babies.

KR: (nods)

SIG: I know it's been played to death, but I'm partial to *Beast of Burden*, y'know? "All your sickness/I can suck it up/Throw it all at me/I can shrug it off" — I can relate.

KR: The heart of that song is C major, love. It tells the whole story.

SIG: (confused) Right. So what was it like getting a blood transfusion to kick your heroin habit? Was it an overnight kind of, BAM! My-shit's-all-right kind of thing?

KR: I'll tell ya, love. Keep away from the horse. Stick with the bourbon. But, yeah, it was like gettin' a second chance, y'know? You saints are big on that one, yeah?"

SIG: I think you know the answer, chief. You came this fuckin' close to being anointed a few times yourself.

KR: (raises glass of bourbon)

SIG: (does the same. They click glasses and drink. The next hour is all about Muddy Waters. Mick's facelifts, how Charlie lays it down.)

*   *   *

Kyle plugged his iPhone into the St. Bobo's sound system and played The Fixx's *Red Skies at Night* to a bedraggled gathering of mortals, zombies, vampires, zombie vampires, angels, and one saint.

"Sometimes the eighties, it hurts," Cate said.

The sunset had provided a red sky, which gave a slight sense of foreboding to an already psychotic, religious, paranormal past twenty-four hours. St. Bobo's was the last respite before the beginning of the vampire blood drive. It was filled with tired souls.

"A little bit of *déjà* vu in the air, eh?" Kyle said, rejoining a table, espresso in hand.

"I'll give you fifty bucks to turn this song off right now," Xavier said.

"Seriously, we've been here before," Kyle said. "Thierry's tavern? The scheming, the plans, the whiskey flowing, us against the undead world?"

"Getting off on this, are you?" Cate asked.

"A little bit, yeah," Kyle said. "Gives me a sense of purpose. I like the feeling."

"If this goes well, maybe you've got a new career in vampire bloodletting," Sylvia said. "Beats advertising."

"Getting blood sucked through my ass beats advertising," Kyle said.

"Thanks for that image," Cate said.

"It's funny. We're sitting here, tanking up on coffee, ready to perform what is probably the world's first vampire blood donation drive in history, us a bunch of misfits, and yet, it all seems to make sense," Kyle said.

"What exactly did you two talk about?" Cate asked St. Irene of La Guardia.

"Chicks," St. Irene of La Guardia said, with a smirk. "Same as what all you mortals want to talk about: what it all means."

"I gave up on that question around the time we started bombing Iraq the hell out of Kuwait," Oscar said.

"So did you get the answers you wanted?" Cate asked Kyle.

"Yeah, it lies somewhere between Stephen Hawking and the Creator," Kyle said. "And that's as good as it gets."

A few moments of deep thought occurred. Coffee was sipped.

"So what's to become of the vampires?" Sylvia asked. "Seeing how I now have a vested interest, along with Cate, Dr. Baeza, Charo, Ricky, and Talia—did I miss anybody?

"Me, the world's first formerly partially paralyzed talking zombie vampire Chihuahua," Dog said.

"Right," Sylvia. "Pardon the omission."

"S'kay," Dog said.

St. Irene of La Guardia rose out of her chair, stubbed out her cigarette, and produced from her robes an olive branch. She held it up for all to see. "Virgil, the Roman poet once wrote: 'High on the stern Aeneas his stand,/And held a branch of olive in his hand,' and yada yada, I can't remember the rest of it but it's pretty fuckin' amazing. It's a classic poem, look it up. Olives, olive branches—they've got a long history of standing for everything from redemption to tenacity. Olive trees are tough little sonsabitches. Droughts, fires, no problem. It's got a kick-ass root system. You can cut one down, the roots will grow another—tenacity. Ask Pliny the Elder, these trees go the distance. Are you gonna fuck with a tree that's twenty-four-hundred years old? I don't think so. And look what these rough and tumble little bastards produce: olives. Pick 'em off the tree and take a bite. Bitter as hell. Nasty. However, a little TLC, some fermenting, brine…"

"Packed in salt," interrupted Noam.

"Packed in salt, thank you, Noam. Are you getting the idea? There are at least one hundred and one uses for olives. Noam, what's a great olive and wine pairing?"

"Uh… marinated olives and Rioja," Noam said.

"Excellent."

"Good with cod, too."

"Let's not be a suck-up, Noam. Anyway. The olive branch. The symbol of peace. There was one in King Tut's tomb. The sons and daughters of Abraham—the dove that brought the olive branch to Noah, letting him know the flood was over? Ancient Greeks? They were batshit for it. Smeared it all over their bodies, don't get me started on why. Mount of Olives in the New Testament? It got seven mentions in the Quran. There's a town in Mississippi called Olive Branch that produced a NASCAR driver. Fuckin' NASCAR, people. It goes on. That's nice, Saint Irene of La Guardia, but why are you telling us all about the mu-fuckin' olive branch when we got vampires to bleed? GOOD QUESTION. It goes like this. We're going to make peace with the vampires. Sure, we're gonna bleed 'em dry, but then we're gonna offer a nice and easy coexistence, just like you kids did with the zombies back on St. Agrippina. For the record, St. Agrippina is the very definition of drama queen. So?"

Nobody said anything, mostly because they didn't know if the speech was over. They all agreed silently to themselves that St. Irene of La Guardia was a bit of a blowhard.

"And the vampires are gonna what? Just go along with it?" Kyle asked. "They like the taste of human blood. There's no getting around that."

"I will admit," Sylvia said, "I did get a chance to sample some human blood and, yeah, it was a-mazing. It would be a tough sell."

"We used to, at least those of us who wanted to just keep living our lives in normalcy, we used to just eat the brains of bad people," Dory said. "Y'know, criminals and such. In fact, I had a plan to create these cruises that went to terrorist training camps where we could dock and feast on dictators, fascists—there's a market for it, but I haven't had time to get it up and running."

"Vampires detest water," Topo said.

"How do they feel about flying?" Xavier asked.

"Does West Indies Air offer ethnic-cleansing vacation packages?" Kyle asked.

"That's sick," Cate said.

"You know what I mean," Kyle said. "There's good eatin' in places like Syria, Uzbekistan, Texas. All kinds of assholes pulling heinous shit whose blood is just as red as ours."

"See there? This is some good spitballing," St. Irene of La Guardia said. "I like that you're all at least giving it a chance. It took me about four hundred years to even be in the same room with a vampire without removing his head from his body. Monks, too. This whole feasting-on-a-neverending-stream-of-evildoers has a nice ring to it. Remember, Kyle, what I told you about this life you live."

Kyle nodded. "Don't be an asshole about it."

"Bingo," St. Irene of La Guardia said.

CHAPTER 14

From Joaquin's drink blog, *Beba!*

La Marseillaise de l'olive

I offer you a moment from one of my favorite movies, Casablanca, *in which the hero (at least to me), Sascha, the Russian bartender at Rick's, intones the following:*

> **Rick:** *Sascha, she's had enough.*
> **Yvonne:** *Don't listen to him, Sascha. Fill it up.*
> **Sascha:** *I love you, but he pays me.*

If your calling is to be a mixologist of the highest order, you must remember two simple rules:

> *1. The conflicts are never your own.*
> *2. You cannot survive on tips alone.*

Having said that, I am here to tell you that I have broken both rules. For those of you that have been longtime readers of my blog, you know that many of my recipes involved the use of human blood when putting together a concoction for a vampire. I did so and was handsomely rewarded with exceedingly large tips, thus I broke rule number two, for I did not only survive on tips, I thrived on them. I came to rely on the generosity of vampires and in doing so became part of their world, the one that dined on blood of which I did not know the origins. I never asked. It was supplied to me and I kept the aperitif glasses, the martini glasses, the tumblers, and ,of late, the copper mugs full of various blood types in addition to the spirits and seasonings that I added. I hang my head in shame for doing so.

"But Joaqiun, if you broke rule number two, what of rule number one?"

As for rule number one, I am happy to report that I have broken it, as well. Oh, I tried not to. I remained in the shadows, letting the events that have transpired on our little island occur without upsetting my routine. But, unlike business and sports, it became personal. Years ago, I became bound to a vampire and spent every day since inventing creative mixtures fit for their kind. Again, I never asked where the blood came from, I knew its source, but I did not know if it was a neighbor, possibly a vacationer I'd struck up a friendly conversation with (and there were many), or the delivery man who brought the fresh herbs before sunrise.

Ah! But now? I have a pretty good idea.

What to do? As you already know, there is, so to speak, a new sheriff in town, and she is a patron saint not for the faint of heart. She brought with her, along with others who shall remain nameless (okay, we shall call them 'The Magnificent Seven' though there are more than seven), a new way of living. Think salt being introduced to Timbuktu—which may not be the best example as Timbuktu's other commodity was slaves. But you get my meaning. Perhaps democracy in the States? At any rate, there is a new way in which to obtain blood, and I will tell you, it is blood taken on an oath. An oath to rid the world of evildoers, one vein at a time. So yes, I will still be mixing your favorite recipes, but the blood will be sacrificed to a higher cause. I have joined the fight thus breaking rule number one. I stand with Victor Laszlo and the other patrons of Rick's café in singing a boisterous version of La Marsellaise, to honor what is right—and delicious.

La Marseillaise de l'olive

1.5 to 3 ounces Thierry Delasix's St. Bertold bourbon
   at room temp.
1/2 ounce of evildoers' blood
A single Galega olive

Mix blood into bourbon in a shot glass. Down the
bourbon. Eat the olive. Watch *Casablanca*.

*   *   *

EPILOGUE

"WHO KICKS ASS ON THE AMERICAN RED CROSS?" Bert Saunders, a program director with the Red Cross office in Lewiston, Maine, wanted to know. He stood in front of a conference table surrounded by a mostly volunteer staff. "We're the American Red Cross. We've been doing this since nineteen forty-one. You'd think we'd gotten a handle on collecting blood by now. Hmm? But look here." Bert held up a spreadsheet. "Looks like there's some newbies who managed to fill every blood bank from Turin to the fifty states, right her, in America, home of the American Red Cross. How'd that happen?"

"It's not a contest, Bert. We should be celebrating the fact that there was a sudden influx of blood donations," said Connie Wilkins, a volunteer.

"Oh, it's a contest," Bert said. "A cutthroat one at that. What do you think happens to an underperforming region? Hmm? They close it down. That puts you all out of a job."

"We're volunteers, fer chrissake," Angus Whittier said. "Most of us are retired. You're the one out of a job, which might speak well to how you run things around here. The coffee tastes like used motor oil and the damned toilet backs up and…"

"This is what happens when some downsized project manager from Google takes over a regional blood donation center. It becomes about the process and not the actual goals," said Charley King, the college student intern. "Who cares where the blood comes from? The world is looking at shortages every day. Urgent medical care is put off because of a lack of blood. People remain sick. People even die. The politics and policies of blood donation are bad enough to make a vampire switch to whiskey. I don't care that there is this tidal wave of blood flooding centers throughout the world, and I don't care who gets the plaque honoring the regional office. The only thing I—we—should care about is that lives are gonna be saved."

"In other words, take your middle-management attitude elsewhere," Connie said. Applause followed.

*   *   *

"There isn't a scenario in this where you come out getting what you want," Cate said. She sat opposite Kyle in a booth at Koufax's, Sari by her side.

"I dunno. You guys can't tell me there isn't chemistry between you two and between me and you, and I'd like to think between me and Sari," Kyle said.

"Ha, you think a couple of well-played jokes gets you in the front door?" Sari asked.

"Doesn't it? It did with Cate."

"It's true," Cate said. "I'm deeply ashamed."

"Okay, I'll admit you have a certain charm and misguided idea of yourself," Sari said to Kyle. "But as far as a threesome is concerned, ain't gonna happen."

"C'mon. I'm picking up a bisexual vibe from you, and Cate doesn't seem to be deflecting it and frankly you've both given me some sleepless nights."

"How do you know Cate and I didn't already get together?" Sari asked. "Would you consider that cheating if we did?"

"I'd consider it crazily hot if you did," Kyle said. "Did you? Tell me, honestly. Was it full on…"

"Whatever you were gonna call it, just don't," interrupted Cate. "And for the record, if I did sleep with Sari, how would that not be cheating?"

"Because you're... both hot and I'd really love to watch you guys pillow-fight," Kyle said.

"What bullshit!" Sari said. "If Cate blew another guy, you'd be freaked out. But if she goes down on another woman, that's okay in your book? It's like you're negating me as a human being. Sexist pig."

"Soooo, you'll think about?" Kyle asked.

"Okay, let's take it down a notch," Cate said.

"Tell it to the Cro-mag," Sari said.

"Sorry, sorry," Kyle said, holding up his hands. "Yet another dream crushed."

"He gets like this when he's stressed out," Cate said. "He's still coming down from everything. Aren't you, *honey*?"

Kyle took the rebuke well.

"So what did you and St. Irene really talk about anyway?" Cate asked, redirecting the conversation and hopefully the tone.

"Nothing much," Kyle said. "Just the little things—why we're here, what God thinks, et cetera."

"Did she give a reason why we're here?" Cate asked.

"Not really. I mean she did in a kind of obtuse way. Why do you think we're here?"

"I'm not sure I am," Cate said. "Look at me. Look at this situation. Everywhere around undead beings roaming the earth, living among the living, mixing with them..."

"Boning them," interrupted Kyle.

"How do you put up with him? Sari asked.

"...and yet there's no explanation about why the undead exist," Cate continued. "I died, Kyle. And then, for some reason, be it a virus or maybe some kind of reincarnation or divine intervention, I'm sitting here, drinking espresso, not breathing, still able to have thoughts and ideas and feelings. Just like the vampire we slaughtered and the zombies last year."

"After learning that Mom was killed by a vampire and that Dad belonged to an ancient brotherhood sworn to protect humanity from vampires, I'm ready to believe in anything and everything."

"That's kinda what St. Irene was getting at," Kyle said. "Believe what you want."

"Sari, where'd you put the tray of leftover kugel?" Noam shouted from the counter.

"In the fridge, where else?"

"I can't find it."

"Gotta go help out the old man," Sari said. "To be continued."

She left the booth. Kyle and Cate sipped their espresso.

"I know I've asked this before," Cate said, setting down her cup. "Doesn't it freak you out to be with me?"

"Freak me out?" Kyle said. He took a moment to think it over, which made Cate a bit uncomfortable as she was talking to a guy who had a penchant for talking before thinking.

"No. It doesn't freak me out," he continued. "It does make me wonder about the idea of being in a state of being... dead. We've talked about this. I'm just happy to be with you. I do find it interesting that, ever since I got out of St. Eligius, what? Eighteen months ago? I've been thrust into this paranormal existence. I learned that undead walked the earth. I learned how to kill them. And I learned that some of them want the same thing as the living. To be happy. Makes me wonder what the next year will bring. Aliens? Werewolves? The Tea Party? Things get weirder and weirder, and you know what Hunter S. Thompson said."

"When the going gets weird..."

"...The weird turn pro," Kyle finished.

They joined hands at the center of the table. Kyle had become familiar with her cold touch, had come to expect it and find comfort in it. He often marveled at what one could get comfortable with. Which was good and bad. But what did anything matter? He loved Cate and would do so to the end of his days, which could be years or centuries if he could only decide here he'd let her take a bite out of him.

* * *

Oscar remarked that even though he got a chance to break out the 50mm gun and mow down vampires, the buzz from re-killing the undead had lost some of its potency. He thought it might be his injury-ravaged body or having finally reached a level of maturity that went beyond blowing shit up. Whichever, he felt it might be time to hang up his warrior ways, take Woman and Dog back to their island paradise, and maybe get interested in trains or building airplane models. Woman smiled and Dog commented that once a dog of war, etc...

There hadn't been much damage to the hotel, which now resided on the rechristened island of Queixa. Some bullet hole repairs, broken chandeliers, but the worst part—some of the tourist dead were returned home, the story being that Somali pirates had overrun the island—had lent a somber note to the reconstruction. The cruise ship *Greta Garbo* was purchased by Dory to be the private line that serviced Queixa and St. Agrippina. Dory didn't need any lawyers to sever her partnership with Rupert Jagger as St. Irene of La Guardia pressed him into service as her new Percy Merriwether. She often referred to Rupert as her "olive pimp," in charge of making sure the local olive farmers' needs were attended to. As for Percy, he decided he'd had enough weirdness and joined the Gampo Abbey in Cape Breton, sitting at the feet of Pema Chodron, learning the monastic way of being. The shaved head worked in his favor.

Noam and Sari continued running Koufax's deli, trying their best to mix kosher classics with the Portuguese palate. It was a challenge they both met heartily. Sari did have feelings for Cate, which she wrote in an email to her. Cate replied with a wistful and warm embrace that an emoticon could convey. For Cate, it was more a sisterhood thing. But why spoil Sari's ideal of what was between them? Besides, there could come a day...

Noam and the Brotherhood decided that, with St. Irene of La Guardia on their side, who could be against them? They officially changed the charter of protecting humanity into a Bocce ball league. They called themselves the "Sons of Irene."

Sylvia and Luria decided they liked each other's style and opened a small consulting firm specializing in blood bank management. They worked long nights, and refused all meetings that mortals insisted happen during the daylight hours, when it seemed that so little was accomplished. Sylvia had enlisted Kyle and Cate to work up some branding materials for them, with Sylvia being relentless in her indifference to the work they showed her, and Luria, because Sylvia Woodcock was an industry badass.

Philomena returned to her life in L.A. on her own. Rolf had decided undead sex with Desmond and island living suited him just fine, something that was not lost on Kyle. Desmond put Rolf to work as the new beverage manager, working alongside Thierry and LeRoi. Working with Joaquin, Thierry had rolled out a new line of aperitif, St. Irene's, each small batch containing an ounce of Thierry and Joaquin's blood. It was included in *Esquire* magazine's "Top 10 Aperitifs You Can't Get Your Hands On." Xavier, when the mood struck, would load up his Grumman and make runs to various ports of call to deliver the new product and to remind himself what being a pilot felt like.

Charo's bookings in the undead circuit kept her busy year-round.

Sid from Toronto had come within hours of death when Dr. Baeza gave him a transfusion of vampire blood. It didn't turn Sid into a vampire, but it did revitalize his body so that Dr. Baeza, Ricky, and Talia could devote their time to research. Ricky and Talia had an easy time getting their parents over the hump of being vampires. They were grateful for the opportunity to have their children with them no matter what state they existed in. Ricky attended a conference on the Singularity, proposing an additional epoch: when humanity merged with the reincarnated cell. Minds were blown. Papers were written. Ricky found himself amidst a confabulation of science versus myth—or faith, as Dr. Baeza saw it.

Topo Bogomil loved Dory and wished to spend the rest of his life with her, however long that might be, with the provision that when Dory finally grew tired of his heaviness, she'd kick him to the curb. It would be a long-distance relationship as Topo could not deny the calling to be the world's vampire cop, roaming the earth, keeping tabs on various vampire communities, and, when necessary, helping out St. Irene of La Guardia with the harvest of blood from whatever dictatorial regime that popped up. Topo was never surprised that no sooner would he lay waste to a collection of fascists with guns, another would emerge.

The life of a saint continued as it always had for St. Irene of La Guardia. She listened to prayers, took orders from the head office, and, whenever possible, sought to ease the suffering of those in need. She checked in with Topo about blood and made the occasional road trip to oversee the wholesale slaughter of evil. She had her days when humanity seemed to be "the single largest collection of halfwit flesh bags that careened off each other like air hockey pucks" she'd ever pitied.

"But what the fuck are you gonna do?" St. Irene of La Guardia said to an angel. "They're like cockroaches and Jehovah's Witnesses. They just keep coming back."

THE END

ACKNOWLEDGMENTS

How many people does it take to put a book together? More than one. Thanks to the folks at Booktrope Publishing who thought, "What's the worst that could happen?" Thanks to my beta readers, Jillian, Mike, Leah and Sonja. Thanks to my genius editor, Jim Thomsen of Desolation Island Editing Services (www.facebook.com/jimthomsen). Thanks to Kathryn Galan for her excellent proofing skills. To those who bought the first book, *Paradise Rot*, and waited for the second. Thanks to Rooster's Café for the table and—coffee. Most of all, thanks to my wife, Jillian, who just assumed the book(s) would be great.

ABOUT THE AUTHOR

Larry Weiner is the author of *Paradise Rot (Book One)* and *Once Again, With Blood (Book Two)*. Larry earned a degree in film from CSULA and was an award-winning art director. And then he got the hell out of Dodge (advertising) and decided he was better at fiction for the greater good (entertainment) than fiction to make people buy shit they don't need (advertising). He'd written two novels and a ton of scripts in his 20s but doesn't really count them, as over twenty years passed since writing *Paradise Rot*. So really, let's call *Paradise Rot* the first novel.

He lives on an island in the Pacific Northwest with his wife, two kids, and a mess of animals.

Social media stuff:

Website: www.larrynweiner.com
Author Page: https://www.facebook.com/larrynweiner
Paradise Rot page: https://www.facebook.com/larrynweiner
Once Again, with Blood page: https://www.facebook.com/pages/Once-Again-With-Blood/1447388282202651
Twitter: @LarryNWeiner
Goodreads: https://www.goodreads.com/book/show/18457307-paradise-rot

ALSO BY LARRY WEINER

Paradise Rot The Island Trilogy, Book 1 (Horror/Satire) A well-crafted, fast-paced comic thriller of pancreas-rupturing hilarity, loaded with heart, colored with sharp cultural observations, and dry-rubbed in the spices of folklore and history.

Hindu Sex Aliens, The Island Trilogy, Book 3 (Horror/Satire) Part meta-fiction, part Metamucil, the cerebrally comic conlusion to Larry Weiner's uproarious trouble-in-paradise trilogy.

www.ingramcontent.com/pod-product-compliance
Lightning Source LLC
Chambersburg PA
CBHW021139130626
46554CB00005B/1585